Neon Dancers

Also by Matt and Bonnie Taylor

Neon Flamingo
Black Dutch

Neon Dancers

Matt and Bonnie Taylor

Walker and Company
New York

First published in the United States of America in 1991
by Walker Publishing Company, Inc.
Published simultaneously in Canada by Thomas Allen & Son
Canada, Limited, Markham, Ontario

Library of Congress Cataloging-in-Publication Data
Taylor, Matt.
Neon Dancers / Matt and Bonnie Taylor.
        p.   cm.
        ISBN 0-8027-3207-0
    I. Taylor, Bonnie.   II. Title.
    PS3570.A946N39   1991
    813'.54—dc20   91-21151
                              CIP

Printed in the United States of America
2 4 6 8 10 9 7 5 3 1

For Rebecca Thomas

Neon Dancers

1

SMUGGLING A WAGONLOAD OF carrots by a rabbit warren would be easier than keeping a secret from Alice Jane Egan. It was barely past dawn and here she was, already snooping around the creaky old double doors of my workshop. Through the crack I spied her — small, energetic, and wearing yellow sneakers.

"Palmer, are you in there?" Fingers scrabbled with the door hardware.

"Forget that. It's latched on this side."

"You sure got an early start," she replied. "Let me in. We can talk while you work. I've got the papers."

Something about the way she said that worried me. I could be in for another one of A.J.'s early-morning surprises. "Go on in the kitchen. There's coffee."

The latch rattled again.

"Just get away from the door, A.J. Damn reporters always sniffing around where they don't belong."

"Oh, for God's sake, Palmer, open up!"

I deliberately dropped a wrench on the concrete floor to annoy her some more.

"Okay. But if you think I'm going to do all that baking you conned me into by myself, you're wrong," she grumped. A.J. is never a cheerful loser.

Cold from the concrete floor picked like crab claws at the fresh scar along my spine as I rolled under the roadster. Flat on my back, I was working on her Christmas present. I wrestled a hand-tooled ball joint into place under the 1939 American Austin — lipstick red with a new white canvas top. Too small for me. I'd look like a buzzard in a robin's nest, but it was just right for A.J. Or it would be when Curly's chrome shop got around to replating the box of hardware I'd sent over.

As I worked, gray scud increasingly blocked the winter sun in the skylight. All the other windows in the warehouse-size shop were painted over to protect the guilty treasures that unexpected and, if the truth be known, unearned wealth had bought me over the last decade: classic cars of the 1920s and 30s. From my low position I glanced down the long row of undercarriages toward the small space heater and wished it were closer. The damp cold blowing in off the Gulf was Florida at its worst – angering tourists who didn't expect to spend three hundred dollars a day for this, scaring the living bejesus out of growers for whom a few degrees make the difference between a bumper crop and disaster, and setting all us under-clothed Crackers to shivering.

But the cold wasn't all that was bothering me. I couldn't keep my mind off work. Well, not work, newsroom politics – the poison that's replacing ink in journalists' veins. The sad truth was that the new publisher at the *Marlinsport Tribune* seemed to like everything about the newspaper, except us reporters and editors.

I was able to get in another half hour's work before the latch rattled again. "You've got a call."

A.J.'s shadow was visible under the doors as she tried to peer through the gap and plumb the recesses of the drafty old cavern. I grasped the Austin's thick, solid fender with my plowman's hands and levered my six-and-a-half-foot frame out from under the car.

"Palmer? Why is this place always locked?"

I laid a hand over the spot framing one violet eye. Slipping the latch with the other, I eased the door back and filled the opening with my bulk.

"Tell 'em I'll call back," I rumbled down at the top of her head, which was gleaming like polished coal and patted with traces of flour.

"You look like an anarchist in his basement," she said. "What's going on in there?"

Even on tiptoe she couldn't see over my shoulder.

"I'm working."

"Try that line on your city editor. Paula is in no mood to chat with me."

Shielding the interior I squeezed out and slid the double bar in place. A.J. watched as I snapped the heavy padlock. "You show a lot of trust."

"Habit, that's all," I mumbled as we walked through the hedge of tropical foliage that mostly hid the ancient shop from view. "You know how I feel about the phaeton."

"The Packard?" she mocked. "What about the others? You could open a museum."

"Humh," I said evasively.

We hurried across the drive. Vapors from the swimming pool rose in swirling patterns in the cold air. At the back of my towering pink stucco casa of indecent splendor we climbed cracked tiled steps. I noted once more that the loose iron railing needed attention. It was always something. But in my defense the 1920s Spanish mansion fell onto hard times and was subdivided into apartments long before I bought it.

My bright yellow kitchen was rich with the aroma of fruitcake, the air thick with sifted flour. Gooey dough rubbed onto my hand as I picked up the telephone receiver.

"What's up?"

"Palmer, why's Kincaid Treaster at the Federal Building on a Saturday?" Paula Prince, newly installed as city editor at the *Trib*, knew as well as I did that civil servants aren't big on weekend duty.

"How would I know? Cop shop's been my beat for twenty years, remember?"

"Come on, Palmer. You once told me the two of you were pals when you were kids."

"No, I said Treaster and I used to hang around together. We were never pals."

It was an important distinction for me, even after all these years. Treaster left Marlinsport in the seventies for Vanderbilt Law School. After climbing the ladder to success as a U.S. attorney, he'd made headlines when the White House sent him back to us on a crusade against corruption. So far I'd successfully avoided seeing him.

"Could the federal grand jury be in session?" Paula asked.

"It's possible."

"But the U.S. attorney himself wouldn't be running it."

"If Treaster's near it, he's running it," I said.

There was a hesitation on the phone. "Can she figure out what we're talking about?"

I eyed A.J. Her little behind was toward me as she stood spraddle-legged, peering into the oven. Floured finger marks spotted the thighs of her faded jeans.

"If you mean A.J., she's taking notes." I get royally pissed having to explain our relationship over and over.

A.J. stiffened, then slipped a rack against the back of the oven.

Paula's words came in a rush. "It's a bit awkward, having her live at your place."

"Not for me."

"Come on, Palmer. How do you think I feel having a *New Seville Times* reporter answer your phone?"

"There's no problem, Paula, unless you make it one. Why don't you let me worry about 700 Island Drive?"

A.J. spun around. "You want me to leave?" she whispered.

She was letting her hair grow, and the limp black strands clung to her neck. When I shook my head, A.J. turned back to her work.

Through the whir of a mixer I heard Paula's half-irritated, half-worried voice. "This is turning out to be a fucked-up Saturday. I've got to get a handle on Treaster. And having A.J. within earshot is really swell."

"What's your problem, Paula?"

"You know she's been churning out those damned zoning stories?"

"More or less." Actually, as with everything else A.J. writes, I'd been following them closely.

"Yeah, well, it's been pretty dry stuff. I thought no one but the city counsel and me were reading them. But you know how these stories can be . . . deadly dull and suddenly just deadly. People get themselves killed and dropped in the bay over deals like this."

I straightened. "What are you talking about?"

"You didn't read her story this morning?"

"Not yet."

"No wonder you're in a better mood than I am. The day after A.J. filed a Freedom of Information request for a bunch of zoning records on that fancy development up by Balders Edge — ."

"Balders Swamp is what we Crackers call that muck field," I interjected.

"Whatever. Anyway the records and an old hand in the zoning office have both vanished."

"Who?"

"Nick Darvin."

Instantly I had a mental image of the short, round guy who rode around the crowded downtown streets on a little Honda scooter. Winter or summer he always wore a yellow helmet with a black face shield, and a bright yellow windbreaker over his business clothes. I'd never said aloud that he looked like an outsized bumble bee squatting on a rail, but I'd thought it a time or two. "Is Randy working on it?"

"Yeah, but there's not a trace of Darvin or the records. The zoning director's dummied up, too. Could you check with the cops?"

"I will," I said, adding cautiously, "You think Treaster's getting interested?"

"Could be the Feds have this Darvin. Questioning him." A short silence. "Goddamnit, Palmer, she's making us look bad again — like we don't know what's happening on our own turf."

4

On this I could share Paula's concern. A.J. works for a big rich newspaper on the west side of Marlin Bay—the quiet side, mostly populated by coupon-clipping retirees. But our rowdy, blue-collar side is her beat. Even with the veneer of sophistication new money's brought to town, Marlinsport's heart is still a rowdy port, rich with mischief for a relentless reporter like A.J. She's capable of stealing the socks off any reporter who goes up against her. I know this all too well, having been left barefoot myself a time or two.

"What do you want me to do?" I asked my city editor.

Paula marked time. Maybe a fear of revealing either indecision or inexperience was working on her. But Paula's good. It didn't take her long to plot things through.

"The very fact that A.J.'s with you argues that the Feds are meeting about something else. I'll keep Randy Holliman camped outside for a while."

"Sounds like you're on top of it," I said.

"Maybe," she replied. "But if A.J. suddenly ducks out on you let me know."

I laughed. "No way, Paula. You're on your own."

"If you and a reporter for the *New Seville Times* are going to live together you gotta expect some conflicts, and frankly I expect the *Tribune* to come first."

"We reside under the same roof. That's all."

"Un-hunh. Sure. She's just one more happy tenant in Palmer Kingston's Taj Mahal."

"Well, it's true."

Paula laughed, but there was ice in it.

"I gotta go," she said, and hung up.

When I put down the receiver I saw that A.J.'s fingers were dancing on the kitchen counter. When the Marlinsport cops sent her to me for an apartment last summer they'd done it for a joke since she was going to work against me on the same beat. But A.J. fell in love with the little attic aerie I showed her and she rented it anyway. We've been trying to balance how we feel about each other and how we feel about our jobs ever since. When she left the police beat for city hall I've gotta admit it took a lot of pressure off me.

"Paula was giving you a hard time about my being here, wasn't she?" The violet eyes leveled on me. "Maybe we should talk again about my moving."

"That's ridiculous, A.J. We're doing just fine." I reached for the

5

butterballs. "Paula was only lecturing me on my many shortcomings."

"Not that one, it's hot," she warned. "Try the other end, and don't get greedy. They're for your Christmas party." She took a moment to eye my considerable frame. "I don't know how you do it, Palmer," she said at last. "You eat like a goat and never put on an ounce of fat. It's disgusting."

"I just took a couple."

"You've got four," she said.

I mumbled a reply and turned to the *Trib* and the *Times* spread out on the kitchen table. A.J.'s story was stripped across the *Times*'s front, along with a photo of the missing clerk. With his round face and big grin, Darvin looked like a man without a trouble in the world.

"Anything in the papers?" she asked idly.

Answering her was going to be as delicate a procedure as picking a sandspur off my socks. It's hard to find stories we can discuss freely. I made a safe comment about hoping the Dolphins reached the Super Bowl.

A.J. put a cup of coffee in front of me, liberally dosed with sugar and half and half. She poured herself a cup and sat opposite me.

"You and those Dolphins." Her indulgent laugh filled the kitchen.

"This is gonna be their year," I declared. "It's all coming together again."

Her smile showed that once more my passion for Miami's football team had gotten away from me. I grinned self-consciously.

"I wanna ask you a favor," she said.

"I'll do it."

"Hold on. It means a trip. My Aunt Tot's farm is going to be auctioned off back in Indiana. I was hoping you'd go with me. Can you get the third Monday in January off?"

"Sure. What's one day?"

"You'll need the weekend, too. It's—" A.J. stiffened at the sound of car tires crunching through the gravel in the drive.

Through the screen door I saw the austere profile of the mayor's limousine creeping into a sheltered spot next to the shop. So did A.J. Her eyes glittered with speculation as she peered at me over her coffee mug. We didn't have to say a word to understand each other completely. Julio Montiega, Marlinsport's political kingpin, wanted to see me awfully early on a Saturday morning. Whatever was up was important.

I got to my feet. She wouldn't ask any questions but it was a cinch that as soon as I hit the door A.J. would call the *Times* to ask whether anything was cooking at city hall.

I gazed down into those violet eyes. "Shall we dance?" I asked teasingly.

"I guess it's time," she answered with the merest hint of excitement in her voice.

I headed for the mayor. She headed for the phone.

$\bigtriangledown$

2

WHEN HE SAW ME Mayor Julio Montiega, with the lanky grace of the consummate Latin dancer that he was, stepped out of the back of the long Lincoln. His unnaturally black hair fluttered in the wind. Above the cabbage palms clouds streamed past like a river at flood stage.

"*Alcalde*," I greeted him, "You're up early."

He gestured subtly for his driver to wait in the car and walked toward me.

"Would you like to come in?" I asked, knowing he wouldn't. "We're baking. A few dozen butterballs will improve your stature in the community."

Julio usually enjoyed my bad jokes, but not today. His dark eyes were troubled as they traveled up to mine. "She's inside, isn't she?"

"Yes."

The mayor spread his long, thin fingers nervously. He was a man under great strain, and not hiding it very well.

"You told me I could see the car Cat Man died in." His words carried on the crisp air. They were meant for his chauffeur, I figured.

"Sure, but it's a mess after sitting in the old lady's garage for fifty years."

"Show me now. Please."

I led the way through the sagging doors, made a skinny belly, and sidled past my yellow '35 Packard, which once belonged to another Marlinsport gangster but was not the car Julio wanted to see. It was my newest possession I was leading him to. It took a while for us to work our way to the northwest corner of the shop, where the 1933 midnight-blue Cadillac town car sat, in desperate need of a lot of attention.

"Ah," I heard him say in a strange way, "that's the one."

"The car's complete in every detail except for a detachable trunk. It's missing."

"May I?" His hand hovered above a rear door handle.

"Go ahead," I replied and settled in the backseat beside him. The door closed with a thunk. The smell of a half century of neglect filled the car.

8

"Solid," he said.

"Sure is."

He tapped on the window. "Thick glass."

"Un-hunh. It's bulletproof. In the old days this is where I'd have wanted to be when trouble showed up."

"Maybe so. Maybe not." His thick fingers stroked the leather seat and found a hole made by one of the few bullets that had missed Michael "Cat Man" Contreras nearly a half century ago when he opened his car door in front of the Casino in Alverez District. "This is not the first time I've been in this car."

"I didn't think so, judging by your interest in it."

He gestured to the silver and leather case built into the back of the chauffeur's seat. "What's in there?"

I touched a latch, and an elaborate bar popped out. Solid-silver-mounted glasses and decanters, black with tarnish, tinkled faintly in their pockets.

The mayor — *el alcalde* to both his friends and political foes — picked up a glass. "A liquor cabinet. I guessed as much but always wondered."

"Fancy bottles for bathtub gin."

"No bathtub gin ever went down Cat Man's throat."

"That sounds a little like admiration."

Montiega's voice had the cadence of a troubadour. "No, a mere statement of fact. I met him."

"In this car I take it."

"We rode through the Latin district and he offered me five thousand a year while I was in school. Running numbers."

"Why?"

"His son — you know him as Joe Sparkles — was a classmate of mine. Three older boys grabbed him outside a pool hall one night and I was cut up helping him. Cat Man wanted to thank me."

Amazing. As much as I knew about my hometown I'd not known these two polar elements in the Latin community, the straight mayor and the heir to mob power, had a connection. A pang of sympathy for A.J. rose in me. It would be damn difficult for a newcomer like her to figure out the tangled skeins of a raw, unruly city like Marlinsport.

"Are you trying to tell me you've been friendly with the mob all these years?" I asked archly.

The *alcalde* didn't look amused. "I turned him down, of course. I wanted to stay clean, go to law school, be somebody real."

I studied his face. "Why are we sitting in this car early on a Saturday morning talking about your past, *Alcalde*? What's going on?"

He looked over his shoulder as if we were tooling down Bay Drive and he was afraid someone was following us.

"Is there any chance A.J. will come in and hear us?"

"Come on, *Alcalde*. You know nothing we say in this car can be overheard—by her or your driver."

I waited. Raspy, whispered words came from the mayor's throat. "I have technically broken the law."

"Technically? As in really? Or certainly?"

"I was approached with a bribe yesterday, but I haven't reported it. Not yet . . . although I must." His eyes reflected a certain bewilderment. "It was a zoning matter . . . I don't even handle zoning matters."

"So report it and forget it."

"It isn't easy to turn in an old friend."

"What old friend?"

"Cesar Armonia."

"Cesar!" I wouldn't have been more surprised if he'd said it was the pope. Cesar Armonia owned a small restaurant that served the Cuban community. I knew he was hot-tempered and proud. I also knew he was honest.

"Why in the world would Cesar try to bribe you?"

"I don't know. But he is in deep financial trouble because the rezoning of a property he bought has been delayed. . . . Still, I can't see him doing this to himself, or to me. Something's wrong. Now with this disappearance of Nick Darvin . . . I am truly alarmed."

I peered hard at his dark, etched face. "Are you telling me A.J.'s series on zoning is drawing blood?"

"She is not the only one snooping around city hall."

"I see. It's Treaster you're afraid of, not A.J. Should I ask if there's a reason?"

The mayor drew himself up indignantly. "You know better than that, Palmer. But any politician who is not leery of a glory-seeking prosecutor is a fool. Treaster came into town waving a crusader's banner but he's achieved nothing and it grates on him."

"You think it's possible he's using Cesar to get at you?"

"I don't know what to think, except that Cesar would never do this on his own."

"You could be fooling around with a piece of dynamite, *Alcalde*. My advice is to run this by the city attorney."

"Not yet. Regardless of my fear, I cannot bring myself to destroy

Cesar so cavalierly. I need somebody I can trust to check this out first. A friend."

I stared at him. If anyone had a call on my friendship it was Julio Montiega. My wife, Betsy, was a legal secretary in his law firm when she became sick. Even after it became impossible for her to work, the paychecks kept coming, and God knows we needed them to pay for those desperate trips to the Mayo Clinic. Then, after she was gone and I'd talked wildly about selling our little farm and leaving town, he advised me to give myself a year or two, that the familiar places and memories that hurt so much then, I'd come to cherish later. I knew he was right the day I was able to walk into the old Tropical Cafeteria on its last day of business and persuade the owner to sell me the neon flamingo in the front window. Betsy had always loved the gaudy thing, calling it the perfect symbol for Florida.

So I had to be careful. Publishers and editors are always self-righteous about reporters getting close to people they cover. I don't argue with that even if I do find it hypocritical. Publishers and editors play golf and slurp martinis with these same people seven days a week.

"You've known me long enough, *Alcalde*, to realize I won't promise anything." I warned, "except to find the truth."

"Palmer" — Julio pronounced my name in a clear, resonant tone — "that's all I ask."

"Okay, give me more detail."

"It's tied up with El Principe de Cordoba. Are you familiar with that old cigar factory?"

I leaned back in the pockmarked seat and crossed my arms. "Oh, yeah, I know El Principe. When we were kids, my friends and I climbed all over that brick monster."

One dark eyebrow raised. "Strange, that's exactly what Cesar called it."

3

AFTER JULIO LEFT I went inside. A.J. was gone, and from the looks of the kitchen she'd left in a hurry. I decided I'd better get a move on myself.

When I walked into the *Trib*'s newsroom, Paula was in the managing editor's office — and on the spot, it appeared. I could see through the glass walls that Bob Wilson's mood was as nasty as a blue crab's in a pot. I ducked my head in the door.

"Any word on Treaster and the Feds?"

Paula's green eyes flashed my way with relief. A diversion had arrived. "No. Randy's here, making some calls."

Without looking up from the *Times*, Wilson waved me off. I went in anyway.

"Reading the wrong paper, aren't you?" I asked, and slumped into one of his cushy blue chairs.

"Humh," he grumbled. "Paula thinks so. She's trying to explain how your girlfriend isn't really making us look like shit on this zoning story."

"A.J.'s blowing smoke," Paula said defensively, tossing long red hair off her forehead. "There's no pattern to the council's zoning votes. All she's written about are a few cases that upset the environmentalists, and hell, everything upsets them."

While she spoke, Wilson struggled, as usual, to keep his gaze on her face. In his early thirties, a few years younger than me, the *Trib*'s managing editor was between marriages and eternally on the make. He forced his attention back to the newspaper on his cluttered desk.

"I bet this guy Howard Ketch pulled somebody's strings so he could put those houses at Balders Swamp."

"All the people moving into Florida have to live somewhere," Paula said.

"Sure, but good God, growth is supposed to be managed." Wilson nodded toward the window. "Look out there. Another damn marina's going in across the river when there's already enough oil floating by the *Trib* to fuel a power plant."

I smiled. Everybody in the newsroom knew about Wilson's binoculars and his periodic checks of the bikinis around the hotel pool upriver.

"On what grounds should their building permit be denied—spoiling your view?"

Paula stifled a laugh as Wilson glared at me. "You Crackers would concrete the Gulf if you could find a buyer."

"And the buyers would all have accents like yours," I replied. "Nasal north."

"If all you want to do is jaw, Palmer, shove off. I want to talk to Paula about finding this zoning clerk."

"So do I."

Paula looked at me in surprise. "Randy says Darvin's probably at a fat farm someplace. He was always threatening to go. There's no reason for us to get worked up just because of a few headlines in the *Times*."

"Worked up?" Wilson growled. "Hell, it doesn't even look like we're awake."

At that moment Paula seemed to me to be the thing she hated most: vulnerable. I loathed siding with Wilson against her, but I had no choice.

"The mayor came to see me this morning. Not only is he sure A.J.'s on to something, he's scared the U.S. attorney is after him. That's why I'm here. I thought I'd look into this zoning stuff if you agree."

Wilson's hazel eyes narrowed on me suspiciously; then he grinned in that nasty way of his.

"Let me get this straight. You're volunteering to shovel through a shitload of city documents and go up against A.J. What'd she do, cut you off? Now wait! Relax. I'm only kidding." He had a hollow laugh at times like these. "I keep forgetting what an old-fashioned gentleman you are, Palmer, and me just a Jersey City street kid."

Paula jolted us both back to the story. "You think the mob's in on this?"

I shrugged.

Wilson leaned forward. "*Could* the mob be involved? I know for a fact that the new marina is bankrolled by one of Marlinsport's finer citizens—Joe Contreras."

I hesitated. Was it only a coincidence that the old mobster's name had come up twice this morning? "Certainly that should be checked out."

"You're damn right it should," Wilson gloated. "Now how's the mayor fit in?"

I repeated Julio's story. "An old friend approached him yesterday on the sidewalk near city hall and said things that didn't make much sense about getting a zoning change."

"What old friend?"

"Cesar Armonia. The mayor claims Cesar took a fat envelope out of his pocket and shoved it at him."

"What was in it?" Paula asked.

"Thousands of dollars."

"I'll be damned," Wilson muttered. "A bribe. Sounds like the mob to me."

"Except it was Cesar passing it. I can't believe that man's connected to organized crime. There's a lot more I need to find out before we have a story."

"Bull. How'd the mayor react?"

"When he realized what was in the envelope, he handed it back, cautioning Cesar that it wasn't safe to be carrying cash like that in the middle of downtown Marlinsport."

"Isn't that nice," Wilson said.

I ignored his sarcasm and continued. "When the envelope was pushed at him again the mayor says he laughed and told Cesar if he was determined to give him money to send a small check to his campaign for governor."

"As a declaration of integrity that leaves a little to be desired," Paula interjected.

"These are two old, old friends."

"Friends! The mayor sounds like an idiot, or a man on the take," Wilson chortled.

"What happened next?" Paula asked.

"Cesar demanded the mayor stop stalling his variance for a derelict cigar factory in Alverez District — El Principe. Julio tried to explain that he didn't vote on zoning but Cesar was livid, ranting 'I did as I was told now I want my zoning.' That's when alarm bells finally went off in the mayor's head and he got away from there."

"Without the money?"

"Without the money. Later Julio did a little checking around and learned Cesar's mortgaged both his restaurant and home to raise enough cash for an option. Now the banks won't give him a construction loan until the zoning goes through. He's on the verge of losing everything."

"So why did the mayor come to you?"

I looked from him to Paula and back again.

"Look, you're both still sort of new to Florida . . ." I began.

"Oh, for Christ's sake, here we go again with old-timer's disease,"

Wilson groused. He and Paula were products of the chain mentality that's taken over American newspapers in general and the *Tribune* in particular. The rotating editors come to town with dazzling plans, use the local readers for applause meters, then move on to the next market, just like TV newscasters lusting for the Big Apple.

I gave my civic lesson anyway. "Julio Montiega is an unapologetic social liberal in what was a blue-collar town, and if the U.S. attorney is after him, there's an excellent chance it's not because he's corrupt — it's because he's in the wrong party."

"If the bribe was a setup, Treaster won't have much of a case," Paula said. Then her eyes opened just a bit.

"Right," I agreed. "So what?"

"I still don't see why the mayor came to you," Wilson interjected.

"He's in an agony of indecision. What if Cesar is just addled? He is in his late sixties. If the mayor goes to anybody with this and Cesar was acting on his own, Cesar's down the tubes. Julio's too loyal to risk destroying a *compañero* on the possibility of a setup. He wants me to check it out."

Wilson cocked an eyebrow. "It's also possible he's using you to cover his ass and is into this zoning mess up to his elbows."

"I'll get the story wherever it leads. But Julio says he doesn't know what's going on in zoning."

"He says . . ." Wilson's tone was mocking, but the light in his eyes told me this story was beginning to look like a horse he wanted to see on the track. "What would make Cesar risk everything on rezoning a damn cigar factory, anyway?"

"Knowing Cesar, he probably acted impulsively when he got a glimpse of the main chance."

"Little old for that, isn't he?" The *Trib*'s managing editor had the smugness of a man to whom success came easy and early. But he lusted for more and I knew it.

"Yeah," I said, "sometimes old codgers make out — like Fred Nettleman."

Wilson's straight brows came together like arrows. Last year when the *Trib* was in the market for a new publisher, Wilson had hungered for the job, but Nettleman, a hometown boy who'd worked his way up the ladder, was sent back from corporate headquarters to take over the paper, even though he wasn't a journalist, only a bean counter. Immediately he'd proved suspicious of all of us in the newsroom, to the point of paranoia.

"Nettleman didn't make out," Wilson rumbled. "He kissed ass. Now tell me what Cesar's got in mind for El Principe?"

"Make a mall out of it. One of those artsy places tourists like. I haven't seen his plans, but it could be the best thing that's happened to Alverez District in a hundred years."

Wilson came out of his seat and slammed his fist on his desk. "God, I'd love to put the screws to the *Times* on this. We've got to get Cesar to talk."

"Hopefully we'll be the first," I said cautiously.

Wilson started like a bucket of ice water had been poured over his head. His square jaw almost quivered. "Christ! Don't tell me Egan's onto this business with the mayor?"

Paula echoed his alarm. "Did she see him this morning?"

"She didn't talk to him," I said.

"What you ought to do, Palmer, is bang that Egan cockeyed," Wilson blurted, "so she won't be good for anything except covering cats caught in trees and Kiwanis conventions."

"Now, by God —" I began, rising.

"I withdraw that." Wilson gestured wildly as I loomed over him. "It was a tactless fuckin' thing to say."

I forced myself back into my seat.

"Especially to somebody who's got both the body and brains of King Kong," Wilson muttered. He loved to live on the edge.

Paula put her face between Wilson and me.

"Can I count on a story on El Principe for tomorrow?"

"I'll try," I managed.

"While you're at it, find this guy." Wilson tapped the photo of Nick Darvin in the *Times*. "If he's alive and has something to say, I want him saying it to us first."

Paula left with me. Out of earshot of Wilson's office she said, "I'm glad you're on this, Palmer. I know you'll get it right. I just hope you'll get it first."

Squirreled away in a cubicle in the *Trib* library I read all we had on zoning. Most of the recent clips on the swamp story were A.J.'s. Nowhere did I find a mention of Cesar's request for a zoning variance, even though I knew from Julio that the city council had delayed it twice for studies. I was getting a bit more optimistic. With any luck I'd find out what the mayor's old friend was up to before A.J. realized he was a player. I checked my watch. It was after eleven. Cesar's restaurant would be open. I slipped out the library door and, bypassing the newsroom, took the back steps three at a time.

"Hey, Smitty, what's happening?" I greeted the *Trib* guard at his station of TV monitors by the back door.

"I was hoping you'd tell me," he said.

"What do you mean?"

"Two guys came running—" He stopped as a *Trib* photo van rocketed through the loading dock tunnel, then Randy Holliman, the stocky young reporter who backs me on the police beat, steamed by in his rattletrap Olds with an unsecured exhaust pipe that waved like a cat's tail. He squealed out onto the street.

Smitty wrote furiously on a pad. "Mr. Nettleman will have their hides for that."

I took off for my Jeep at a dead run.

The radio scanner crackled with the reason for all the haste. I caught a glimpse of Smitty's astonished face as I roared away after the others.

$\triangledown$

4

AT THE COURTHOUSE THE Saturday matinee produced by the Feds was already under way. Pulling up to the curb was the marshal's van, the same one that had passed me a couple of times while I hunted for a place to park. Obviously it was driven around long enough for all the TV cameras to be set up. There was quite a crowd. Treaster's office must have alerted every reporter in the Bay area, except me, about the impending arrest.

When Julio Montiega emerged from the van, photographers elbowed each other for full-length shots showing the chains. Each step the mayor took up the long walk to the side door of the federal courthouse diminished his reputation. The image of that shivering, gaunt figure in handcuffs linked to a chain around his waist was devastating. It would not soon be forgotten by the millions who were seeing it, thanks to the TV satellite links that enmesh Florida like spider webs. Even if Treaster's charges came to nothing, Montiega's long-cherished hope to run for governor was destroyed.

I grimaced when he hesitated on the steps and raised his manacled hands to screen his eyes from the bright lights. It looked as if he were trying to cover up, to hide his shame. I wanted to call to him not to do that, to stand straight and tall and face the cameras head on, but of course I didn't.

Shouts filled the air as reporters vied for his attention.

"Were you in this alone?"

"Have they offered you a deal?"

"Are you going to resign?"

The mayor lowered his hands and blinked. His mouth opened, but no words came out. Randy Holliman, who had been in such a hurry to get here, was furiously taking notes. Beside him A.J. stood quietly, her eyes darting around the scene as if she were looking for someone.

"Mayor! Mayor!" The voice of one TV reporter carried over the throng holding up mikes. "Any words for the voters?"

His lips trembling, Julio tried to smile. "Tell them I am innocent. To have faith in me."

A few laughs broke out.

"Merry Christmas, Mayor," a mocking voice called.

The *alcalde*'s dark, haunted eyes swept the crowd, found me, and seared my soul like lasers. After an eternity one of the Feds took his arm and pushed Julio through the door. All the other agents disappeared inside after him, except for Ed Priestly, a buzzard-nosed FBI agent from the Hoover era whose career Treaster had salvaged. As if he couldn't remember seven words strung together, Priestly fumbled in all his pockets for a piece of paper and at last announced there would be a briefing at three. Not willing to wait, pushy reporters pumped him for information.

I turned away and found myself face to face with Cy Betz, the former strike force prosecutor who was demoted when Treaster returned to Marlinsport.

"The stink of that deal keep you back here?" I asked him.

Cy rocked toe to heel, toe to heel, and sucked on a scorched briar held in strong teeth. His thin brown hair tossed in the growing breeze. "Does the reek come from the government or the press, Palmer?"

"It's symbiotic," I admitted. "But putting Julio in irons is a travesty. Without saying a single word Treaster's destroying a reputation built over fifty years. The *alcalde* will go in the side door in chains and out the front on his own recognizance."

"Surely you're not offended by a little showboat justice," he said. "You know we always use the cuffs. Most reporters love it."

I hunched my shoulders against the cold. "Is Cesar Armonia involved in this?"

Cy blew the rich aroma of Bond Street tobacco my way. "Could be."

"What about Nick Darvin?"

"We're looking for him."

"That's a piece of news. I thought maybe you had him." I pondered a moment. "Would anyone profit from harming him?"

"That's a good question, Palmer. I could only guess. Why don't you ask Miss Egan at the *Times*. Maybe she knows."

"Very funny. At least you can tell me if Treaster has anything real against the mayor."

Cy squinted against the sun and the Bond Street. "Why else would we be here?"

"It occurred to me the great prosecutor might be playing politics."

"With RICO?"

"Right."

Cy stared at me without speaking. We both knew that the Racketeer

Influenced and Corrupt Organization law was a stinker. It had been perverted from a federal anticrime tool to a political weapon and a means of seizing people's property by ignoring the Bill of Rights.

"I'm not going to watch the poor son of a bitch come out for another hassling." I started away. "See you later."

"How much later?"

I turned around. The pipe bowl trailed smoke into the wind, and Cy's ash-gray eyes had a veiled look I'd seen a hundred times before on as many different faces.

"Whenever you say. Wherever."

"I hear blue crabs are taking anything you'll give 'em down at Bayles Point. I'm gonna catch the nine o'clock tide tonight." His thin eyebrows were a question mark.

"I could eat a washtub of crabs," I said.

As I left, Cy stood there, a distant, lean figure staring bemusedly at the maelstrom of journalists with no one to interview but each other and the dour-faced Priestly, Treaster's junkyard dog.

▽

5

THIS WAS NO LONGER a typical *Trib* Saturday of long coffee breaks and desultory conversation. The atmosphere bristled. As I made my way to the city desk I passed a political reporter on the phone demanding that a press aide in Tallahassee contact the governor, who was off somewhere for the weekend. Others were calling city council members for comments, as well as party bosses, Julio's family, his business associates, and everyone who'd ever run against him.

"Palmer!" Paula spotted me across the sea of desks. "I need you to write the main story tonight."

I motioned her away from the crowd and into a small conference room.

"Wilson's upstairs, pushing for extra pages in the A section," she said, edging a hip onto the corner of a table. Her red hair was puffed in straggly clouds. "Treaster didn't waste any time, did he?"

"No." I sat down. It's one way to minimize my size when talking to a woman. Some might say that's sexist. I call it polite. "Listen. You ought to get someone else to do the story. I have a conflict."

"What's that?" Her voice was doubtful. She'd already made up her mind how to handle this story.

"Somebody in Treaster's office wants to talk."

"Great god almighty, Palmer, you've already got a snitch? I never saw anybody have stuff fall in his lap the way you do."

The new-era itinerant journalists, even the good ones like Paula, don't understand that two decades on the same beat in the same town just might lead to a few dependable sources. I shrugged off her undisguised amazement at my dumb luck.

"Wilson's expecting you to handle the story," she said. "He's already seething big-time over not getting to break it, and by the time he gets through in Nettleman's office his mood will be – oh,well, it can't be helped."

She glanced through the glass wall into the newsroom, her eyes darting from desk to desk. Like Paula, I also began to think of reasons why first one and then another of the reporters out there wouldn't do.

"Get Moses for me," she called at last to an assistant.

It was a good choice. Moses Johnson, the *Trib*'s fretful intellectual, had the skills in spades to do the rewrite job. Like me, he was one of the few old hands still around since the chain took over the *Trib*. Once the city editor, Moses was over fifty and too deferential to fit into Wilson's belligerent style of management. Last fall he was eased back onto the streets, and Paula moved up.

"He'll be better than me anyway," I said.

She cocked an eye. "The flow will be smoother, but I'd rather have a hard edge on it. Can you stick around long enough to put background in the system, plus *A* matter for a profile of the mayor?"

"Sure, I can do that."

At my desk I tried Cesar's restaurant, but he wasn't taking any calls. I can't say I blamed him. Whatever his motivation, he'd just ruined the career of an old friend who was doing his best to help him. I began to feed the terminal.

Twenty minutes later Paula leaned over my shoulder. "Wanna see the art?"

She dropped a stack of eight-by-ten glossies before me. There in stark black and white was Montiega in chains.

"You gonna crop it from the bottom so the cuffs don't show?" I asked.

"Not a chance. This is what happened. This is what we show."

"Treaster's playing us like a cheap organ," I growled. "You'd think he captured John Dillinger."

"If Montiega can't take the heat . . ."

"Don't give me that, Paula."

"We don't make the rules."

"Oh, yes, we do."

"Only the rule that says, 'If the mayor gets indicted, lead the paper with it and use big type.' "

She had a gleam in her eye that made me smile in spite of my mood. Although we differed on how to cover Treaster's staged performance, I couldn't help but like her enthusiasm.

"Paula, I'm telling you something's not right. Ken Treaster's smart, and he's devious, but he's not so smart he could build a real case against a man like Julio Montiega that quickly. Not if Cesar's all he had."

"Treaster's been stumbling around city hall for months."

"Stumbling's right. And getting nowhere. Suddenly, bam, he's got the mayor? I don't buy it."

Her green eyes flashed merrily. "Chase your hunches, Palmer.

22

That's fine. But bring me facts." She tapped a polished fingernail on the mayor's picture. "That's a fact."

When I finished writing I tried the restaurant again. Cesar's oldest son, Don, told me his father had stormed out but should return soon because the lunch crowd was building. I said I'd call back and hung up, realizing I was getting hungry myself.

It's only seven minutes from the *Tribune* to my place on the island, if the bridge isn't up. As I zipped down Bay Boulevard, by Marlinsport's stately old family homes, I could see it was in place. On the far side of the channel sailboats and cabin cruisers berthed under tall new condominiums were pitching hard in the choppy swells.

Long before I reached home I could see A.J.'s arched Spanish windows through the wind-whipped palms. Her tiny apartment was perched at the top of my pink castle like the adobe of a cliff-dwelling Indian. Hoping she was there, I chugged into the big brick circle out front and parked beside the gnarled mosaic fountain.

A couple of tenants greeted me as I sped through the fern-lined reception area and up two flights of ornate wooden stairs. With the grace of a Clydesdale on a trapeze I swung into the narrow passageway that went up to the attic, and A.J.'s. My big feet thundered so on the narrow steps, I wasn't surprised that her door opened before I could knock.

She was tucking a blouse into a pleated ivory skirt. A four-in-hand tie and burgundy blazer were draped over a chair. Her heels were under it.

"Montiega looked awful," she said, closing the door behind me. "I wonder if he's guilty."

"I'd like to see the evidence," I said. She had to be curious about the mayor's visit to me earlier but would never say anything about it.

Water was boiling on the little stove in the alcove across the room. The door to her bedroom was open and I caught a glimpse of downtown and the bay through the oversize windows. A.J.'s compensation for cramped quarters and a long climb was the most spectacular view in Marlinsport.

"Getting ready for Treaster's press conference?" I asked.

"Yeah. He called me himself to be sure I was coming."

"Probably figures he owes you because of your zoning investigation."

"What Treaster thinks he owes females of the press is not a news story."

My eyebrows shot up as I watched her slip on her heels.

"Oh, he's smooth," she said. "No hands. No lewd propositions. Mainly smug self-assurance."

I laughed uncomfortably. "He's had that a long time."

A.J. smiled, but there was tension in her straight, thin lips. "I shouldn't have said anything. It's my problem. Or was. For the last few weeks he's shifted attention to my intern."

As she talked, A.J. spooned instant coffee into two cups, dosed mine with sugar, and brought both over. Tucked in a wicker chair, she nervously swung one leg as she sipped her coffee.

"I'll be working late," she said. "Montiega's arrest may be a disaster for him, but it's a break for me." I opened my mouth, but she hurried on. "Up until now there's been no smoking gun. Just some odd zoning decisions. The Naturalist Club is incensed about those eagle nesting grounds destroyed in Balders Swamp. It was their calls that hooked me into this story in the first place."

"A.J."

"I found out the original zoning change was turned down. Once. Twice. Then zap! Marlinsport loves the deal."

"A.J."

"Here the mayor get's arrested, and all this time I thought it was the Alliance. I wonder if he's in —"

"A.J.," I said louder.

She glanced at me, waiting.

"I'm on the story."

There was an audible intake of air. "What?"

"I'm investigating these zoning deals."

Those violet eyes were full of hurt, but her voice was indignant. "Why? I've been working this story for months!"

"I know."

"I was perfectly happy on the police beat, Palmer, but I got off it so we could avoid this kind of thing." As her voice rose I found myself slouching lower in my chair.

Guilt made me want to forget what I'd heard, but the word "Alliance" kept repeating itself in my brain.

"It's this business with the mayor, A.J. I can't let it go."

"You should've told me that right off."

"I tried."

"Damn it, Palmer. Everything was going so well. For a change we weren't tiptoeing on eggs around each other."

"I'm sorry, A.J."

The narrowing of her eyes and further compression of her lips suggested I'd be a whole lot sorrier as soon as she could manage it. The only sound in the room was the steady tick of A.J.'s little hand-painted cuckoo clock.

"How about grabbing some lunch?" I suggested. "We won't talk shop."

"No, thanks. Finish your coffee." Her voice was even, controlled.

"Throwing me out, hunh?"

"You got it."

I plodded down the stairs and, after failing again to reach Cesar, fixed a banana sandwich. While I ate, I looked up Nick Darvin in the phone book. His address amazed me. Balders Edge Drive. I'd never been out to the new development, but I knew from the Sunday ads in the *Trib* that prices there for single family homes began in the six figures. Some sleeping quarters for a zoning clerk, who, from what I heard, was already spending half his salary in Marlinsport's best restaurants. His appetite and his girth were prodigious. I tried his number. A machine told me he was on vacation. So why did A.J. and the U.S. attorney's office figure he was missing, I wondered as I hung up.

Curly stopped over around one o'clock with the Austin's chrome in the back of his pickup. Stacking it carefully in the workshop I considered getting started on the reassembly job before going to Treaster's press conference. But with the *alcalde*'s march of shame on my mind, and A.J.'s anguish, my heart wasn't in it.

On my way to the Federal Building I stopped by Cesar's place in Alverez District. His three sons were much in evidence, but Cesar still wasn't back. Don walked with me outside.

"Last week Papa was raving against the *alcalde*. But this morning, he turned deathly pale after seeing him arrested on TV. He made a telephone call and left. Probably walking it off somewhere."

This confused me. "Why's that?" I asked. "I figured he'd be glad to see Julio in chains."

"Who can figure these old guys, Palmer? Even dressed in their Sunday white suits they'll jump in a mud hole to save an enemy's mule."

I smiled. "Do you have any idea why your father thought the mayor was holding up his zoning?"

"Papa had a sudden need for fifty thousand dollars cash."

"You're telling me Julio Montiega asked your father for that kind of money?"

"That's what I'm telling you. We could lose this place because of him. And our family home. Can you believe it? My father's oldest friend. But it's a new day. I hope the U.S. attorney puts him away for a hundred years, and you can quote me on that."

"Have you talked to Treaster?"

"No . . . why?"

"I just thought he might know where your father is."

"Not likely, but it's worth a try."

I checked my watch. "I've gotta go. Treaster's press conference about all this starts in a few minutes. If I catch up with your dad on my own, I'll pass the word that you'd like to hear from him."

Don wiped his hand on his apron, then extended it to me.

"You tell him if he's not here in an hour I'm gonna make the *empañadas* myself."

$\triangledown$

6

THE GRAY FACE OF Ed Priestly contained a bare touch of color, evidence of the satisfaction he felt at being in charge, however briefly, of a room full of journalists. He wore his FBI identification on his suit jacket, but it didn't help. Nobody paid him any attention as he tried to jockey us to the back of the Federal Building conference room. The TV camera guys in their ragged pants and baggy shirts prowled around, putting duct tape on the cables they'd strung under our feet. At last Priestly shouted for us to stay behind a yellow line painted across the floor.

"You people check those lights and mikes now," he said grittily. "While the United States attorney is speaking there'll be no turning on or off of equipment, no smoking, and no shouted questions."

"Kiss off, *tonto*," an older reporter from the Spanish weekly grumbled. "He's not the president, for god's sake."

"No follow-up," Priestly shouted back.

"Go piss up a rope," somebody called from amid the pack.

"Who said that?" Priestly's face turned foxy. "If you're not a coward, step up here and say that to my face."

His only answer was an uproar of derision. The man's excessive loyalty to Treaster was already well-known, if not well appreciated. Most reporters thought it was ludicrous. But to my certain knowledge he was not the first to venerate Kincaid Treaster. There had been my best friend, Raymond. As we waited my mind went back to the first time I met Treaster. I was a scrawny, awkward boy, tall enough to play with the Celtics but so skinny a well-tossed basketball could move me backward a step. They called me Spider in those days. I belonged to a small band of sorts that gathered before dawn at Station 500 in Alverez District, a drop-off point for the *Trib*'s circulation department. My buddies and I delivered papers, but that was only an excuse to get away from home and roam the old brick streets of Marlinsport's Latin section.

Early on, we discovered that nights lit by neon hold many secrets. There was a thrill in being part of it, scaling forgotten fire escapes above sleazy bars, running across rooftops in the dark, jumping gaps where a misstep meant death. I will always remember the sense of power that came with each leap but no one was as daring as Raymond Chancey. I've seen him walk a four-inch ledge at the top of a tall building for the hell of it. Gaunt like me, but shorter, Raymond radiated nervous energy. His fingernails were always chewed down to ragged lines that made me cringe no matter how quickly I looked away.

"You'll like Ken Treaster," Raymond said the morning we were waiting for him to show up at the *Trib* station to see about his own newspaper route. "He's smart. He even reads Aristotle."

"Aristotle?" I'm afraid the word had a nasty roll to it getting out of my mouth.

"Yeah," Raymond said. "I saw the book in his room." Then he laughed in that strange way of his. "Ken had to tell me who Aristotle was. How dumb can you get?"

"You're not dumb," Deanna Weldon, the only female in our little melange, said. "Who cares about some dipshit Greek?"

Raymond blushed, even though swearing was Deanna's usual way. She cussed to make us forget she was a girl in a boy's world of paper routes, although all that did somehow was accent it.

When Treaster finally arrived Deanna was ready for him.

"Well, I'll be damned. So this is what an honest-to-God scholar looks like." She checked him over good. "Shi-i-it. You coulda fooled me."

Color spread all the way up Treaster's thick neck to his short blond hair. I guess if Deanna had been a boy he would have slugged her. It was the only joke I ever heard anyone make at his expense.

A couple of years ahead of us in school, Treaster had the air of sophistication suitable for a boy from Charleston moved down to Marlinsport. His father was some sort of a functionary with a fruit importer, although Treaster acted as if he were president of the Cunard Line.

"Palmer Kingston," he repeated when Raymond introduced me. "That's a princely name for a guy with bird legs poking out of his pants." It didn't matter much to me when he laughed, since my old jeans did have holes in them, but when Raymond laughed, too, that was different.

My dislike for Treaster began at that moment, but Raymond practically fell in love with him. Not queer, as we called it in those days, but close enough. Hero worship was what it was. Extra tall and strong, with flaxen hair, Treaster was right for the role. He looked like a tackle in pads. But he wasn't in pads. Treaster mocked Raymond as much as he did the rest of us, but my old friend was self-demeaning enough to think he was getting no more than he deserved. It made me so mad I thought about giving up my paper route and getting out of the gang altogether. It was Betsy who convinced me not to, even though running across rooftops had no appeal to her. She spent her evenings studying. I dropped by her house as often as her father would let me. That bright, resourceful girl was already the strongest influence in my life. She was the one who told me Raymond needed me for a friend even if he didn't know it. As for Treaster, I eventually came to tolerate him, but just barely.

In spite of the heat of the TV lights my skin prickled as I remembered a fierce rainstorm and the miserable night we crouched in neon shadows on the roof of the Casino—Treaster, Raymond, Deanna, and me. God, what a night . . .

"Okay, you guys, quiet down. He's coming!"

Priestly edged back as Kincaid Treaster stalked heavily into the room and made straight for the array of microphones at the lectern.

"You were told to stay behind that line," he said to a TV reporter—one of the stars in our local constellation of anchor people. Treaster's voice had resonance, but more than that it had the innate authority that came from the powerful personality behind it. Here was a man who didn't equivocate. The TV star jumped back to his place.

"A sealed indictment issued by the federal grand jury sitting in Marlinsport was served today by U.S. marshals on Mayor Julio J. Montiega for extortion. This crime is covered under RICO, the federal racketeering conspiracy statutes."

Looking at Treaster dispassionately, I had to admit that although his waist sagged a bit, there was an abundance of muscle in there. His wide-footed stance gave evidence of his bull-like determination. Changing this man's mind would be like trying to push a steam locomotive on its side with your hand. His spiky blond hair hadn't changed much in twenty years. It was longer than an old-fashioned crewcut but reminiscent of one. The dark blue pinstripe suit he wore combined with the white broadcloth shirt and red-patterned tie to give him an assertively patriotic air.

"I suppose I need to say—although as members of the press you should know—that because it is before the court I will not comment further on Montiega's indictment." His sonorous voice, although not loud, filled the room. It came to me that many a tinny-voiced lawyer over the years had probably gone crashing to defeat against Treaster on little more than the effect of that voice on a jury.

He looked slowly around the room, as though he wanted each of us to know he was recording our presence. When he reached me he paused. But there was no raised eyebrow. No greeting. His icy blue eyes went on in their visual pat-down.

A young woman seated beside A.J. raised her hand tentatively to ask a question, and A.J. tried as discreetly as possible to talk her out of it.

"Well?" Treaster's voice cut through A.J.'s hushed protest but without the impatience I'd expected.

The college-age blond got nervously to her feet. Tall, she wore a business suit and little makeup. Wide blue eyes looked at the big U.S. attorney.

"Isn't it a fact, Mr. Treaster," she began in a voice as sweet as a kitten's purr, "I mean, you wouldn't be announcing this and arresting the mayor unless you had a really good case?"

The groan in the room was heartfelt. Even the newest TV reporter knew not to ask questions like that.

"Get the bat and gloves," somebody mumbled, "we're playing softball."

"I mean," the young woman insisted, "you're doing a job that has to be done."

Treaster could handle anything. He put a big smile on his slightly reddened face and said, "I'd like to go on the record as giving an unqualified yes to that question."

There was a wave of nervous laughter through the room, except for A.J. She was redder than Treaster.

"And I owe it to the public to add one thing more . . . ," Treaster said louder. "We're going to clean up Marlinsport — give good government a chance here. It's a tough job and not made any easier by reporters who would rather hide behind the First Amendment than join the effort to root out this evil."

"What the hell does that mean?" Randy yelled. Good old Randy.

"We all know who's been playing supermarket tabloid with titillating tales from 'anonymous sources,' " Treaster responded, staring icily at A.J. "Information about criminal activity ought to be shared with those who can *do* something about it."

A.J. sprang up. There was enough lightning coming from her eyes to split a tree, and I could see her thin fingers trembling with anger.

"What kind of a crack is that?" she demanded. "We're not paid to do your job!"

Treaster grinned. "Did I mention any names?" he asked, adding quickly, "But make no mistake. You and every other news person here have the same obligations as any citizen to report wrongdoing to the proper authorities."

"Now just a minute," A.J. shouted above the uproar.

Treaster stared at her. "You have my statement."

He turned and left, outsmarting us all. His views were on film, his accusations were made, and the reporters were left with nobody to interview but each other.

"You may turn off your lights," Priestly said mockingly.

We were escorted out of the Federal Building.

On the sidewalk the reporter from the Spanish weekly congratulated A.J. for doing what he implied he'd done many times before, standing up to the Feds. It was all gas. The old fraud dealt in gossip and smears. He didn't know news from nasturtiums.

"You be careful," he warned. "If you don't give him what he wants that man's tough enough to put you in jail for obstructing justice."

"If Treaster thinks I'll make his case for him, he's got a lot to learn about me." A.J.'s eyes darted my way ever so briefly, then returned to the other newsman. "And I won't be chased off."

I let her go without a word. With her intern trailing, she walked toward her old VW Bug. As much as I wanted to there was nothing I could say to help A.J. It was her editor and probably the *Times*'s lawyers she wanted to talk to now. And I had an old pal to call—someone who might know more than Treaster did about what was going on at city hall . . . maybe even more than A.J.

$\triangledown$

7

THE TOMBOY SHARPNESS AND the cocky laugh that I once knew were gone.

"What are you doing here?" Deanna Chancey, holding her front door only half open, said in a throaty voice. "This is a long way from that island mansion of yours."

"Hi, Deanna. Would you believe I got a craving for one of those pickle and peanut butter sandwiches you used to make?"

"Do better than that, Palmer, or I'm closing the door."

"Okay. I need to talk to you. For some advice."

"I'm not in real estate anymore."

"I know where you're working."

"I see. That's why you've come."

" 'Fraid so."

"Why don't you see me there Monday?"

It was sort of a rude thing to say but no ruder than me showing up on her doorstep after years of silence between us.

"I'd like a chance to talk away from city hall's rumor mongers."

"City hall?" There was an odd intake of breath, then a long pause as she processed the significance of something that escaped me. "Well, I suppose we can talk now but you'll have to wait while I get dressed."

The door closed. I paced the small front porch. I'd always liked the bungalow's solid brass side lamps and the thick glass door panels of etched blossoms. Paint was fresh and crisp on the clapboard siding but the old wooden glider was still in place. In my youth I'd spent many an hour on it. That was when Raymond's parents were still alive, and long before he married Deanna. Because his home was only a half block from the bay and within walking distance of downtown we'd used it as a congregating point. A shady, quiet workingman's neighborhood, the small homes now sold for twenty times their cost to newcomers who wanted to be close to the water. The slats in the glider groaned as I sat down. While I pushed back and forth, I wondered if Treaster had tried to see Raymond or Deanna since he came back to town. Memories stirred once more of that stormy night the four of us first went out on a ramble together. We'd waited for Treaster right here.

* * *

Thunder was already rolling across the dark sky when we reached Alverez District. Along one side of Ida Street three-globed streetlamps cast spheres of light on the tiled facades and rows of iron-rail balconies. Six stories up, a rainbow of colors flashed from a roulette wheel. Beside it blazed "Casino." Down the block ballroom dancers, glimmering in blue neon, protruded into the night sky. The Rhumba Academy occupied a walk-up, and sometimes we would watch classes across the street — from the rooftop of El Principe. Even in those days the sprawling factory was deserted and gloomy. Tiers of small windows laced its flat brick face like the eyes of a mythological ogre. In the huge clock tower by the boarded-up entrance unmoving hands read three fifteen. Every so often, like the idiot teenagers that we were, we'd shinny up and change the time. But not that night. Because of the approaching storm Raymond led us straight to the narrow passage beside the Casino. When he reached a metal ladder mounted in the wall he motioned us to hurry and scurried up. Treaster gaped at the steel rods stretching more than a hundred feet, then laughed and started after Raymond. Deanne and I followed. At a ledge five levels above the street we dashed for a catwalk angling to the base of the club's blinking sign. A second ladder ran beside it to the roof. As I grabbed the pencil-thin rungs hand over hand behind Deanna, wind gusts swiped at me. Swaying, I brushed the cracking and buzzing neon. Its warm power vibrated against my arm.

Above the fleur de lis at the top of the sign I eased over the parapet onto a narrow flat roof by the Casino's courtyard. More rumbling from the sky was accompanied by cold drops of rain. As always I scanned the blackness for Raymond. That boy had a ghostly talent for disappearing in a blink. It was as though the very streets and buildings had secret passages only for him. But he was still on the roof. While Ken and Deanna watched he poked a nail into the lock on a dilapidated shed. I swear the little burglar could make a pry bar out of a cat's whisker. Within seconds the door swung open.

Inside we huddled beside the air conditioning system and peered out through the cracks in the wall. Across the courtyard some serious card playing was under way in the Casino's private room. The mobster who was in high school with the *alcalde* a generation earlier, Joseph Contreras, "Joe Sparkles," was dealing to a pair of well-dressed hoodlums and a couple of local politicians. Even at our tender ages we all knew what that was about. Cigar smoke floated toward the green

33

hanging lamps. Three women in shiny dresses served drinks.

"That room's got more tits than a holstein convention."

Raymond and I both started at Treaster's words. We'd always been a bit self-conscious about dirt road talk around Deanna. But she laughed and said, "Those broads are all wires and stuffing," and Raymond joined in like he'd just seen the joke.

Treaster glanced boldly at Deanna's scant chest. " 'Cause you don't have it doesn't mean nobody's got it."

"For Christ's sake, shut up," I said.

Treaster grumbled and turned back to ogle the women below.

The storm swept in with a fury. Sprays lashed us through the cracks, but we could still see the slow drama of cards. One of the women circled the room and, pausing at the window, seemed to peer right at us. My heart pounded.

"The lightning's getting close," I murmured. "Let's get out of here."

"Screw the lightning," Treaster said.

"Sit tight," Raymond told me. "It's moving over fast."

The space we were crouched in smelled of lubricants and rubber belts. Huge palmetto bugs, undisturbed by either the storm or us, crawled along every crevice. When one, its antennae testing the air, wandered over to explore my shoe, the thought of it disappearing up my pants leg made me shiver.

"To hell with this," I said.

When I stepped into the rain dancing on the roof, Treaster angrily called me a son of a bitch for spoiling his fun and the woman at the window pointed my way. The card players scrambled toward her, and I thought I saw a gun in the split second before I started down. Running footsteps told me the others were in headlong flight behind me. We clambered down the ladder, slick with rain and clattering loosely in the brick wall. As I crossed the lower roof at a dead run Raymond passed me.

One by one we dropped onto the wood and plaster cover over the sidewalks of the promenade. From there it was a short jump to the street. Raymond led at a trot, using every shadow and angle so that it was hard to keep him in sight.

"Ken says he's gonna brain you," he called over his shoulder. Then, quietly, as though he hated to say it but loyalty to his new idol required it, "You've got it coming."

He dodged up a sloped cellar door at El Principe, then dived through a broken window. Treaster's hand was on my shoulder as I followed.

"You motherfucker," he shouted and slammed his knuckles into the back of my skull. When I spun toward him another blow landed on the hinge of my jaw. I collapsed.

When my eyes opened Raymond was over me. Care and reproach were on his face. "You okay?"

Groggily I glanced around. The brick room was like a gigantic red cell. Light from the Casino's sign flickered through dirty windows and danced across an image on the back wall. I blinked. While I was out on the floor Raymond had sketched a big cartoon on the bricks. He was always swiping chalk at school and drawing pictures everywhere. In this one Treaster was ogling Joe Sparkles's girl. Her chest filled up most of the red wall. It was kind of obscene, but funny.

"If my head didn't hurt so bad I'd think I was in Hell. And there's the devil."

"Don't say that, Palmer. He's my friend."

"Where's Deanna?"

"She and Ken went home to dry out before the *Trib*'s truck comes. The rain's stopped." He returned the chalk sticks to his pocket. "We'd better get to the station."

I rubbed my head. "Your big lousy friend sucker-punched me."

"Don't start putting off on Ken. He got mad 'cause you were dumb. You coulda got us all killed."

"The guy's twice my size. Why'd he hit me from behind?"

"You're the one that messed up, Palmer. There's no changing that."

"Yeah. I messed up his chance to drool over Joe Sparkles's girl-friend. What a moron!"

"Come off it, Palmer. Ken's smart. Smarter than you and me put together."

"His brain's in his dick."

Raymond looked mad. He didn't get mad with me very often.

"He's not the one who screwed everything up."

I locked eyes with him. "If you feel that way how come you didn't go on? Why'd you stay with me?"

He squirmed uncomfortably. "Somebody had to. A rat might have eaten your face."

The door to Raymond's house reopened. "Sorry to take so long. Come on in and I'll fix you a cup of coffee. But no peanut butter sandwiches. I can't stand the stuff anymore."

35

Deanna had slipped into a pair of jeans and a safari shirt. Maybe there was a little tomboy left in her after all. She was tanned and angular with short dark hair, a long jaw line, and distant gray eyes. She wore no lipstick. Time and a child had filled her out in a nice way, and she carried her height well. The biggest change since her teen years was not her figure, nor her voice, but the frowning sadness of her mouth. It drooped as though someone had just disappointed her greatly.

She led me into the living room and pointed to a snow-white sofa—one of those stuffed things marketed not for comfort but for its lines. She chose to sit on a footstool across a marble table from me. On a shelf behind her were two framed snapshots, a faded one of Raymond in full-dress Marine uniform and the other of the two of them at sixteen or so at the Chanceys's cabin on the headwaters of the Teach River. Next to the pictures was a little clay Indian figure that Raymond called the God of the Wilderness. It, and the snapshots, seemed out of place in the modish room.

"How's little Lynn?" I asked, feeling a bit out of place myself.

"She's not little anymore, Palmer. What can I do for you?"

I suppose her coldness was to be expected, but it still bothered me.

"I'm trying to get a handle on Nick Darvin. You think something's happened to him?" I didn't mention Montiega's arrest. My guess was she didn't know about it yet and there was no sense risking our getting sidetracked.

"All I can tell you is Nick was always talking about going on a trip. Maybe he finally went. I don't know. We may have worked in the same office but we were hardly buddies."

"But there are old zoning documents missing?"

"So I hear. Maybe it's coincidental. They could have been misplaced a long time ago. As far a I know no one's looked into those closed files for years—before that *Times* reporter." She smiled. "Looks like I'm not much help."

"Were you surprised by her zoning stories?" I asked as nonchalantly as possible.

"Surprised? No. Impressed, maybe. I didn't think there were any reporters in Marlinsport smart enough to tackle it."

I ignored the inference. "So you think she's on target?"

Deanna laughed. "Even with this frigid weather I imagine she's got some folks in town sweating."

I took a chance and used the name A.J. had let slip. "You mean like the Alliance?"

It was as though I'd ground out a cigarette on Deanna's white sofa. She sprang to her feet.

"What makes you think I know anything about them?" she demanded.

I gazed up at her. "You're in zoning."

"Don't lie to me, Palmer. I could lose my job. Who's been talking to you about me and the Alliance?"

Her words had trajectory like artillery rounds.

"No one. Look, all I'm trying to do is find a place to start so I won't have to bother you at city hall next week."

She cocked her head. "If you want to see me next week, it won't be at city hall. The U.S. attorney's office requisitioned me and a clerk weeks ago. We're interpreting city codes and plat books for Ken, and if he finds out you're here, I'll be in big trouble."

"Why?"

"I swore that you and I haven't talked in years and that I wouldn't see you."

"Treaster made you swear that?"

She smiled that sad smile. "Is it so amazing that he doesn't trust you?"

"Maybe not . . . What zoning cases is he investigating?"

"Un-unh, Palmer."

"Come on, Deanna. I know about Cesar Armonia."

"Cesar? You know what about Cesar?"

"That Treaster's checking out his zoning problems."

Her eyebrows arched slightly, then she shrugged. "Look, Palmer, I'm not discussing what's going on in Treaster's office with you. So forget it."

"Okay. But won't you at least tell me which city councilmen are in the Alliance?"

"You don't know who they are?" She was incredulous. "You're here on a fishing trip?"

"I told you I needed help."

"Good God." She stared at me as though she wasn't sure if I was cagey, or just stupid.

I decided to plunge ahead anyway. "I can't seriously believe Rebecca Reed would be part of any conspiracy to take bribes. That old lady does come down on the unpopular side of some controversial issues, but that's probably personality."

When there was no response I went on. "And it doesn't seem likely that a bunch of Crackers would let a black college professor in on a deal like this, so I can eliminate Rupert Sandstrom. That leaves Jerry Stack, Link Garland, and Max Jones."

"You said that, I didn't."

"But those three don't always support the same projects. How could they be in a conspiracy when their votes don't correlate?"

Her expression grew angry and then softened with a shade of disappointment around the edges. "That's the puzzle, isn't it?"

"I could use that cup of coffee now, Deanna."

I followed her into the kitchen. She poured the coffee and, shoving a stack of college textbooks aside, sat me down at a table.

"I sure wish I knew how to buy a zoning change," I tried.

"Are you talking about in general?"

"No. Marlinsport."

"I can't say."

"In general then."

"The most direct way is to bribe someone, but . . ."

"But . . ."

"You could look for a consulting firm that guarantees results for exorbitant fees."

"Sort of a zoning-for-dollars company?"

"I've heard them called that."

"How does it work?"

"Oh, I suppose the firm might have a few public officials for secret partners."

"Do you know if there's an outfit like that in Marlinsport?"

"Not on your life, Palmer." Her smile was as plastic and cold as a beauty contestant's on swimsuit night. "It's bad enough having Ken use me. I don't need you doing it, too."

That hurt, but I guess I had it coming. "I'm sorry, Deanna."

Her eyes found a neutral corner of the ceiling. "Actually I'm halfway glad Ken's nosing around. These high rollers would put a liquor store in a Sunday School building if the right bagman came around. I oughta know, I sold houses for them for a long time."

"Who's the right bagman?" I couldn't help myself.

This time the laugh was cocky.

"Go screw yourself, Palmer."

It was a flash of the old Deanna. The rooftops, the paper routes, the crackling of neon came back to me again.

"How's Raymond?" I asked.

"He's fine," she responded, then added, "I guess. He's not too good at keeping in touch since he took up fishing full-time."

Despite what Deanne said, I knew Raymond slipped into town fairly regularly to check on her and Lynn and deliver seafood to Ortega's cafe and a few old-line bars. I'd catch sight of him every couple of months.

"Tell him I said hello . . . and to come see me."

"I'll do that. You know, Palmer, you're one of the few people on this earth that he still trusts." She sounded defensive, although no one, especially me, ever blamed Deanna for what happened between her and Raymond. When he left the service a few years ago he was still too restless to settle down. Within a few days he'd departed once more, buying an ancient boat and heading for the Gulf.

I finished my coffee and rose to go.

"Thanks, Deanna, for seeing me," I said. " 'When our paths cross in the next few days I promise to look right through you."

Her mouth was downcast. "I'm counting on it," she said.

$\triangledown$

8

THE MOON WAS RISING on a blustery winter night when I tossed the crab nets in the Jeep, along with the washtub, chicken necks, and string, and took off for Bayles Point, fifteen miles south of Marlinsport. I was late because of my efforts to find Cesar. Don was now half-worried, half-angry at his father for not coming back to work. Treaster, he learned, had no idea where the old Latin had gone and was as eager to find him as we were. If it wasn't for Nick Darvin I wouldn't have been so concerned, but when two key men in an investigation don't show up for work there's reason to wonder.

I parked near the pier and paid my two bucks. At the shallow end of the wood decking, where a lone figure was fussing over his lines, I plopped down my gear. A steady wind had turned wet on its journey across Marlin Bay but Cy Betz was well insulated in an old-fashioned navy pea jacket and overalls. With the sloppy hat pulled down over his eyes I barely recognized him, which I'm sure is what he had in mind.

There are two kinds of Florida Crackers. Three really. The synthetic kind is found mostly in the state legislature in Tallahassee. These guys (they are always guys) may have been born in Florida — or not — but they all love their contrived folksy phrases, mostly made up on the spot. "It doesn't take me long to look at a horseshoe," I remember one saying about a proposed law he didn't like.

Cy wasn't one of them. He was an ordinary Cracker, one of those whose speech — the *ya'lls*, the *eatin' supper*, the *cuttin' the fool* — are genuine idioms. I'm the third kind, a plain Cracker who got a break and was now alienated, at least partly, from my roots. It was the same as if I'd won the lottery.

As I laid out my lines Cy checked his in the water a couple of times.

"Whoever said the blue crabs are running told a lie," he complained. "It's too damned cold."

"Hell, Cy, you've got to give them a chance. You can't pull your bait up every two minutes."

Bond Street whipped past me in the darkness. Way across the bay the lights of New Seville glowed low on the water like a bar of light under a door. I knelt on the dock and began tying the bait with stout cord. Cy spoke.

"The U.S. magistrate was antsy this afternoon when Treaster marched Montiega before him."

I looked up. "Why?"

"He thinks a federal judge might drop the charges."

"He actually said that?" I asked, lowering the bait over the edge of the pier.

"Sort of. Privately. He only bound Montiega over because Treaster said he was developing a criminal conspiracy case at city hall." Cy leaned forward on his knees beside me. "But that's so much horseshit."

"Treaster smells smoke and can't find the fire, you mean?"

"Yeah. It's more like the fireman who axes his way into a house." His words sounded brittle in the cold. "The house survives the fire but not the fireman. The truth is, since he got into town he's worked hard and played hard and not much good has come of either one."

Cy's face immediately fell into a self-critical frown. "Strike that last, Palmer. I'm not here to gossip. And nothing I know about his personal life rises above that level."

I nodded, remembering what A.J. had said, wondering what kind of moves Treaster tried on her.

"What about this missing zoning employee?"

"Nick Darvin? His brother called city hall today and said he forgot to notify the department his brother was called out of town. It looks like the *Times* was reaching on that one."

"Did he say where Darvin's gone?"

"No. Said it was a personal matter."

"Do you believe him?"

"I figure if he's lying we'll find out when the body begins to rot."

"Do you have to be so damned graphic?"

"You asked."

"What's the evidence against the mayor?"

"You named it earlier. Cesar Armonia. Treaster has video and audio tapes of the two old Latins in a sidewalk confrontation."

I wondered if the *alcalde* had told me everything. "Saying what?"

"Saying whatever you want to hear," Cy mumbled around his pipe. He turned to me in the darkness, his eyes level with the necklace of lights from New Seville. "The tape isn't much evidence, but if Cesar can be encouraged to say what it means . . ."

41

"How could the mayor help Cesar?" I asked. "He doesn't even vote on zoning."

"Tell Treaster that and he'll remind you the mayor has a lot of influence. Marlinsport is a rat's nest of liberal politicians led by Julio Montiega." Cy was tugging on his crab line as he spoke. "Look at that devil. Give me the net. Damn!"

"That was a fish."

"That was a blue crab," he said, pulling his bait up and letting it fall once more into the swells. "Don't get me wrong. Montiega's not my concern. Marlinsport would be better off without him. He throws federal money wildly at every social ill he can come up with, real or imagined."

"Then why are you risking your job talking to me?"

He stoked up his pipe with a couple of deep puffs. For what seemed like a long interval there was no sound except the water against the pilings.

When Cy finally answered, his voice was full of emotion. "For the criminal justice system, corny as that may sound. What Treaster's got against Montiega smells fishier than a trawler. He's using the courts for political leverage. They told me at the University of Florida that's not the way it's supposed to be. Damn, Palmer, I worked hard to get a hold on the dirty deal makers here. You know that. We convicted a few, too. It was our case against the public housing director that brought Treaster down here. Washington figured Marlinsport's bag of garbage was about to split open and wanted a more adept political hand to preside over the outflow. But it's a tough old bag and Treaster's getting impatient. He's hoping the arrest of Montiega will shake up the city enough that someone else will get scared and make a mistake, or talk."

I couldn't believe what Cy was saying. "You mean he's using Montiega as bait?"

"Treaster's convinced the mayor's a crook, and he wants to get him, even with a shaky case. But the answer to your question is yes, he's dangling Montiega on a hook to see if the smell of blood will stir up any other sharks."

My moment had come. "That's a hell of a way to go after a phony zoning-for-dollars company."

"My God, you've already heard about Z Corp?" He was astonished.

"It's come up." I tugged on my line. The name Cy had just given me was what this whole crabbing-under-the-moon excursion was about. If

I was lucky nobody else outside Treaster's office, meaning A.J., knew it.

"That's one slick outfit," Cy said.

"I take it you can't tie Z Corp—the name rolled from my lips so naturally—to the mayor?"

"No, or to anyone else at city hall. Only Zandell's name is on the corporation papers. Whatever money changes hands is all in cash under the table, and happy developers aren't about to tell us who they're paying off."

"So you guys are scrambling for a case against Zandell?"

"We were, up until this morning. I don't know what Treaster's next move will be now. The shame is it won't matter how shoddy his law is on this one, he'll have the emotions of the community with him. Particularly the old-timers like you and me. Marlinsport was once a damn fine place to live. As far as I'm concerned every national ad on Florida should be withdrawn and the borders barricaded."

"You trying to say we're loving it to death?"

"Exactly. Hell, you and I drove way down here and still paid two bucks to stick a crab line in the bay. Balders Swamp is the last piece of wilderness left in the city limits and it's going. Acre by acre, they'll get it."

"You think the zoning deal for Balders was rigged?"

"One way or the other, I do. But we can't prove it. All we've got is a half-assed case against Montiega." He pulled the pipe from his mouth, tapped out the dottle, and slipped the pipe into his inside coat pocket. Patting it, to be sure it was secure, he spoke to me in mocking tones. "Of course, there's always a chance that little reporter from the *Times* will find the evidence for us."

"It sounded at his so-called press conferences like Treaster wants to throw her in jail," I said.

"No way will that happen. Treaster likes her." He raised his bait. "There's no crabs left in the bay."

"You said there was a big one a minute ago."

"No. That was a turtle."

We fell silent. I began to brood over what he'd said. When I was a boy I could walk for an hour in sand dunes around Marlin Bay and never cross a fence or see another soul. Now condos lined the waterfront like damned sentries and the area beaches were so strung with walls I'd need an army tank to crawl over them. The last time I crossed the causeway to New Seville's beaches I'd driven up and down for an hour trying to find a place to park, and when I finally did, there was nowhere on the beach to be alone. I left after ten minutes and haven't been back.

Now Balders Swamp, refuge of the blue heron, coots, cowbirds, and egrets, was being swallowed up. Damn developers. Before they were through the whole bay area would be chopped into seventy-by-hundred-foot lots, all connected by miles and miles of asphalt.

Then I thought about my own place on the bay. And how I'd fixed up the ironwork fence so it was strong and shiny, and intimidating to trespassers.

A couple of small crabs crawled onto the chicken neck, but I shook them off. The truth was I no longer felt like crabbing. After a few minutes we agreed to call it quits. Cy left first. I fooled around for another ten minutes, throwing chicken necks as far as I could into the bay.

Zandell. A new name to the case. And to me.

∇

9

I COULD TELL WHEN A.J. was working against me. Really working, I mean. We always shared a certain tension because we were reporters for competing newspapers. We could deal with that. But when we were on the same story – well, she was as elusive and devious as a Florida panther.

She ignored my knock for a long time, but I persisted. I knew she was up because I'd seen lights in her aerie when I drove home. Finally her door opened a crack and she peered up at me. She was clad in a granny gown that covered everything from her chin to her bare toes. God, I wanted to hug her.

"I'm asleep, Palmer," she lied.

"Can't I come in for a couple of minutes?"

Her nose wrinkled. "What'cha been doing?"

"Crabbing."

"You smell like it."

"I didn't catch any."

She sniffed. "Did one catch you?"

I backed up.

"Hell, A.J., I didn't get near a crab."

"You got near something," she said, closing the door. I caught a last glimpse of one sad violet eye before the dead bolt shot home.

I sniffed my hands. She was lying about that too. Not caring about the noise, I clumped down the stairs and across the tiled entry to my part of the old Spanish mansion. There was some mail, nothing special. Passing through the gloomy banquet hall I hesitated. It was not a room to hurry through. Pale moonlight passed through the overhead clerestory windows and reflected on exotic patterns of glass.

The real estate baron who built the house had ordered six huge crystal chandeliers strung down the room, to hang over a banquet table that must have been fifty feet long. When the Florida real estate bubble burst in 1926, he was among the first to collapse with it. His table and chandeliers were lost in history – probably providing firewood during the Depression. But I had turned the room to a purpose of my own. Old cars were my treasures. But this room . . . this room was for my obsession.

I opened electrical panel doors and flung switches rapidly with practiced fingers. In a blaze of pastel and garish glory the collected neon of Marlinsport's decadent past sprang to life. Signs for fresh fish nipped at the Seminole Hotel's Indian chief; a cocktail glass fizzled up to a Palace Theatre marquee; the Casino's old sign leaned into the room. All the pieces of bent glass, huge and small, recreated a kaleidoscope view of the city, especially Alverez District, in the 1930s.

So much soft light made for wonderful parties, and I had them often. But they could not cure loneliness, not tonight. Not any night.

The polished rosewood beams far above reflected the magical hues. As I passed into the kitchen my gaze lingered — as always — on the first piece I'd collected, the pink neon flamingo standing in a wave of blue by a bent green palm.

A.J. had cleaned up the baking pans sometime during the day. Wrapped bowls of cookies now lined the counter. I found a can of cream of mushroom soup and microwaved it. The result was tepid and lumpy but close enough to edible so I didn't bother to get up and zap a few more watts into it. The telephone saved me from eating very much.

"Palmer?"

"Yeah."

"I was beginning to think you'd never get home." It was Emilio Salgado, the diminutive police chief of Marlinsport.

"Well, I'm here now and about ready to hit the sack."

"Look, *amigo*," he said in a tense voice, "if I were a police reporter I'd forget about bed and go take a ride."

My halfhearted attention turned to full alert. The city's tough, straight chief was giving me a tip. It wasn't the first time, but it also wasn't the way things usually worked.

"I might snoop around a bit. But where do I begin? It's a big city."

A long pause. Thinking.

"In the district. Maybe around Ida Street."

The soup hit the disposal and I dashed for the Jeep. The west end of Ida Street was quiet. I drove east for thirty blocks with fading hopes of making the deadline for tomorrow's paper even if I did find whatever Salgado had sent me after. As I flashed across the Habana intersection swirling lights off to the south caught my eye. Laughing out loud, I slammed on my brakes. Emilio had made damned sure I didn't go straight to the scene. Habana, not Ida, swarmed with vehicles and blue lights. It really would look to anybody on the sidewalk that I'd just stumbled across the action.

46

I looped back and rolled slowly past the medical examiner's wagon and two squad cars. Somebody was dead, then. I was puzzled.

This was Emilio's turf. Why was he so coy about telling me to come here?

As I passed the familiar small restaurant ablaze with light I saw late-model, nondescript sedans gathered in a knot before it. The Feds, too, had quite a presence. I was beginning to understand the tone of Emilio's call. I swung the Jeep in beside the last car and jumped out.

"You can get right back inside that thing and haul your ass out of here."

I eyeballed the slumped figure of Ed Priestly moving toward me.

"You've got about as much authority here as Whistler's Mother," I said, stepping around him.

He muttered, and his car door slammed. As he drove away I scanned the entrance to Cesar Armonia's old Spanish Club. FBI agents and assistant U.S. attorneys were milling about. Looking a little crowded, a couple of Emilio's uniformed cops stood to one side. In the window neon beer signs glowed.

Like Priestly, the Feds wanted to keep me out. I ignored their comments. This was one of those times when being so big was an advantage. I simply shouldered my way by and, seeing the chief of detectives inside, called, "Hey, what's up?"

Bennie Mills, Emilio's right hand and a hound dog on a case, motioned me in. He was issuing orders to a couple of uniformed cops.

"Cover every inch of this restaurant. If he left a note, find it."

I glanced around. There was no sign of disorder. The worn wood floor was polished. Chairs were neatly stacked upside down on the metal tables. But Bennie looked grim.

"How'd you get here in such a hurry?" he grumbled.

"Just passing by. What'cha got?"

"You don't know?" He brought his owl eyes to focus on me. "Come on . . . ," he said. Then, in a different inflection, repeated, "Come on."

Bennie led me through the half doors at the back, through the kitchen, which smelled of peppers and old grease, and stepped aside so I could peek inside a small door. It was the office. Two detectives were brushing a huge rolltop desk for prints. It took up almost half of the narrow room. Stacked on it in disarray were papers and bills and penciled menus. On one corner was propped a glossy rendering that showed the drab brick buildings of El Principe made over into an array of shops, with decorative lights and greenery.

I absorbed all this instantly, my attention shooting to the back where, swinging from the ceiling, the rope making a creaking noise as it slipped back and forth on the exposed fire sprinkler pipe, was the body of an elderly, chubby little man.

His swollen jowls hung over the manila rope biting into his neck. Even the distortion and the purplish flesh didn't prevent me from knowing who that was — or had been.

"Cesar Armonia," I breathed.

"Oh, yeah. You got that right," Bennie said. "Body's barely cooled. Hasn't been there long. No sign of foul play — except the window's been jimmied."

"Suicide?" I could feel my own skin turning cold as I looked at the delicate pendulumlike swing of the body. The long scar on my back felt like crab claws were picking at it again.

"Too soon to say. There's no note. At least we haven't found one yet. He could have jumped off the desk. Or he could have been pushed. The Feds are adamant that we treat this as murder of a federal witness. But we get to call it, and they know it."

I pointed to the desk. "You been through that?"

"The obvious places. When the forensic team's finished we'll take him down and go through it drawer by drawer. But it's not likely he'd hide a note, is it?"

A Fed stuck his head in the door and snapped a few pictures.

Bennie frowned. "We've already got plenty of shots. You can see them later."

"Hey, relax, okay," the man said. "We've got a job to do here, too."

Bennie followed me back into the kitchen.

"Who found him?" I asked.

"It was a phone tip."

"Anonymous?"

"Yeah. A man."

"What did he say?"

"He said there was a dead guy here."

Powder, spray, and preservatives blossomed suddenly as the finger-print crew moved into the kitchen.

One called, "Hey, Captain, you can take him down now. Tell the Feds to stop griping. It was their own man who messed us up."

"What's he talking about?" I asked Bennie.

"Oh, that FBI guy Priestly came ham-handing his way in here like a cleaning woman before I stopped him. He left smeared prints all over the place."

"Why'd you bring the Feds in anyway?"

Bennie laughed. "We didn't. They got the same tip we did. That's one reason I'm not ruling out murder. Who in the hell gives anonymous tips to suicide?"

"What about his family? Have they been notified?"

"Chief Salgado's taking care of that personally. He knows the Armonias from way back."

I excused myself and hurried outside. It was still possible to make the final edition if the desk could get the pressroom to cooperate. This was big stuff. As the Jeep lurched away from the curb I checked around and then smiled for half a second. There wasn't another reporter in sight.

10

TENSION FILLED THE ROOM. Not ten minutes before, decked out in a fleecy blue running outfit, A.J. had come downstairs on a peace mission, gathering up the Sunday papers off my steps. Her eyes had a sort of dreamy look when I let her in, and she was relaxed, even detached, as I offered to fix omelets and ham. Absently, she'd let the papers slip out of their plastic wrappers onto the kitchen table and reached out to touch me on the waist as I opened the refrigerator. Then A.J. patted me gently on the back, unconsciously avoiding the termination point of my long scar. The blood began to course through my body and I turned to sneak a kiss since she was in a better mood. But in that brief moment she'd casually reached out and flicked open the papers on the breakfast table, and the truce between us ended.

On page one of the *Times* was A.J.'s arrest story, paired with a thumb-sucker — "Ethnics fear mayor's fall is their fall" — no doubt put together by the *Times*'s smug young "writers" straight out of Harvard. Unfortunately for them, it included a melodrama on Cesar, fighting for both El Principe and his honor, and very much alive.

In the *Trib*, stripped over the photo of Julio in chains and the solid profile of him by Moses, was my story on Cesar, hanged and very much dead.

Head down, hair covering her face, A.J. read it silently. Then she refolded the *Trib* so that the two front pages were side-by-side.

"Well!" She forced a smile, but it was tight enough to cut off circulation.

"I was sort of driving by and saw the commotion," I offered.

Her eyes ran down to the address of Cesar's restaurant.

"I didn't know you rode around the district that late at night . . . Well."

There it was again. And there I was, wishing the papers were still outside on the steps.

She headed for the door. I trailed along, trying to think of something to change her mind.

"What about the omelets? It's only ten."

"I'm not hungry anymore," she said gloomily. "Anyway, I may as well get on over to the *Times*. Something tells me there's gonna be a general clock-cleaning, even if it is Sunday."

My own appetite wasn't too hot when I went back into the kitchen. Sounding like dobbin, I crunched my way through a bowl of Grapenuts and was making a cup of instant coffee in the microwave when the telephone rang.

The voice of the *Trib*'s publisher was deep and raspy with the strain of too many cigarettes. "Palmer, the United States attorney is in my office. Have you got a minute?"

Those last words were Fred Nettleman's code for a command performance, whether it was to chide a reporter for an extra mile claimed on an expense account, or to badger Wilson over the newsroom's budget.

"There's one problem. I just got up and look like a politician from the Persian Gulf," I said, even though joking with him was a bad idea. Nettleman was too suspicious of reporters and editors to share in a good joke with them, and mine never rose to that level anyway.

"If I can make the time to come down here on a Sunday morning surely you can, too," he said in his bassoon voice.

"If you need me now I'll come now."

"If I didn't need you, I'd never have called." He hung up.

Like a schoolboy ordered to the principal's office I sped over to the *Trib*. I told myself that it wasn't personal between the publisher and me, but the truth was I didn't like him any better than Wilson did.

Smitty gave me a sympathetic look as I approached the guard station at the back door. It couldn't be good news for me to show early Sunday after Nettleman and Treaster. I detoured into the newsroom, empty except for Paula bent over her desk and a couple of copy kids reading the wires. It was one of those rare quiet times. In years past Teletype machines provided a nice background clatter day or night, but no more. Now all I could hear were computer terminal fans, buzzing like pesky flies. I checked my desk for messages and then went on up.

On the third floor I passed through a red mahogany door with polished brass scrolls into the executive suites. To my surprise there was a grating underfoot. I glanced down. Grime spotting the thick beige carpet gave witness to the newsroom scuttlebutt about Nettleman's spy network. Obviously workers from the back shops were dropping both tales and steel filings in his office.

"Well, he's finally here," the publisher cracked as I appeared in his doorway.

I must have been a sight. Dressed in faded jeans and a Dolphins sweatshirt, I needed a shave, a shower, and a real cup of coffee. Treaster's eyes took me in, but he said nothing in the way of a greeting. I stood over the two seated figures like the Cardiff Giant until Nettleman waved me to one of the scratchy cheap chairs he'd moved in. The fine furniture personally selected by the old publisher, Walter Hammersmith, along with his mirrored bar, had been banished to storage, if not Carrie Nation's hatchet. In their place Nettleman stuck up profit charts and advertising awards.

"You were saying?" he asked Treaster, suited up and sporting a starred red tie.

Treaster still sucker-punched hard. "We're only a half step away from sending that thief Montiega to the federal detention center at Eglin."

Nettleman snickered coldly through a cloud of cigarette smoke. "Make it Atlanta."

Treaster laughed with him for a polite second before he turned on me. "My comments are off the record."

"I'll tell you when we're off the record," I corrected him.

Nettleman pulled the stub of a cigarette out of his drooping mouth. "Make no mistake. I called this meeting. Anything said in this office is off the record."

Holy Christ, I thought, the bean counter is going to play editor. I said nothing.

Nettleman's pout changed to a Cheshire smile. "We all know slick Latins and fast dealers have surrounded Julio Montiega from the day he was born over at Centro Asturiano."

I couldn't let that pass. "It's okay to indict the mayor because his friends speak Spanish?"

Treaster almost came out of his seat. "Montiega's getting what he deserves and you know it. The only unfairness in all this is by you." He snatched up the newspaper spread out on Nettleman's desk and read out loud. " 'The case against the mayor may have died with Cesar Armonia. His interpretation of evidence was essential to the U.S. attorney's case.' " Hard blue eyes appeared above the paper. "That statement, John Palmer Kingston, is a gross misrepresentation and reveals you've compromised someone in my office."

I stirred inwardly. Treaster's use of my first name, which wasn't on the story, suggested I'd been on his mind a lot more than I'd ever have guessed.

"Or" — "his eyes met Nettleman's — "Montiega knew we had him yesterday when he visited a certain *Tribune* reporter and fed him a bunch of malarkey."

The chair legs slipped back to the floor as I pulled myself upright.

"Oh yes, Palmer, we know the mayor spent the morning in your garage." There was an annoying smirk on his face. "What'd he tell you?"

"Never to trust self-righteous crusaders."

Nettleman's watery gray eyes blinked rapidly as he peered down the ridge of his bony nose at me. "Your attitude is inappropriate and unprofessional. We're talking about corruption here, maybe even murder."

"Whose murder?" I asked.

"Cesar's, of course!"

The picture of these two jokers concocting theories about the *alcalde* and murder rankled me. "If the U.S. attorney's office knows Cesar was murdered, and who did it, why are we sitting up here chatting? Let's lead the paper with it."

"You're in bed with Montiega, aren't you?" Treaster said tightly while Nettleman's head of thick gray hair bobbed in agreement. I said nothing.

Treaster leaned toward me, almost conspiratorially. "Take this as a friendly warning, Palmer. Talking someone in my office into leaking information that damages this investigation is not very smart. It borders on being a crime."

"The newspaper would never be a party to anything like that," Nettleman exclaimed piously.

The lump in my stomach was as heavy as granite. It was obvious the man in charge of the *Marlinsport Tribune* didn't have the first notion of what was good journalism and, worse, didn't seem to care.

We sat in silence.

"Well?" Treaster asked.

I shook my head.

He looked to Nettleman for support.

"Palmer, I don't want to use my power as publisher — "

"Then don't," I interrupted, "because it won't get you a thing but a vacancy on your reporting staff."

Treaster chuckled. "What's one reporter?"

Nettleman's wavering eyes betrayed him. One of those petty tyrants for whom office is everything, the *Trib*'s new publisher knew enough about me to realize I'd fight him if I had to.

"Of course, we want to cooperate with your office, Mr. Treaster, but I believe both Palmer and I need to consult with counsel, since a question of journalism ethics is involved."

Nettleman had it wrong, but he had it right. I didn't need a lawyer to tell me what I was going to do about confidential sources, but by calling for legal advice he could drop the curtain on this little scene, which he suddenly wanted over as much as I did. Treaster tried to play on Nettleman's patriotism one more time, but he couldn't get the flag to fly again. The meeting that should never have been was over. Treaster left and the *Trib*'s publisher lit his seventh cigarette of the morning and did not look up as I exited.

Downstairs I stopped by the cafeteria for a cup of machine coffee and took it with me to the library to see how the other papers in the state were handling Montiega's arrest. Later, when I passed the newsroom, I glimpsed Treaster sitting across from Paula. He was postured in one of our small stenographer chairs, turned backward, with his football linesman's legs spread wide. Paula was laughing. I decided to go home to make my calls.

▽

1 1

MY MORNING OF CONFRONTATION didn't end with Fred Nettleman and Treaster. In fact, it got worse.

Trammel Zandell was fifty and portly. But with a golf club held threateningly in his hand he looked potent enough.

"You outsized son of a bitch," he cried, waving a pitching wedge at me like a tomahawk, "you push me any harder and I'll call my sons. I tell you I won't be followed. I won't be questioned. I won't be threatened."

"I'm not doing any of those things," I replied calmly. "There's a story going in tomorrow's paper that is in your interest to comment on."

"A story?" Despite his menacing stare, he followed me away from the sand trap where I'd caught up with him. "About what? And you damn well better be specific."

"As I told you on the phone," I said, keeping at least a putter's length away from him, "Z Corp's name keeps cropping up in reference to questionable zoning decisions."

"Questionable? Questionable to whom? Just because some pussy at the *Times* is crying over the loss of a few acres of swamp the *Trib* isn't going to call economic growth questionable, is it? That's ridiculous! You stupid reporters never understand anything about growth or money."

"If you give me a second I can lay out the facts —"

"Didn't hanging up on you twice tell you what I think about your facts? You put any fucking story in the paper with my name in it, you're talking libel suit, mister. I'm a member of the bar and I make more money in a week than you do in a year. So take it as a warning. You mess with this and the cost will be extremely high."

I kept plugging away. "Z Corp has a remarkable success rate in getting rezonings for clients. That's a fact, not libel."

The club head was waving dangerously close to my head.

"You put Z Corp or Trammel Zandell in that sheet of yours and I'll own it," he threatened.

"All right," I said, "I'll take that as a 'No comment.' If you change your mind you can try to get me at the *Trib*."

He grunted, looked at the club like he'd just discovered it, and turned his back on me. I watched as he tramped into the sand trap. "Get my boys on the damn mobile phone," he barked at his caddie. "A man can't even have a damn peaceful Sunday on the damn golf course. God, I hate the press."

For some reason his foul mood improved mine. I found myself whistling on the way back to my Jeep and thinking about rescuing the rest of the day. It's against policy for a reporter to drink while working but seeing Deanna yesterday had given me an idea, and since it was officially my day off, my next stop was one of Marlinsport's famous dens. Also its worst.

Zacharia's Oyster Bar is seedy—not genteel seedy, but downright seedy. Some really nasty characters hang out there, along with a lot of *Trib* staffers. It's the kind of place where a boy can get his first drink—no matter how old he is. Mine had come at fourteen.

It's also the kind of place a boy can get the shit beat out of him for nothing more than the wrong expression on his face. That came at fifteen.

Zacharia himself was still around, mean as a three-legged alligator and with a mouthful of teeth not wholly unlike a gator's. Sitting there on his ragged-assed raised chair, he didn't speak to me. He glowered. I took it kindly. He never spoke to anybody unless he was mad, and most folks did everything they could to keep him from getting that way. The Dolphins game, of course, was on TV. The outside of the bar bristled with antennae and earth-station dishes that gleamed like clean teeth. If the Miami Dolphins were on a bus in Cleveland I think old Zack could get them on his wall-wide set.

Despite its shameful service the place was packed. I wasn't the only former teenager in Marlinsport who couldn't resist the double dose of Dolphin football and the chance to prove he's still man enough to go there. Once past old Zacharia I paused to let my eyes adjust to the lack of light and then headed for a lean, shadow-cloaked figure seated at a plate-sized table in the back. This was what I'd been hoping for. I slid quietly into the chair across from him.

A sketch pad was propped against the table edge. Like always, his jeans were ragged enough for a rock star, and he wore a faded military dress shirt. I'd long ago decided Raymond Chancey still wore pieces of his old uniform as a badge of defiance.

Not taking his eyes off the screen, his hand moving rapidly over the pad, my old friend greeted me. " 'Lo, Palmer."

"How they doin', Raymond?"

"Stompin' Seattle."

"Great. So it's on to the Super Bowl!"

"Could be. There's still the play-offs."

I ordered a beer with my bucket of oysters and watched the set with him a while.

"I saw Deanna," I said.

"She told me. You're workin' a story."

"Yeah."

"Well, keep her out of it, will you? She doesn't need any more trouble."

"Deanna's got trouble?"

His flitting green eyes swept to me for the first time. He put a thumb to his chest. "I was talking about me. We're still married, you know." It sounded like a confession. This was territory I tiptoed through. Raymond joined the Marines the day after we graduated from high school, and I hung around the *Trib* so much they finally put me on the payroll full-time. When Raymond came home from boot camp all tanned and decked out in his blues he and Deanna went out a few times, but I didn't realize how hot their romance was until Raymond dropped in at the *Trib* and asked me to put a wedding announcement in the paper.

"You're kidding," I'd said. "You and Deanna?"

I'll never forget that hurt look in his eye. "Yeah, me and Deanna. She's going with me to Panama."

Betsy and I stood up for them. Four years later Deanna, and Lynn, came back to Marlinsport to live with Raymond's ailing parents while he did a tour in the Middle East. And then another somewhere else.

He was still away, but Deanna stood beside me when I said good-bye to Betsy. She opened her door to me when I dropped by, not knowing what to do with myself. She was there when I sold the farm, there when I bought the old house. I was grieving too deeply for a long time to see what was happening. We almost made a big mistake. That's when I quit going over. Things have been awkward between us ever since.

"Are these oysters from your secret beds?" I asked, drowning one in horseradish. They weren't Appalachicola oysters but they were good.

Raymond nodded. "Can you spot this woman?" he asked.

I peered at the drawing, trying to get into his world. His nail-chewed fingers, the flesh puffy at the tips, did a four-count dance on the paper.

The drawing was as ragged as the stubs of his nails; the jagged lines stuttered across the paper.

A furtiveness in the eye of his penciled image helped me pick the living model from the room.

"That blonde. In the red polyester pants suit."

"What can you tell me about her?"

I looked back, remembering the game Raymond and I used to play. Along with planning careers as either a cat burglar or a film stunt man he'd become obsessed with reading the deepest secrets of people's lives from the clues they provided on the surface.

"She's having a good time. She likes football."

Raymond smiled. "She's faking it."

"Faking what?"

"Faking everything. Faking her life."

"She whooped loud enough on that last play."

"Didn't you notice that she glanced first at her husband? Checking him for clues of what to do. Her eyes are watery and glittery—scared. She lives her life a heartbeat behind her husband. She probably hates football. "

"You think he bullies her?"

Raymond shrugged. "One way or the other. Life in the big city."

"Well, now, goddamn, Raymond, there's more to life than one woman with a scared expression."

"Her husband's not doing so well, either."

"You just said he bullies her."

"Yeah. But it's like dominating a sick dog. He avoids eye contact with her. He's ashamed."

"You can't tell—"

"Sure, I can. He's playing the tough guy to prove he's virile."

"Raymond, you're making far too much of a couple of strangers in a bar." I sounded gruff, I knew, and added hurriedly, "How about coming to a party?"

"Party?"

"Yeah. At my place, Christmas Eve. Lots of old friends, lots of *Trib* staffers."

He sketched on.

"I could invite Deanna."

Raymond looked sideways at me. "You having the party in that big room with all the flashing neon signs and potted plants?"

"That's the one."

He went back to stabbing at the woman's drawing. "I won't be around."

"I wish you'd try," I said, standing. When he didn't respond, I squeezed his bony shoulder and left.

So Raymond, my nervous, reclusive old friend, liked my house and my neon signs, I mused on my way to the paper. And he knew what my parties were like. Emotion surged in me — regret and melancholy and deep pity. Raymond had never been inside my house. I visualized him standing on the seawall, peering inside my windows for long, lonely minutes before he disappeared into the night.

As I pulled into the parking lot a Saab cut across in front of my Jeep and I jerked to a stop. I glanced over in time to see Treaster lean toward the woman in the seat beside him. I didn't see her face but that long red hair left no doubt who it was. I hoped to Christ Paula knew what she was doing. It was my guess Treaster had conned her into going out with him on the pretense of improving relations with the *Trib*. But I'd bet his idea of improved relations differed in substantial degree from Paula's, or at least I hoped it did.

I spent the rest of the afternoon on the phone and at a computer terminal, cranking out two stories — one on Z Corp and its list of clients who'd had shaky zoning variances approved, and the other outlining an old man's passion for a building and the questions concerning his death. Cesar's family was in seclusion and the restaurant was closed, so the story was too short and too sketchy for my tastes, but last-minute calls to the medical examiner's office and the police helped. Cesar died by strangulation as a result of hanging. If the poor old Cuban did try to end his own life quickly by breaking his neck, he'd botched it. But the question of murder or suicide wasn't settled. Even though both the Feds and Cesar's family were pressing Chief Salgado for a ruling of murder he wasn't ready to call it that.

"The only trauma to the body was from the hanging," he told me. "Nothing indicated a struggle or attack."

"What about those marks on the window?" I asked.

"Oh . . . you know about those? Well, they are a puzzle. One of several, I'm afraid. The sweet old man had no enemies. Who would kill him in such a vengeful way?"

His voice trailed off. I could just see Salgado staring across his austere office to the wall of photos of family and friends. I knew one of them was taken at the chief's fiftieth birthday celebration at Cesar's restaurant.

"Still no suicide note?" I asked.

"No suicide note."

"He was worried over El Principe, you know."

"More fighting mad, his sons tell me, at least until Julio was arrested. For the life of me I can't understand what happened there. That's personal, Palmer," he added hurriedly.

I used what I could of the chief's remarks and hit the save key. The wall clock verified what I'd suspected all afternoon. Paula wasn't coming back in. I yelled to Moses that I'd wrap up my stories after supper. What I really wanted was to walk awhile and mull over whether it was by chance or by design that someone broke into Cesar's restaurant the same night he'd suffered a slow, agonizing death with a noose around his neck.

12

THE TWO CHARACTERS WHO were waiting outside the *Trib* would have liked me to take them for a couple of old-time gangsters. They talked tough and dressed flashy. But they were a tinny echo of the old days and the old movies. Just the same they had a job to do — take me to Joe Sparkles. They probably realized when I got into the car with them without protest that it was curiosity, not fear, that prompted me. Anyway, they looked disappointed.

Through the tinted sunroof I briefly saw Marlinsport's office towers, rising in the dim daylight like black monoliths. We moved at a fast clip away from the belt of green and prosperity along the river and cruised east through drab brown pods of public housing, then along narrow sign-cluttered streets where the poor shop. For many blocks whatever wasn't asphalt was dirt. The only ground cover was trash. My escorts maintained a silence that could have passed for contempt but which I suspected came from the same mind set — empty.

The scenery changed abruptly as we crossed into Alverez District. Not that the poor don't live here, too. But there's something about the seediness of the old Latin district that's almost noble. Ancient stucco and brick buildings whisper of exciting days long past when Cubans inside made cigars and bread, and revolution. Stout bougainvillea vines, planted in those earlier prosperous times, today struggle to survive in a patchwork of concrete and dust.

But more than anything else what gives Alverez pathos and character are the aging faces peering out from behind rusty wrought-iron fences. Once they were flirtatious and bold, now they are suspicious, and lonely.

We bounced across railroad tracks past rows of battered shotgun houses, one room wide and as long as the lot, and turned onto Ida. It was nearly deserted, but that was not surprising. Not until nighttime, when the bigger restaurants and clubs opened, would the street in any way regain its old glory.

Long shadows from a slipping sun snaked out in front of the heavy limousine, shimmying along the rough streets. When the familiar building appeared, images from my youth surged in me. It was like encountering a triceratops in the Everglades — driving up to this red dinosaur fighting the weeds and vines of subtropical Florida, so near yet so far from the popsicle buildings of downtown Marlinsport. We came to a stop at the curb before El Principe.

They walked me down an alley behind the three-story factory and into a vast courtyard. A million oblongs of dull red clay pressed in upon us. The patch of sky was a dead gray.

My guides stopped at a decrepit shipping dock and motioned me to go in. I levered myself up. The dark, rusty interior yawned before me like a cave.

"An empty factory is a grim place, is it not, Palmer?" The words came at me in a quaver.

I stepped inside. The air was different. Not just colder, but like an ice pack laid on bare skin.

Joseph Contreras stood in the shadows. I recognized him, although he hadn't been around the day I bought the Cadillac from his mother. His was one of many photographs she was packing away, preparing for moving out of the family house.

The slight man was right for the role of an aging, prosperous don, especially the aging part. The years had burrowed his face like strong winds, eroding away any softness that had ever been there, leaving a network of trenches across a field of coquina. He and Julio were contemporaries. But the *alcalde*, up until a day ago, had looked like a man still having a good time. Joe Sparkles, in his tailored silk suit, looked as if he didn't know what a good time was.

"Come over here," he said in a softly accented voice. His tight smile revealed a few of the gold-capped teeth that had earned him his nickname.

I towered over him a good eight inches as we stood alone in the middle of the monstrous room. He'd sent his associates away without a word or gesture that I could see. I didn't know if that meant he trusted me, wasn't worried about me, or had me covered. It was a strange meeting: an elderly mobster who still had a world of clout, me, and a ghost of a building that smelled of toil, rot, and tobacco.

"I thought under the circumstances we ought to talk here." His words echoed as he strode a hundred feet into the dusty atmosphere. "This is the assembly room."

He pointed toward empty space as if he were seeing a scene of machines and workers. The nails on his dark-skinned fingers were edged in sienna, all around.

"Many a man labored his life away here . . . on a stool, rooted to one spot like a tree . . ."

He tapped the floor between his shoes where a tin patch was tacked over a knot hole in the broad boards. "Here, Julio Montiega toiled as a boy."

"The *alcalde*'s told me about you growing up together."

Joe Sparkles stared at me. With his liver-colored face and bloodshot eyes he reminded me of a rattlesnake coiled on velvet. "Is that so? Has he also told you my father offered to help him? He could have made Julio a man of wealth and respect in this community."

I shifted uneasily. "The *alcalde* is respected."

"Your paper showed this morning how much respect he gets."

I felt the blood rising to my face. "This business will not end there."

"No, it will not. That I can promise you."

Wind crashed through loose shutters in the courtyard. I looked out a dirt-caked window. The two hoodlums were standing side by side, their backs to us, watching the street and their car. Beside me Contreras lit a crook, a very expensive old-time Cuban cigar. I waited. Whatever the reason he'd wanted to see me, and in this place, it was about to come out. "After my father passed on and I took over the business I, too, offered Julio opportunities, perfectly legitimate ones, but he refused out of his own sense of principles."

The car in which Contreras senior "passed on" was in my garage. I wondered briefly if he knew: all my dealings had been with his mother. Then I realized he had to know.

His eyes narrowed on my face as if he were sizing me up in a scope. "But the time has come for me to step in. Wouldn't you like to know why Cesar went after his old friend?"

"Do you know?"

He drew on the cigar and smoke curled up between us. "Cesar was set up, too."

My thoughts went straight to the U.S. attorney's office.

"Treaster talked Cesar into this?"

"He used Cesar, and I will not forget that, but he was not the first."

"Who was?"

"A lot of people like to gamble . . . even family members of prominent citizens who might choose to avoid my club themselves."

I looked down into his hard eyes. He couldn't have made himself clearer. The mayor had had trouble with his brother-in-law's boozing and gambling for a long time. Still, I was puzzled. Al Rojas's gambling debts might embarrass the mayor, but what possible connection could they have to a zoning bribe?

Joe Sparkles took the cigar out of his mouth and answered my unspoken question. "Al Rojas lost much more than he could afford in a private poker game with Howard Ketch."

I knew the name. Ketch was the Balders developer and one of Z Corp's biggest clients.

"And?" I prompted.

"Rojas was a regular at Cesar's restaurant. If he said, 'You pay me this, the mayor will do that,' Cesar might have believed him."

"Maybe. But why would Cesar go to Treaster instead of confronting the mayor? They were close friends."

"Exactly. That's what infuriated Cesar. Don't forget he was a desperate man, hot-tempered and desperate. A dangerous combination. He went to Treaster in a blind rage."

"Any proof?"

His look was condescending. "I've marked the trail for you. You should be able to find what you need."

"What about Cesar's death?"

"Was he murdered, you mean? That I do not know. It is interesting to me, though, that the FBI and several assistant U.S. attorneys arrived at Cesar's almost simultaneously with the police. You could agree that's odd?"

I could and I did.

He seemed amused. "Apparently there is still a division of loyalties in the police department."

"It's possible the leak to the FBI didn't come from inside the police."

"Yes?"

"Whoever tipped off the cops about Cesar could have also called the FBI."

His laugh was a rustling of dry palmetto. "Maybe you should come into business with me, Palmer. You possess a subtle mind."

I smiled at the intended compliment. "I'd rather think of it as healthy skepticism."

"In any case, your observation brings up an interesting question — who could profit from calling both?"

"That is an interesting question. Here's another. Why did you choose me to tell about Rojas?"

There was a glint in his eye. "I believe our talk is over."

He walked me back to the lattice door. At our appearance the two hoods crunched through the oak leaves toward us. As they escorted me across the patio the old mobster called from the red, gaping doorway. "Palmer."

I turned back. "Yes?"

"Watch your running around on rooftops to spy on people. And stay out of the rain."

A rattling laugh came from the brick doorway.

Christ. An incident on a rooftop more than twenty years ago, nothing to anybody except a bunch of raggedy-assed teenagers, and the old mob boss of Marlinsport not only knew who it was, he remembered.

All I could do was stare at him, then walk away.

$\triangledown$

13

BY THE TIME I finished reworking my stories on Z Corp and Cesar and headed home, night and the temperature had both fallen hard. It was the coldest Florida winter in a decade, and the forecast was that it wouldn't let up. Icy air seeped in through the Jeep's canvas doors. My heart filled with the old sadness as I turned onto the island and caught sight of the twinkling lights of Christmas and the glitter of twisting tinsel.

Number 700 Island Drive was ablaze. The blue and white lights I'd strung in the tall podocarpus on both sides of the formal arched entryway were on, as were decorations in a number of apartments, and high up, A.J.'s tiny tabletop tree sent out a soft glow from a dark room. I figured she'd fallen asleep with it on. You could have worse company.

The shower was steamy, washing away aches I'd accumulated at the frigid old cigar factory. I pulled on a flannel hunting shirt, sweatpants, and thick woolen socks. I was heading for the bar off the banquet hall when the telephone rang.

"Been takin' a shower, hunh?" It was A.J.

"How'd you know?"

"This isn't the first time I called. You dressed?"

"Sort of."

"Good. Come on up. I've fixed hot toddies with Myers's rum."

God, I was glad to hear the warmth back in her voice.

"Give me five minutes. I'm kinda thrown together."

"Take your time," she said. "But I'm locking my door in sixty seconds and turning off the stove under the tea kettle."

"I should change."

"You've got fifty-five left. Fifty-four."

I dashed out the front door through the cusped archway and pivoted on the filigreed iron banister. The freezing air passed through my single layer of clothes and circulated like refrigerator coils. I sprinted up the second set of stairs and then the narrow crooked set leading to her place.

A.J. laughed as I lurched to her doorway like an orangutan in a clown suit.

"That's some getup," she said, pulling me in.

She was carefully put together herself in off-white pajamas, a burgundy robe, and moccasins with white leather flowers and crystal rhinestones.

I plopped on her little sofa and watched as she added dollops of basswood honey and cinnamon sticks to the steaming cups. She brought me one and settled into a wicker rocker. The room was cozy, with heat churning out of the old-time electric heater in the wall. The only light was the one over the range and the spectrum from the bedroom tree.

"Oh, that's just right," I declared.

"There's enough cholesterol and calories in these drinks to strangle a goat," she replied.

"Yeah," I agreed, "but he'd die a very happy goat."

She crossed her ankles contented-like on the stool. "So, how'd your day go?"

"Oh, morning to night mostly. Yours?"

"You know the cop shop. Always something to keep you going."

"You're back on cops, hunh?"

"Sure am. Thanks to your story on Cesar. Poor Tim's going to spend a year in the Fort Loam bureau for penance."

There was no denying she was in a good mood. I couldn't believe how my luck had turned.

"Salgado welcomed me back like a daughter. He hugged me in the middle of the squad room."

I decided the best way to keep her in a good mood was to get her off work. "What do you want for Christmas? How about something warm? Maybe a jacket."

She knitted her long thin fingers together, then flexed them toward me palms out. "That sounds nice. I was thinking a power tool would make a good gift for a closet car mechanic like yourself."

I was wondering if she'd been poking around my garage when I realized she'd spoken again.

"What?"

"Did you get that Monday off?"

"I got it."

Her eyes were level and serious for an instant. Then it was gone. Apparently my answer was satisfactory. She held up her mug. "Another?"

"Sure." I sprawled out further on her settee.

She picked up my cup, went to the stove, and fiddled with the makings. I suddenly realized she was looking my way. Dumb as a stump I arched my eyebrows, questioning why.

"Don't you have on any underwear under those things?"

Red-faced and fumbling, I jerked upright on the settee and adjusted my attire like a sixteen-year-old under the cop's light at the drive-in.

"Goddamn it, A.J., you wouldn't give me any time to dress."

Laughing, she said, "It's late and I don't have much time. I've gotta get up with the chickens tomorrow."

"Am I in your way?"

"You're never in my way, Palmer, but I won't sleep if you're here."

"You're stirring the glaze right off that cup."

She looked down, set one cup aside on the counter, and walked with the other to the zigzagging hallway that passed from the living room to her bedroom.

"The city's all lit up and cold as ice," she called. I went to her.

She was standing by the small tree and looking out. I placed both my hands on her shoulders and began to rub gently.

"You know, Palmer, I was glad when I got off police because it meant we wouldn't be competing anymore."

"Me, too."

"Do it lower . . . to the left. I can't stand it when you beat me, and I don't feel all that swell when I beat you. It's sort of a victorless contest."

"I've never noticed much sorrow from you when you're on a roll, A.J."

She turned in my arms. A big innocent smile was on her face.

"Maybe I hide it."

We kissed. Her body was lithe against mine.

"Palmer!" she exclaimed. "You really don't have any underpants on!"

"Sorry."

She laughed.

"Why don't you pipe down, A.J., and invite me into your bed."

"I might invite you but I don't know about that."

"We're a team."

"Oh." She slid laughing between the sheets.

"Damn, A.J., you act like this is the most amusing thing that's ever happened to you."

"It's those damned drawers you've got on."

I fumbled my way in beside her, feeling big and ungainly and an object of ridicule.

She saw that, I guess. The laugh left her lips, but it lingered in her eyes.

"Take off your shirt," she said. I struggled out of it with the grace of an alligator in spats.

"Turn over."

I sighed. That again. "Oh, A.J . . . let's don't . . ."

"We'll get to the rest, Palmer. Roll over."

I did as she asked, the best I could. Her finger found the shoulder blade and the beginning of the long scar. Her touch was as tentative as the brush of a bird's wing.

"It's looking pretty good," she said. "Nice and pink."

"How in the hell can you tell whether it's pink or chartreuse in this Christmas-tree light?"

"It's pink. And no writer who's any good says hell in the same sentence with Christmas."

"That's the silliest damn thing I ever heard."

"I'm telling you. Publishers look at stuff like that. You still working on that book?"

"About how I got this scar? Yeah. I'm not very far into it though."

"Use active verbs."

"What?"

"You gonna tell 'em you got this scar by trailing a kidnapper to a deserted circus train?"

"Maybe."

"And that you were too dumb to carry even a stick to defend yourself?"

"I wasn't gonna put it exactly that way."

A long quiet spell. The finger moved to the middle of my back, tracing the scar.

"Every reporter in America is writing a book someday, Palmer."

"I know."

"What makes yours different?"

"I'm gonna finish it."

"Is that right? At least you're not claiming you're a great writer."

I found I could now lie flat on my stomach without difficulty. "Yes, A.J."

"You've got a lot of energy. I can see that in your news stories. But you're not a 'writer.' You know what I mean? Like Moses is."

"Is your inspection over?"

"In a minute. Don't be so grumpy. Is there gonna be any sex in it?"

"Jee-sus. It's only a little mystery story."

"Nobody'll read it without sex in it."

I shifted slightly onto one hip.

"The doctor didn't do a good job on the stitches here. Because it's so close to your spine, I guess."

"Un-hunh." I'd heard that one about a million times since the night I was knifed in the back trying to rescue the *Trib*'s old publisher from a killer.

With a soft rustling she moved closer to me.

"Am I in your book?"

"Well, no, A.J., not yet. I've only done a couple of chapters."

"But I will be?"

"Sure."

"Tell me about me."

"You're you."

"Now there's a great piece of writing."

"You're a reporter. You're smart. You almost beat me to the story."

The finger was gone. "I beat your patronizing ass plenty on that story, Palmer, until the very last, and then you were so dumb to go in that train alone . . ."

"You're right, A.J. I'll make you the star."

She moved closer. Her hand dropped to my side, near the kidney. "Oh, quit squirming. I don't know how anyone as big as you can be such a baby. What do I look like?"

"So that's it!" I turned angrily to lecture her on her feminist shortcomings. But somehow she'd managed to shed her clothes while needling me. The violet eyes were hooded—vulnerable, but with a real appetite in them. Her dark hair clutched raggedly at her throat and shoulders. Shadows played at the hollow of her neck and at the soft curves beneath her breasts, where her skin was a rich creamy color.

"Lie back down." There was a catch in her voice.

When I was on my side again, my back to her, one finger moved to my waist and tugged at the elastic in my jogging pants. With a pull in the rear and a little careful engineering in the front by me they were gone.

"Socks, too," she said. "I'm not making love to any Norwegian farmer."

"You don't know what those Norwegian farmers have got."

She laughed and pulled my backside to her. I felt the tips of her breasts against me as she snuggled close and warm.

"We're not going to get very far this way, A.J."

"Why don't you be quiet," she whispered.

Her hand found my chest and made wandering circles. Then it found my ribs, and my stomach. And everything.

"Tell the truth in your book, Palmer. Sex and all. Don't make us look like Hansel and Gretel."

She gave me a squeeze. I turned to her and found her arms outstretched, her eyes languid. A smile crossed her lips.

"You could give me a figure – well, statuesque – if you wanted to."

I had the good sense not to tell her she didn't have the frame for it. Instead, I said, "I'll make you irresistible."

She stretched, fragile as a soap bubble, but pliant, and accepting. Her dark head nuzzled the hollow at my breast bone. I was careful to support my own weight. Her hands left my hips and went to my shoulders, above her head, pushing me and, with her palms, rolling me upward as though she really had the strength to support me. It was a beautiful long time together. At last A.J. pulled air in through flared nostrils because her mouth was clamped shut in modesty, and then the last lungful was expelled with a laugh. I gave way, full of regret and satisfaction, and gritted my teeth to hide my almost tearful pleasure. A.J.'s eyes fluttered down, ready for sleep.

I stroked her cheek softly. Turning away from me, she cocked one eye at her bedside clock. The deep line of shadow that curved from the base of her spine to the deeper shadows between her thighs was the most erotic thing I had ever seen.

She touched my hand and after slowly extricating herself, padded, naked and a little dazed, into her bathroom.

When she came out, she was A.J. Egan, crime reporter. Well, almost.

"You better go, Palmer. I have to be at work in five hours."

I struggled up.

At the door she gave me a last, long affectionate hug. "When you put me in your book," she whispered on tiptoes, "make me feisty like Katharine Hepburn."

"You're feisty enough on your own, A.J."

"Just say I'm like Katharine Hepburn – nerves of steel."

"Good night, A.J."

"Remember," she said and pushed me out into the hall.

Cold reached out and grabbed me. I ran downstairs, shivering.

14

DAWN WAS STILL A blustery hour away when the telephone roused me with its nasty electronic buzzing.

"I want to thank you, Palmer, for the story in this morning's paper. I always thought you'd look good in prison blues."

I blinked awake. When a sorry lawman is pleased it's a bad omen. "You sure do your reading early in the morning, Priestly. What do you want?"

"The U. S. attorney's waiting for you in his office."

I sat bolt upright. Treaster was at work — and reading the *Trib* — before six in the morning? I looked outside. Sleet slashed at the windows.

"Too bad. I'm going back to sleep."

"He told me to get you down there right now. You meet me outside the Federal Building in a half hour."

I laughed just to annoy him. No way on earth would I miss such a meeting, but lawmen on horseback grate on me.

"Don't make me come after you."

"You come banging on my door you better bring a baseball bat with you."

"I can bring a subpoena. You want that?"

I threw back the covers. "Don't bother. I'm awake and in a lousy enough mood to want to see Treaster."

While I showered I briefly considered calling Whitey Smythe, the bespectacled First Amendment expert who represented the *Tribune* in times of legal stress, but there was no sense in our both losing sleep. First I'd see what Treaster had on his mind. At least this time he was talking to my face, instead of trying to hit at me through Nettleman.

The temperature was right around freezing, and the night rain was gathering in sleety patches on the drive. A.J.'s windows were dark as I cranked up the Jeep and coaxed the balky engine. The time with her came back to me with a warm rush and I tried to hold on to it as I drove downtown, but the gloom in the air and the rude awakening worked against me. Early morning can be full of suppressed excitement if you're starting out on an adventure. But it can also overwhelm you with melancholy. All reporters know this is the time of the worst accidents — the ones that smell of blood and alcohol — the time of the cruel crimes, and the time of execution when the anonymous hooded man at Starke pulls the handle of death.

My mood was getting way too morbid. I turned on the FM radio and got a station of old-time rock and roll. It helped.

The street in front of the Federal Building was dark, but a smoky ambient light presaged the dawn. For once I didn't have a problem finding a place to park. As I tugged on my raincoat I caught sight of a bearded man with shaggy clothes huddling in a stone niche. Only an old tarpaulin over his shoulders kept out the wet and cold. The downtown streets were spotted with lost souls like him. Through the huge glass doors of the Federal Building I also could see the back of a woman in a bright pink raincoat, talking to a shirt-sleeved security guard. In leaving the warmth for the sleet she slipped the hood over her hair and, head bowed, passed the derelict in his niche without a sideways glance. The incongruity struck me: the homeless man trembling in the elements paid dues on his wine, making him as much a taxpayer as anyone else, but he wouldn't be tolerated inside this government building to use the urinal or even to warm his hands for a minute.

Priestly's car pulled in behind mine. As I ran to the building I could see him stuffing his shirt in his pants and fumbling with his tie. A tie at a dawn meeting.

"Good morning, sir." The security guard pushed the logbook toward me and thumbed several pages ahead to a blank space.

"I'm with him," I said, gesturing over my shoulder.

Ed Priestly's thin frame sidled into the warmth. He stamped his feet and snapped his raincoat, flicking drops of rain over us and the logbook.

The guard, grim-faced but clearly outranked, dried the pages and offered the book to Priestly. He scrawled his name without looking. His eyes, red-rimmed in their sagging gray pouches, indicated he could have used more sleep this morning and less alcohol last night. We entered an elevator without further word and rose to the offices of Kincaid Treaster.

Thick glass covered the receptionist's window beside a small waiting area. My envoy produced a key and a plastic card to open the heavy door to the inner office. Threading our way in the dark past a phalanx of desks, we could see ahead the open varnished doorway of Treaster's sanctum. Light poured through it.

Priestly tapped on the door frame in passing, then eased onto one end of the leather couch facing a broad, massive desk and pointed me to a chair. Treaster, making notes on a legal pad, did not look up. I presumed this was calculated. His spiky hair was askew, as though he hadn't combed it and the golden stubble on his jaw told me he also hadn't shaved. The rumpled white shirt he wore was open at the collar, his red-starred tie undone.

"Stop stalling, Treaster," I said, "I'll give you ten minutes."

He didn't react, but as quickly as he could do it and save face he laid aside his notes and looked at me with what I think was supposed to pass for a friendly smile.

"How long has it been since we've seen each other, Palmer? Twenty years?"

"It's been a while — except for yesterday."

The smile broadened. "I'd hardly help your career along by making you look like a crony of the big mean D.A."

"I don't think there's a soul on earth who'd call us cronies."

A flicker of irritation crossed his eyes.

"You guys know each other?" Priestly asked.

Today was his turn to be ignored. Treaster didn't respond to Priestly with so much as a grunt. His attention was all for me. "Seen anything of Raymond lately?"

"Not much."

He waited for more, then said, "I thought you all were still buddies."

"No one sees much of Raymond Chancey since he got out of the Marines."

"Nasty shame him leaving Deanna and his kid that way."

My response was a glare.

"I understand Raymond now messes around in the woods like a goddamn coyote."

"There are no coyotes in Florida."

"Wolves then. Or, goddamn armadillos. Florida's got plenty of them, I know."

"Yeah. We got armadillos."

"And Raymond's no better than one, scratching around in the piney woods, eating roots and seeds."

"He loves the outdoors. So what?"

"Nothing. I was just remembering those trips we made up there."

"Did you call me over here at dawn to talk about old times?" I uncrossed my legs. "If so I think I'll go."

The friendly face turned hard. "You always were a prick, Palmer."

A chuckle marked Ed Priestly's presence in the room.

"And you were always a royal pain in the ass," I said.

Priestly's chuckling stopped. "Who do you think you are, talking to a U.S. attorney like that?"

"Maybe I should have run up my colors first," I said sarcastically.

"Better make them Atlanta Penitentiary blues," Priestly shot back. Treaster laughed. "Or yellow."

"So," I said, "the real Ken's decided to surface."

"Don't be so serious, Palmer." His voice was mocking. "I was only remembering the night you panicked at the sight of a few hoods and I had to cold-cock you to calm you down."

"You like to try it again?"

His blue eyes, amused at my anger, dropped from my face to my torso. "You have put on a little weight, but it never was my size that licked you. It was my mind."

"You got me there. Somehow I never could think like you."

There was silence in the room as Treaster decided how he would take my words. His eyes went to a wet copy of the *Tribune* on his desk. "All right, Palmer, so much for the old days. You want this to be strictly cut-and-dried you got it." He jerked up the damp front section. "Why did you alert those dunces on city council about my investigation?"

"What investigation? I thought you were only interested in dragging Julio Montiega around in chains like a triumphant Roman with his slave —"

"Wait just a damn minute. This story about Z Corp and Trammel Zandell is far beyond your ability to dope out. Somebody in my office is leaking stuff to you and I want to know who it is."

"You're grasping at straws. I'm a crackerjack reporter, remember?"

"Oh sure. You worked your ass off since Montiega's arrest two days ago and came up with this data on Z Corp. That won't fly, Palmer. We've spent months going through thousands of documents to put together something on that bunch."

I jerked upright. "Are you saying you've found voting bribes involving Z Corp?"

"I'm not saying anything like that."

"No? Are Z Corp and Zandell clean?"

He leaned across his desk. "Don't piss me off. And what we say here is off the record."

I shook my head. "I'm not going off the record with you."

He finally acknowledged Priestly's presence. "You want to put him in the county lockup?"

The old Fed grinned. "I'd love to."

"On a charge of not letting you go off the record?" I asked with disdain. "They'll love that in Washington."

"No. For witness tampering."

I stared into Treaster's angry blue eyes. That was an interesting threat. "The only way you can have a witness list is if a case involving council members and Z Corp is before a federal judge. Are you saying one is?"

Treaster shook his head. "You can't refuse to go off the record and still pump me for information. As it is we may never get Montiega into court because of your meddling."

"That's bullshit. You moved too fast against the mayor on a political vendetta and if I can prove it, I'll write it."

"So you admit you feel free to attack my office as an institution of justice." His irritation turned to cold calculation before my eyes. "Since you play dirty, the U.S. government will take steps to see just how dirty you are."

A chilling wave worked its way up my spine.

"Look at it from my point of view, Palmer. I knew you as an impoverished street urchin. Now you've got a house William Randolph Hearst could get lost in, and you're still only a police reporter. It's occurred to me the IRS could have a field day with your financial dealings."

"Next I guess you'll promise me a visit from the Gestapo."

His laugh was hollow. "No, the IRS will do. Your real estate dealings alone will keep you and them tied together for years."

"Be careful what you say, Treaster. This sounds a whole lot like harassment, and there's a witness here."

"Is that so? Did you hear anything like harassment, Ed?"

Priestly shifted in his seat. "Hey, what's that? I wasn't listening."

"Treaster, you'll be vegetating in a broom closet in the back of the Justice Department before any of your cronies turn up anything on me. Forget it."

He locked his fingers behind his head. "I don't think so. By the time you clear yourself that little fortune of yours will be gone. Why don't you keep me happy and tell me who's feeding you information. Deanna? She thinks she knows a lot, but she's only a clerk. I found that out in a hurry. It's got to be one of my assistants. He's only a source to you, to me he's a traitor. Think about it long and hard. I mean business."

I stood to go.

"Now, that A.J. Egan," Treaster said.

"What about A.J.?" My voice was no longer steady. If Treaster was going after her as a way to get to me he'd just gone too far.

"She's one smart cookie. She figured out the city council's voting pattern on her own."

He leered as he saw me glance to the soggy pile of papers on his desk.

"Oh, haven't you seen it yet? She makes you look bad. Here she is working for the paper on the other side of the bay, and she digs out a real piece of information while you play guessing games."

"What story?" I asked involuntarily.

"Oh-ho! Got your interest, hunh? Did Ed drag you down here before you saw the papers? Then let me have the pleasure of telling you. A.J.'s broken the rascals' code. I can assure you the three city council members in the Alliance are going back to bed this morning with bad headaches."

The look on my face was obviously satisfying to Treaster. He roared with laughter.

That damned A.J. No wonder she'd been in such a good mood last night. I stalked out with Priestly right behind me, no doubt to see I cleared off the premises.

Deanna was arriving for work as I got to the elevators. She was soaked and brushed past without a word.

"That broad looked mad enough to steam her clothes dry from the inside," Priestly muttered behind me.

I stepped into the elevator.

For once Priestly was right. Deanna was furious. I wondered if my story on Z Corp had upset her as much as it had Treaster. I couldn't help but feel sorry for her. Working in the U.S. attorney's office today wasn't going to be much fun for anyone.

15

SINCE I WAS UP so early anyway I decided to make good use of the time and run down the mayor's errant brother-in-law. As it turned out I spent several hours getting nowhere. You'd think a man who lived as loose as Rojas would be hung over on a Monday morning and easy to find, but that was not the case. He was not at his boardinghouse, or club, or any of the district dives he normally frequented. I left cards all over Alverez with scribbled requests for a call when Rojas surfaced. If he hadn't struck out for Key West, where he spent half his time working both the bars and the games, I should hear something when he got thirsty again.

Hoping at least to get something together on Cesar, I drove to the family home, a neat bungalow surrounded by thick red poinsettias. A.J.'s Bug was in the driveway. I went on by. Maybe my luck would be better at the restaurant. The front was dark, but I decided to give it a try anyway. Don Armonia let me in the back door. He looked terrible. His dark eyes were bloodshot over a heavy growth of whiskers.

I followed him through the kitchen. The door to his father's office was closed. In the front he pointed to a table and said, "Coffee?"

"Sure," I responded and sat down. This was going to be tough. I'd known Don most of my life. He'd worked for his father all the way back to the first Armonia restaurant, a stand-up lunch counter down on El Prado.

The cup he brought me was fixed the only way he knew how—Cuban—which happened to be fine with me, half rich, strong coffee and half cream to make it even richer.

"The pieces don't fit, Palmer. We're going to bury my father tomorrow, and I can't let myself grieve for the outrage. Who'd kill him in such a horrible way?"

I slowly set down the delicate cup. "That's the question we all have." Visiting grieving family members is the hardest thing a journalist does. New reporters either go overboard in gushing sympathy or act like emotionless icemen. Neither way works. All you can do is be honest and try not to take advantage of their grief and shock. "Anything missing from his office?" I tried.

He shook his head.

"Any idea yet where he went Saturday?"

"No, none of his friends saw him. And Papa didn't come back here until after we closed."

"At ten?"

"The clean-up crew works for another thirty minutes or so." Don's voice turned hard. "Chief Salgado came dancing over here this morning with a lot of bull about going slow on saying this was murder."

"He doesn't have any choice," I said uncomfortably. "I understand your father had money problems, big money problems."

Don's chair scraped back and his face leaned into mine. "My father would not kill himself. Maybe he was impulsive but he would not do that. Ask Treaster. He'll tell you. This was cold-blooded murder."

"Your father was a fine man," I said evenly. "A good man. Whatever happened Saturday can't change that."

Don sat back and his gaze dropped to his hands, pressed rigidly on the table. "We may lose the restaurant, Palmer. I don't even know if we can meet the mortgage payments on Mom's house. I tried to talk Papa out of buying that old warehouse, but he had his damned dream and risked everything for it. Everything."

"If you got the zoning, would that help?"

"The option's up next week. There's no way any bank will negotiate a loan for the project with his estate tied up in probate."

As I left, Don was holding his head in his hands.

A few blocks from the *Tribune* the radio scanner began to squawk about a protest at city hall. I headed for the tiered green and pink granite building that was Marlinsport's stab at Art Deco in the thirties. Every few years the cry goes up to replace it. I hope that never happens: it's my favorite city landmark. An anachronism. Not unlike me, in some ways.

The commotion was caused by six women and one bearded man whom I recognized as the operator of a bird sanctuary that received national TV coverage about twice a year for rescuing gulls and pelicans entangled in fishing line or sick from pollutants. But what the protesters lacked in number they made up for with audacity. They'd slung a shrimp net over two councilmen and were shouting questions at them. I pulled into an unloading zone and jumped out.

Link Garland, the high school soccer coach whose pinched nose and beady eyes always gave him a sullen expression, was holding both hands up in mock surrender. Jerry Stack, who'd perfected his rueful smile as a funeral director, also seemed unruffled, except for his curly brown hair caught in the coarse line. They stood patiently, waiting. The sound of police sirens was growing.

The one arguing with the picketers was Rebecca Reed, the sole woman on the city council. Hands on hips, she was standing on the top step above the confrontation. With white hair piled in a bun on her head, blue eyes, a stubborn chin, and an energetic ring to her voice, she reminded me of an irate osprey.

"This is no way to act," she admonished the small group. "Why, Mr. Garland didn't even vote for the Balders Swamp project. I did. And I can tell you why. Ten years ago — when it was cheap — the voters turned down a bond issue to buy that land for a preserve. Well, Mr. Ketch owns it now and we have no right to stop him from developing it."

"No right!" one of the women shouted. "He's destroying the only piece of wilderness left in the city."

Mrs. Reed shook a tiny finger at her. "Where were you when I was pleading for support to buy not only the swamp but a dozen other parcels suitable for parks? All I heard then was 'No more taxes, no more taxes.' Well, now the price of the land is so high the city couldn't afford to buy Balders even if Mr. Ketch would sell it. Be grateful he's agreed to set aside a few acres for a greenbelt. That may not be much, but I'm telling you that's the best we could hope for."

"The state should buy the land," a chorus went up.

Mrs. Reed stared at them. "Your effort is too little, too late."

I watched as the police car came around the corner and slammed to a stop. The nets were removed and Jerry Stack, straightening his hair the best he could, laughed easily and thanked the police for coming but said he wouldn't press charges if the demonstrators would go on home.

Garland nodded in agreement. "No hard feelings," he said glibly. "Hey, I love nature the same as you. But folks have to have homes."

The protestors were still angry, but they'd not expected the men they'd targeted for attack to be so amiable, nor the white-haired grandmother who always supported environmental issues to be so fierce. They were totally disarmed. While the police wrote me out a parking ticket I walked down the street with the demonstrators far enough to reassure myself that their anger over Balders Swamp didn't mean they had knowledge of any zoning corruption. Since I already had a ticket I took a few minutes more to go into city hall. It was obvious after watching them in action that Stack and Garland were a couple of mental lightweights. If there was a city council enclave conspiring to take zoning payoffs its leader had to be young Max Jones. He was not only smart, he had something that in his home district, Marlinsport's prosperous northern neighborhoods, counted for a lot more: he looked good on billboards and he was not Latin.

"I'll be glad to straighten out this misunderstanding on zoning," he said brightly when I appeared at his office door.

"Thanks," I said. "I could use straightening out."

"It's simple. Smart businessmen appreciate dealing with Trammel Zandell. He advises which real estate projects would be acceptable to the city. What's wrong with that? The truth is Z Corp's saved a lot of time and money not only for its clients, but for the city too."

"You don't think it's unusual that various zoning requests were turned down until Z Corp was brought in?"

"So Z Corp scrambles for its clients. Since when is a little initiative a crime in America?" He laughed heartily as if we were sharing a joke. "But don't get me wrong. I'm not complaining about the press. I know the mayor's arrest for taking a bribe makes zoning the hot topic of the day for you guys. But I've got to hand it to you, Palmer. At least your story wasn't wildly speculative like the one in the *Times*. All that rag's trying to do is sell a few more papers on our side of the bay. Right?"

Jones couldn't know how that hurt. If he preferred my story on Zandell to A.J.'s on how the council voted that could only mean hers was better.

"That's not the way the U.S. attorney sees it," I said. "Her voting pattern scenario interests him greatly."

"Voting pattern, my ass. That's wild and irresponsible reporting. There's not one shred of evidence against anyone on the council. You know that, Palmer." He made us sound like drinking buddies.

"Has the federal grand jury subpoenaed you to appear?"

"No, of course not."

"Any interviews with the U.S. attorney's office?"

"Nope."

"That could be good for you, or it could be bad."

"What do you mean?"

"It's possible Treaster doesn't want to risk immunizing you from prosecution by calling you before the grand jury."

"Is that right?" he chortled. "Good thing I play it straight then, hunh, sport?"

When I left he was still laughing. It was a little early for lunch, but I decided to head for the restaurant anyway. About once a week A.J. met me at Jasper's Glass House on the causeway halfway between Marlinsport and New Seville. The view was great there, and so were the steamed mussels. For an Indiana girl raised on country fried steak and sausage, A.J. had developed quite a taste for seafood. Not that she didn't miss Hoosier fare. Every now and then she spoke longingly about sliders. Dumb Cracker that I am, I'd once asked if she meant oysters. That was good for a laugh before she told me a slider is a small square of beef pounded as thin as a playing card and placed on a moist bun with tons of grilled onions. It sounded damn weird to me, but A.J. promised to buy me a bag of the things if we ever got to Indiana. I hoped they'd slide down fast.

I located a bar stool by one of the barrels of roasted peanuts and helped myself while I waited for A.J. Through the misty window low clouds slithered across the wide horizon of churning waters. White seagulls, their wings vibrating, rode the air currents. Every two minutes or so an airliner with blinking lights ghosted past on its final approach for Marlinsport Airport. It was a scene that combined the best of the old with the best of the new in Florida.

When A.J. arrived she started talking in a hurry about how good my Z Corp story was.

"Thanks," I said, "but the big news today was your finding that voting pattern. That was a fine piece of reporting."

She waved my compliment aside. "I can't claim credit for that. I was told how to find it."

"Oh?" I didn't know what else to say.

She thought a moment, her violet eyes locked on mine. "I was tipped, 'Don't read the vote. Listen to it.' And that's what I did. Several years ago the clerk began polling city council on a rotating basis. Records only show how the members voted, not in what order. Each one votes first every fifth time and last every fifth time. That means if an issue has enough votes to pass or fail—whichever the Alliance wants—the guy or the two guys on the end are free to vote the other way."

"And the Alliance members can avoid an obvious pattern on paper while still pocketing their bribes for a job well done."

"Yeah, but without proof to those bribes there's not much meat in the story." A.J. grew a bit wistful. "As my city editor pointed out, you're the one who offered up a possible explanation as to how they did it."

I looked at her somewhat sardonically. "Does that mean you've been to see Zandell today?"

She smiled. "Yes, but the only comment he'd make was an estimation about the size of your brain."

"Yesterday he wanted to measure it with a golf club," I said, then added after a moment, "I wouldn't be at all surprised to see Z Corp fade away."

"And some new company start up?"

I had to admire her quick insight. "That's how crooks stay in business."

"I bet the two of us could keep them on the run." Color rose on her cheeks. A.J. knew she was revealing a wish for us to work as a team rather than as rivals.

"We'd eat 'em up alive," I declared, even though we both knew that was impossible and always would be. Newspapers just don't go for mixing personal and professional lives.

We ordered more mussels, and by the time we'd downed them A.J. was antsy to get back to work.

At our cars we agreed I'd grill steaks for supper, and we sped off in opposite directions.

At the *Trib* Randy Holliman leapt up as soon as he saw me.

"The governor's suspended Montiega," he said excitedly. "I went over to get his reaction, and he shouted at me in Spanish and slammed the door. All I could pick out was 'Treaster.' You wanna try?"

"Sure," I said and went to my desk. There was a stack of telephone messages. Mostly they fell into two categories, those who supported Julio passionately and those who wanted the old Latin finished off. I spent a few tough minutes on the phone pulling quotes from the *alcalde* for Randy's story, and then turned my attention to the real question at hand.

There's a basic rule about reporting on political corruption: follow the money. No matter what or who the cash touches, it taints. Whether as a "consultant's fee" or a "speaker's honorarium" or even an exchange of significant sums at a gambling table, following the cash leads inevitably to the cold heart of the deal. So I next called Howard Ketch, the Balders Swamp developer, a steady Z Corp client, and if Joe Sparkles was leveling with me, the man behind the confrontation over money between Cesar and the mayor.

He refused to talk to me. I left a message with his secretary. "Tell him I was asking about his poker game with Rojas."

There was barely time to sort through my notes before Ketch was on the line.

"If you're writing a story about my playing cards with the mayor's brother-in-law you must be damn hard up for news," he fumed. "The truth is I wouldn't even have played if I'd known Rojas was going to show. I hate to play with drunks."

"Did he pay his debt?"

"What do you mean?"

"He lost to you big."

"That's between me and Rojas."

"Okay. Let me ask you about something else. There's a rumor going around that shortly before Cesar Armonia died Rojas approached him on a business matter in your behalf."

"Rumor! You called me over a damn rumor?" His Boston accent was so heavy I wondered if he'd crawled out from under Plymouth Rock. "What kind of reporter are you?"

"The nosy kind. What business did you have with Cesar?"

"Ask him."

I hesitated.

There was a snicker on the other end of the line. "You have any more questions, call my attorney. He'll want to know why you're trying to ruin my reputation on the word of an old drunk. That oughta play well in court."

I hung up. The call hadn't produced anything that I could print, but it was fascinating that Ketch thought Rojas knew something damaging to his reputation. There was no way the developer could have gotten that from what I'd said on the phone. It was beginning to look more and more like Joe Sparkles had leveled with me.

16

"TREASTER'S GOT A NEW itch about El Principe," Cy Betz murmured to me in an empty hall at the Federal Building near quitting time. I'd gone there after spending the afternoon looking for Rojas. It was time I didn't have to waste. My plan now was to run into Deanna Chancey and ask her to meet me after work.

But she wasn't there. Cy was, his pipe in his mouth.

"Treaster's over at the old factory doing a little reconnoitering," he said. "He wants to see if there are other buildings that could be developed and connected to Cesar's mall."

"Why's he doing that?"

"Desperation. Cesar's death has him so worried about his case against Julio that he sent to city hall for the plat book of Alverez District. I believe there are a couple of new property owners near El Principe that Treaster is trying to link to the mayor in some grand scheme to push Cesar aside."

"Who are they?" I asked.

"You'll have to find that out for yourself," Cy mumbled and slipped down the empty corridor.

On deadline for the early edition, I first went to the *Trib* and fiddled with a story that didn't say much. Suppositions count for zero when it comes time to put one word after the other into the computer. Frustrated, I gave up and drove to El Principe.

I pulled up behind a nondescript sedan at the same back gate where Contreras's half-baked hoods had brought me the day before. Even though it was barely past five, darkness was setting in. The golden glow of the district's street lamps was diffused by leaves swirling in the wind.

As I peered out the Jeep's window at the gloomy old mausoleum, I realized that Cesar, poor hanged Cesar, had been right. Without a doubt El Principe possessed a rich aura of history. It was a perfect location for an ethnic, arty shopping center.

I fished my K-Lite from the glove box and passed through the rusting gate to the courtyard. Scraggly weeds between the bricks danced in the night air and palm fronds clashed like distant castanets. I threw a sharp circle of light against window after window but saw only cracked glass and cobwebs.

A chilly current thundered through the partly open dock doors as across the skin of a drum, giving off a hollow sound that intensified the loneliness of the place. I flashed the light inside. Something about the red bricks, lost in the gloom, then springing ruddily to life in my beam, made me think of spilled gunpowder. Walking through the first floor was a fruitless venture. There was no one about and closed shutters blocked whatever view there was of the surrounding buildings. When I worked my way back to the doors without seeing anything out of the ordinary I considered calling it quits. The circular stairs leading to the floor above didn't look all that stable, especially for me. I'd be a giraffe on a foot bridge.

Then something up there made a fluttering sound, like paper in the wind. Cold bit my hand as I gripped the rail. It was shaky, but still anchored. At my first step the metal framework creaked loudly and lurched to the right. When nothing else happened I ventured another step, and then slowly worked my way around the center pole, my weight tilting the stairway like a carnival ride.

At the top I saw an instant too late that the metal frame had settled away from the ceiling beams, leaving a gap. I jumped and landed with a thump on the second floor.

My eyes went straight to a nearby window framing a startling sight. A full moon, huge and ghostly, was rising behind the Rhumba Academy's neon sign. Lights flashed in waves as the two ballroom dancers moved back and forth across the bone-colored face of the moon. The word DANCE in the sign was dark, and shards of glass tubing glittered on the sidewalk below.

I traced the outline of an enormous room with the flashlight, the place where workers once rolled coronas and panatellas to the steady voice of the lector, reading from, among other things, the *Marlinsport Tribune*. The beam cut past a pile of rags at the far end. My mental perception of burnt powder was sharper. Was that the sound of breathing that I heard? It wasn't my own. I listened. Surely it was only the wind twisting through the derelict building.

The plank floor groaned under my large feet. Cloth fluttered in the distant mass upon the floor. I cast an arc of light across it again. Finally I realized the lung-biting smell of gunpowder wasn't my imagination, and the dark form wasn't a pile of rags.

Long-time police reporter that I am, I still approached the body reluctantly. My white beam swept up the crumpled pin-striped pants to the open vest, across the crimson-soaked shirt, and up the silky tie lying askew. His left hand, red and glistening, grasped at his neck. The right arm was sprawled almost straight out. A small pistol rested inches from the curled fingers.

I shifted the circle of light slowly to the angry, twisted face of Kincaid Treaster. His eyes stared at the last thing they had ever seen, bare pipes crisscrossing the ceiling far above us. Great pools of blood surrounded his neck and shoulders. Nearby, spread open and soaked with his blood, was a plat book page.

Cold air poured in the window, stirring the spiky blond hair above his forehead and drying the perspiration on my own. Kneeling, I put my hand before Treaster's mouth and nose, but there was no warmth. As I felt for a pulse I noticed a small mole at the corner of his left eye that I'd never seen before. There was no pulse.

I rocked back on my heels and stared out into neon-hued space. The neon dancers performed their eternal turn to silent music. I forced myself to look back at the earthly remains of a man I'd never liked. His blood, like mercury, oozed across the slick plat sheet toward a series of penciled notations in the margins. I dropped to the floor for a closer look. As Cy had indicated, it was a plat of the blocks around El Principe. I recognized Cesar's name, but some words scrawled over it were unclear in the weak light. On one large building were two names I knew well. Howard Ketch and Trammel Zandell.

Suddenly every creak and sigh of the old building was an alarm. Turning around, I swept the room with the flashlight but confronted only empty space and vague shadows. I stood and made my way to the leaning staircase. A vagrant impulse almost caused me to ask Treaster to wait, for I'd only be a minute. Strange thoughts come in the presence of the dead.

Outside, I spied a pay phone across the street at the foot of the stairs to the old dance hall. Broken glass crunched underfoot as I ran toward it. My quarter clicked in the phone's innards, and I told Paula where Kincaid Treaster was and how he was. It took maybe thirty seconds.

Then I called the police.

Emilio Salgado, Marlinsport's stocky, straight-arrow chief of police, shook his head in disbelief.

"Look at your palm prints around the body, Palmer. It's like a damn seal's been up here!"

Beside him, Cy Betz's ashen face was contorted with anguish and indecision. His jittery eyes flitted from the powdered floor to the winking neon across the way, its colors augmented by the flashing blues and reds of the vehicles clotting the street. I couldn't help but wonder if he'd set me up, then dismissed the sickening thought. This was no time to doubt him. Around us words whispered into handsets were passed along outside in the foggy cold by the electronically amplified voices of uniformed officers with bull horns.

"Let the medical examiner's wagon through immediately," Salgado growled, and his words came back to us from below.

There was an odd, movie-set atmosphere in the cigar factory's upper room. The ghostly powder formed an almost luminescent aura around Treaster. A slew of investigators and I — their only witness — milled in a loose circle starkly lit by floodlights set up on the outer rim. Drifting up to us were the voices of reporters below being held at bay by police. A brief visit by Ed Priestly was peculiarly touching. Arriving in the second wave of officers and investigators, he knelt reverently beside the body. I would never understand the attraction Treaster had for some people, and why he'd always been hardest on them. Priestly, almost staggering in his grief, soon left.

"Are we going to find your prints all over this place?" Salgado chided me once more.

I thought of Joe Sparkles. His prints, as well as mine, could be on the doors downstairs. What a story that would make — a mobster's prints at the scene of Treaster's murder. How the reporters would love that! Only I would know that it didn't mean a thing. Or at least I supposed it didn't.

"Maybe downstairs, and on the railing. From the sounds below I'd say by now you've probably got a dozen other prints on top of mine."

Salgado shot me a hard look, not made any softer by the long climb from his eyes to mine. Pulling at my arm, he led me to the far window.

"What were you doing up here tonight?" His voice was barely loud enough for me to hear — and for Cy, who dogged us. This was the question I'd been dreading.

"I was told to come."

"By whom?"

"I can't say."

"Your editor?"

"I can't say."

"Treaster?"

"No."

"Now we're getting somewhere. Were you tipped he was dead?"

"I can't say."

"My God, Palmer, this is no ordinary case. I can't play the First Amendment game with you. That's a U.S. attorney stretched out on the floor!"

"I know."

"Do you also know I'm to the point of sending you to headquarters?"

"I'd like to call the *Trib*'s lawyer," I said reluctantly, knowing Salgado was under an enormous amount of pressure himself in this thing, but I had no choice.

The chief's mouth twisted, and his dark eyes lit in anger. "Not on your life. You're not calling anybody, because I'm not charging you with anything — yet. Bennie!"

"Sir?" The balding detective moved in beside me.

"Take Palmer Kingston downtown and question him as a material witness. I want to know every move he's made, every telephone he's been near, everyone he's talked to in the last twenty-four hours."

Emilio Salgado glared at me, then bent a little, but not far enough. "Give him a chance to think this through, Bennie. I don't want to be diverted into a side issue on the freedom of the press. But we've got to move on this case — you, me, even Mr. Betz here — or it'll be rolled right out from under us by Washington."

Cy finally stirred. "Murdering a U.S. attorney is a federal offense, Chief." He glanced at me out of the corner of his eye. "But we'll want your help. Go ahead and take him in."

"Come on, Palmer," Bennie said. Betz gestured and an FBI agent moved to my other side.

"What if I won't go?" I grumbled.

"Oh, you'll go," Salgado said. "Flatly refusing to cooperate in a murder investigation would be plain stupid, Palmer. The judge would be happy to leave you in jail while he sorts through the technicalities."

"Okay," I said grimly, "but I don't know anything about Treaster's death that will help you. Your investigation would move a lot quicker if you took my word for it."

"Sorry," Salgado said, and motioned to Bennie.

At the foot of the stairs the camera lenses were like stubby black spears pointed up at my face. My two escorts, using me for a ram, shoved and battered us through the crowd. I was surprised at the questions hurled by the backward-running reporters. I felt under attack and I didn't like it.

"Are you arresting him?" I heard loud and clear.

"Does this clear up Treaster's murder?"

A tight-lipped Bennie and the FBI agent said not a word, and I certainly wasn't going to give them a story.

Once outside the courtyard I was stuffed in the back of a city patrol unit, one of those rolling cages with steel mesh and no inside door handles. I tried not to blink at the glaring lights or reveal my anger. But I'm sure I failed. I got a glimpse of A.J. staring at me from the crowd. She looked numb.

The ride to the station was silent. I'd known the two guys escorting me for years. But they had jobs to protect and I had a secret to keep. I concentrated on the night lights outside my window. It's amazing how good even a dilapidated part of town appears from the backseat of a police car.

At the station we went into a little green room — Bennie, a second detective, an assistant federal prosecutor, the FBI man, and me. I recited my piece, that a tip led me to El Principe, then told what I'd found there. That was it, repeated quite a few times. I was beginning to wonder what was detaining Whitey Smythe, the *Tribune*'s lawyer. I had a long, exhausting time to wonder before he finally appeared at the door about one in the morning. I perked up immediately. Good old Paula, I thought, she'd not left me alone to the wolves after all. At least I thought this until I glimpsed the solemn expression behind Whitey's wire-framed glasses. Evading my eyes, he demanded to speak to me privately. Bennie scratched his bald spot and then agreed.

"God, am I glad to see you, Whitey," I said as soon as we were alone. "Put these guys in their place and get me out of here."

Whitey sat down heavily across from me. He looked ill. "That's not how it's going to work, Palmer," he said tensely.

My stomach gave a turn. "You are representing me, aren't you?"

"I'm here representing Mr. Nettleman."

"You mean the *Tribune*."

"In this case, no, I mean the publisher."

"Whitey, don't play games with me. Are you saying the paper isn't behind me on this?"

He spoke hesitantly, a lawyer lost for words. "Mr. Nettleman saw the late news . . . and he, ah . . . doesn't like what he saw."

"I guess I don't make a fetching media star, hunh?"

"He says the newspaper has an obligation to do everything it can to bring Treaster's killer to justice."

"How's keeping me here going to help justice?"

"He wants you to cooperate."

"By revealing my source?" I asked in disbelief.

He nodded painfully.

"Never."

Perspiration popped out all over Whitey's tall forehead. I could see he was nearly as upset as I was about this.

"I thought you'd say that, Palmer. But it was my duty to convey Nettleman's position." He leaned over the table toward me. "But, frankly, you don't have to worry about jail — at least not at this point. They'll screw around with you awhile and then let you go."

This may not have been as big a shock as Treaster's death, but it was way up there. I found my voice, but it wasn't one I recognized. "What you're saying is I'm going to take the heat for protecting a *Tribune* source while the paper rolls over."

"I tried," Whitey said hurriedly. "So did Wilson and Paula. They were practically on their knees pleading your case. But Nettleman was adamant. It's his view the community won't stand for the *Tribune* protecting a murderer."

I was so mad I could only laugh. "It sounds like the four of you sat around discussing if I knew who killed Treaster, or even if I did it myself."

Color rose above Whitey's starched white collar, and it hit me like a pistol shot that that was exactly what they'd done.

"My God, Whitey, I haven't the vaguest idea who killed Treaster."

He eyed me solemnly. "I want you to know that even if I can't go stomping into Salgado's office on your behalf you're in a pretty good position. The Florida press associations, SPJ, even the *New Seville Times*, won't tolerate them holding you for not giving up a source."

Suddenly I felt a deep yearning for my own lawyer.

"Thanks," I said dryly. "I really feel great, knowing it's going to take the *Times* to keep me out of jail."

Whitey stood. "I'll do what I can," he muttered.

I didn't bother to look up when he left. In the next minute the inquisition began again.

As it turned out, Whitey was right. They screwed around with me until a little past dawn and then opened the door and let me go.

$\triangledown$

18

A WONDERFUL AROMA OF percolated coffee and maple-cured bacon greeted me at the back door. Along with A.J.

"Jesus, Palmer, did they work you over with a hose?" She gaped at me. "Your eyes are as black and oily-looking as a busted transmission."

"You got that line from me," I complained, keeping her at arm's length. I knew I smelled of the Marlinsport jail.

A.J. was in bleached, nearly white jeans and one of her father's white shirts she'd stolen on her last visit home to Indiana. She loved big shirts, but in any of mine she looked like a parakeet in a laundry bag. She led me toward the breakfast table.

"I'm not kidding, Palmer. You really look bad. When did you sleep last?"

I just stared at her.

"Oh," she said. "That long ago."

She pushed me down before a stack of pancakes and began stirring enough sugar into my coffee to turn it to fudge.

"You need carbohydrates," she said, catching my look.

"Where are the papers?" I asked, then spotted them tucked behind the toaster.

"There's plenty of time for the papers. Eat. You don't want to insult the cook."

I recognized a stall. My hand reached toward the counter.

"Here's your eggs!" A.J. deftly slipped a hip between me and my goal.

"That bad," I groaned, and sank into my seat.

I went through the eggs, bacon, and pancakes like Diamond Jim Brady. When A.J. couldn't think of anything else to stick before me I grabbed the papers and flipped the *Trib* open on the table.

"Ohh . . . shit." My coffee cup sagged, as I'm sure my face did.

"I had no idea the *Tribune* would . . . ," A.J. started.

I carried the paper to the window to read it in the gathering morning light.

"It's not all bad," A.J. tried again. "Look at the bottom. There's a disclaimer in that news story on behalf of you and the First Amendment."

I recognized Moses' touch in the short statement, and I was sure it was levered — or hammered — into the paper by Paula and Wilson.

But the rest of the page was hard on my digestion. Over all was a headline that screamed: "U.S. Attorney Slain Here; Reporter Refuses To Talk." In the old days of Ludlow type I'd have called it one hundred twenty point, but anymore I can't tell. Below was a stark, grainy picture of Treaster's body — hidden mostly behind the wide shoulders of detectives and technicians — and a nasty one of me in a police car peering through the mesh.

A "Statement to the Citizens of Marlinsport" ran down one side, with a secondary head saying: "Responsibility of the Press in Times of Lawlessness." Its words burned into my soul:

We are not going to turn our streets over to murderers or decisions concerning our civic responsibilities over to reporters. The *Tribune* is now in a process of review to determine if Palmer Kingston should be suspended for withholding vital information from the police and federal authorities in the investigation of Treaster's murder.

It was signed by Nettleman.

"I can't believe he'd stoop that low," I muttered. "He's going to destroy the *Tribune*."

"Did he talk to you at all, Palmer?"

"No, he sent the *Trib*'s — his lawyer."

I felt A.J.'s hand on my shoulder. "It isn't over yet. You know the newsroom is behind you."

I turned and faced her. "Yeah, well, my phone's not exactly ringing off the wall."

A.J. looked a little sheepish. "That's my doing. I unplugged it. This was all so — well, I wanted to give you a chance to absorb everything."

I nodded. "Leave it unplugged."

After A.J. dosed another cup of coffee for me I asked to see the *Times*. She nudged it toward me and sat down, her hands clasped tensely on the table.

Her paper covered the hell out of me, too, but not with the meanness of my own. The photo was of me coming out the door of El Principe instead of squashed down inside a squad car. I looked like a lineman punching open a hole on fourth down at the goal line. The cutline used words like "veteran" and "honored" and mentioned my Pulitzer and damned near every other journalism award I'd ever won.

"You've got friends all over Florida," A.J. murmured. There was worry in her violet eyes. "If they try to jail you—"

I reached over and touched her cheek. "It's not the prospect of jail upsetting me."

"I know."

She got up and busied herself at the sink, her back to me.

"Anyway, if I go to jail over this I can have my pick of jobs—the *Miami Herald*, the *New York Times*—even CBS. How'd I look on the tube? Good, hunh?"

Even though she knew I'd never leave Marlinsport, my joking at least got her to turn around.

"Forget it, Palmer." She tried to smile. "You were all over television last night, and I don't think any of it qualifies as an audition tape."

Her voice trailed away as I looked back at the *Times* and began reading the main story; her byline was on it. After dealing with the murder scene and how I found Treaster, she matter-of-factly outlined the controversy developing over my refusal to reveal why I was at the old cigar factory. There were already speculations by the police and federal authorities, she wrote, including one that Treaster himself called the *Tribune* reporter to meet him. She quoted Salgado, repeating my brief statement that I had no knowledge of how or why or who killed Treaster and that my being in the cigar factory had nothing to do with his death.

Next she quoted the *Times*'s lawyer:

> There is a long-established precedent for Palmer Kingston's refusal to reveal why he went to El Principe and who told him to go. The *Tribune* reporter acted responsibly and quickly in reporting the death to the authorities.

It was the story that should have appeared in the *Tribune*. I skimmed through her outline of Treaster's career and suddenly found my eye riveted to one paragraph. I read: "A source close to the zoning investigation says Treaster had indicated Monday afternoon he was going to El Principe to meet someone in connection with the bribery scandal."

A rather broad hint Treaster was set up. And not what Cy had told me. I glanced A.J.'s way. She was watching me closely.

"You must have worked half the night to get all this," I said.

"Frankly, I'm at a loss for words. Would it be appropriate for a *Trib* reporter to tell one from the *Times* he's grateful?"

Her face softened. "I just followed the story."

I was getting up to hug her when the doorbell rang.

"Too bad you couldn't unplug that too," I said and moved stiffly toward the front of the house. My night with the police would linger in my bones until I got some sleep.

I crossed the polished wood floor of the banquet room, which, with the small rosewood library off it, was the heart of my apartment. Overhead, sunlight streamed through the stained glass and sparkled on the highest neon sign, the one from the Casino. Fourteen feet tall, it loomed under the cathedral ceiling like a giant grandfather clock.

Paula was at the front door. She explained quickly that she'd been trying to call but couldn't get through.

"Come on in," I said.

She and A.J. exchanged greetings in the kitchen. They were about the same size, although Paula's figure was fuller. They were casual acquaintances, these two, crossing paths mostly at my parties. I knew they had a lot of respect for each other, and it was too bad that circumstances kept them from being friends. Here they were, anthracite black hair and campfire red, standing side by side a little below shoulder high on me. They were a lovely sight. But not for long. A.J. beat it out the back door, saying she had to get ready for work. She knew Paula couldn't talk to me in front of her.

"I've got lots of news," Paula said as soon as the door closed.

I pulled out a chair for her. I was too beat to stand.

"Any of it good?"

"Leland Hines is flying down from headquarters today."

That was a piece of news to savor. Leland Hines was the editorial director of the group that now owned the *Tribune*. Although he seldom took a personal interest in Marlinsport, Hines was highly respected as a journalist. My initial delight in his coming began to dim, however, as I considered the possible reasons for it. "Who jury-rigged that deal?"

"Wilson."

"Why?"

"Because the *Tribune*'s in danger of losing its managing editor, city editor, and probably half its reporting staff."

I hesitated. "I'm sorry."

"Palmer, we did what we could last night with Nettleman, but he was impossible. Wilson had no choice but to call Hines."

You mean your jobs are on the line on this?"

"If Nettleman suspends you, yes." Her voice wavered with emotion. "Oh, it's not just for you . . . it's for all of us. I'd sure be a piss-poor city editor if I didn't stand up for a reporter with your reputation when he's attacked for taking a professional stand by a pathetic excuse for a publisher like Nettleman."

"That was a mouthful, Paula. Strunk and White would tell you to break it up."

Paula gave me an exasperated look and then laughed. "Wilson wants to see you, but not now, later."

"How about Hines?"

"I don't know. Stay handy just in case. But my guess is he'll talk to Wilson and Nettleman, make a decision, and get right back on his jet."

"You think he'll turn Nettleman around?" I gestured toward the lurid front page spread on my table.

She leveled agitated green eyes at me. "Nothing's for sure in this business, is it, Palmer? But I haven't started packing yet."

That brought a smile to my tired face. But hers was clouding up.

"There's more?" I asked.

"I thought I ought to tell you about me and Treaster."

My heart began to speed up. "You and Treaster?"

"I spent Sunday with him." She blushed. "Thought I might learn something. He told me what great times you two had as kids. How you did everything together."

"Be serious."

"I am. He also wondered if there was an ethical problem with your reporting on his office—because of your friendship."

As weary as I was, that was good for a laugh.

"One more thing, Palmer. I want to know who your source is. Is it that snitch in Treaster's office who's been feeding you stuff?"

"Think what you're asking me. If I give up the name you'll have to tell Wilson, and a lawyer or two. If Nettleman gets hold of it he may compromise us all with his abominable judgment."

She sighed. "Okay, we'll let it ride for now, but I'd still like to know the circumstances."

"I was told Treaster was going over to El Principe with a city plat book to work on his zoning case against the mayor. It seemed a good idea for me to drop by."

Her eyes narrowed. "Sure sounds like somebody in Treaster's office, or city hall."

I didn't answer.

"I guess, then, we're down to waiting."

I nodded.

"You'll be doing me, Wilson, and yourself a favor if you don't go poking around today until Hines has his say."

"My only plans in the next few hours are to take a shower, finish reading the papers, and get some sleep."

"That reminds me," she said. "There's something that didn't make either paper you need to know."

I raised tired eyes.

"Treaster's office and apartment were broken into last night or early this morning."

"Both? Anything missing?"

"Hard to tell. When the police went to secure his condo on the Point they found a balcony door ajar. Nothing was out of place, but Salgado's sure the drawers were searched."

"And the office?"

"An FBI man named Priestly went back there after you were arrested and found his desk jimmied. Some papers were scattered, but nothing's missing as far as he can tell."

"What kind of papers?"

Her eyes sparkled as red eyebrows rose.

"Not evidence. That's kept in a special locker. It was receipts for his expense account and personal stuff."

She was teasing me somehow. I could see it in her eyes.

"What?"

"He had a shit list."

"Everybody has a shit list."

"I mean he kept a list. Actually. In a calendar book. He marked down names of staff members, and others, who said things he didn't like. Randy was there when the cops found it."

"Did Treaster write anything yesterday?"

"Nothing. Maybe he never got around to it."

"The day before?"

"He called you a son of a bitch."

"So much for our great friendship," I mumbled. "I suppose the police liked that."

"You were one of many. Even Salgado and Betz got a mention. Fascinating, huh?"

"Yes, fascinating," I agreed, "particularly if the one who killed him's in there."

Paula stared at me across the table. "Un-unh, Palmer, forget it. At least for today." Her chair scraped backward. "Go to bed. You look awful."

It sounded like good advice to me.

$\triangledown$

19

T HE NASTY DRIZZLE LET up by late afternoon, but the cold lingered. I was lying down, not in bed, but on a wheeled crawler in the workshop. One of the *Trib*'s handsets, turned up loud, was on the concrete floor beside me. The call from Paula, telling me whether I was on the story or off the payroll, hadn't come yet.

I wiped my hands and surveyed what I'd accomplished on the little red car. It was gorgeous. Nervous energy had propelled me to work on the Austin after only a few hours of fitful sleep. With nowhere to go while my career was settled over coffee or scotch somewhere in town, I'd seized the time to finish A.J.'s present. Or hoped I had. If the engine ran, and the steering was right, and the suspension was as solid as I thought, it would be ready by Christmas day. If. Always if.

I wandered to the end of the garage and stared at the classy midnight-blue Cadillac Cat Man had owned. It was too bad, at least for me, that Mrs. Contreras hadn't yet been able to find the missing traveling trunk that fit on the back bumper. If my job with the *Trib* wasn't over, one of the things I needed to investigate was the possibility her son Joe Sparkles was involved with both the zoning corruption and Treaster's death. That could lead to the kind of story a mother never appreciates.

I went back to work on the little Austin. The last of the running gear was fastened into place when the radio squawked.

"That you, Palmer?" It was Paula's voice, scratchy but hers.

"It's me."

"You still on hold?"

"I am." The whole damned city could listen to our conversation. Especially the TV news teams. They monitored everything.

"Call me." It was a standard instruction in the business.

I went to the kitchen phone.

"We don't have any idea here what's happened," she said when I got through. "I just thought I'd give you a holler."

"Been at it a good long time, haven't they?"

"Don't get teed off. It's the stupidest things that always take the carefulest handling."

"Carefulest? And you're a city editor."

"Don't start in on me, Palmer. Carefulest is perfectly good English."

"You mean perfectlyest good English."

"And I'm the Metro Editor."

"Yeah."

"Anyway, you don't sound mad."

"No, I don't."

"Besides, you're the last person I'd accept English lessons from."

"Shouldn't that be I'm the last person from whom you'd accept English lessons?"

"Fuck you, Palmer. I take it you're going to survive this, one way or the other."

"I'll survive . . . but I don't want to leave the *Trib*."

"If you do we all do. You gonna offer me shelter in your palace if I'm out on my butt?"

"You'll have to sleep in one of the towers."

"Ohhh. What about Wilson?"

"He can sleep in the garage."

She laughed. "You've got a phone message. A doozy. It says, 'The blue crabs are running at seven.' No name. No phone number. Marge took it on the switchboard at two thirty-six."

"One of my fishing buddies must think I'm gonna have a lot of time on my hands."

"Sure, Palmer. Keep the radio handy. I'll let you know when I know."

I walked slowly back to the garage. The sun was giving up its feeble attempt to shine for the day, and I thought it would be a good time for a ride. The roads would be wet, but I had to test drive the little machine sometime or A.J. might be left at the curb while it took off.

After some maneuvering of my gleaming hoard I made room for the Austin's exit. Other jobs presented themselves in the process: a Lincoln needed work on its starter and the Cord's engine sounded like the beginning of valve trouble. I'd fix them one day.

Getting into the tiny Austin was a hell of a problem. In fact, I never really made it. I had to put the top down and sit sideways to drive. My rump was mostly on the passenger side, my big feet toeing the pedals and my torso thrust up out of the minuscule interior. If I ever rode in it with A.J. we'd look like Ferdinand and Minnie Mouse.

I gave a good look around to make sure A.J. wasn't about, then crept her present into the gloom, unwinding from my cramped quarters to lock the doors behind me. Peering left and right as carefully as any first-grader I made my way off the island, silently blessing any intersection at which I didn't have to down shift since that involved reaching my left hand across my legs, and trying to find strictly by feel a clutch pedal about the size of a daisy.

As I drove, my delight in the car—the forerunner to my much beloved Jeep—was spoiled by a stupid limerick, which rolled through my head no matter how hard I tried to concentrate on something else:

> There was a young man from Boston
> who bought himself a new Austin.
> There was room for his ass
> and a gallon of gas
> but his balls hung out and he lost 'em.

I hoped A.J.'d never heard the silly damn thing.

The traffic was bumper-to-bumper until I was nearly all the way to Balders Swamp. The country road was deep in twilight. I turned on the headlights. They worked! At the entrance to Howard Ketch's ever-growing development I swung right and drove down several streets of gigantic homes and found the area where Nick Darvin lived. It was a narrow winding lane of walled terrace townhouses, one right after the other with only enough room before each one to park a couple of cars. I stopped in front of Darvin's. The sole window on the second floor was dark. It seemed likely enough that a twenty-year city employee could afford one of these on his salary. There was nothing distinctive about them.

When a car pulled into the slot next door, I kind of broke my promise to Paula and called to the exiting driver, a middle-aged woman whose shoulders drooped with the weariness of a long day at work. "Have you seen Mr. Darvin around?"

"Darvin?"

"The man who lives here."

"No." She turned to go.

"Do you know him?"

"We've hardly passed the time of day."

"Is he a good neighbor?" I called after her.

She laughed. "This wall makes him a good neighbor."

I didn't call anything else. Heads turned on the drive back to town. I wanted to think it was because of the crimson jewel I was driving, but I suspect the looks were for the moose looming out of it. At my garage I was carefully working the Austin back inside when the handset squawked beside me. There was no mistaking who it was.

"Haul it on in her, big guy. I've saved your jumbo ass again."

I put the Austin's top back up, double-bolted the garage doors, and sped away for the *Tribune* in my Jeep.

"You may kneel and kiss my ring," Wilson said as I joined him and Paula in his office. He even had the gall to rise and extend the top of his hand to me.

I plopped down in one of his cushy blue chairs. "What happens now?"

"This." He shoved a proof toward me. It was Wednesday morning's editorial page. "Fastest flip-flop in newspaper history. If his turn-around time's half that good in the bedroom they'll bury Mrs. Nettleman with a smile."

"We've still got Cy Betz to worry about," Paula said.

"Screw Betz! He fools with one of my reporters and I'll nail his hide." Wilson was almost giddy. I felt it a bit myself.

"I assume this means I'm on Treaster's killing."

"Of course, you're on the damn story," Wilson shot back. "Nothing's changed. I'm still the managing editor of this fucking newspaper, and you're still the investigative reporter. In fact, I want a first-hand account of what you saw in El Principe."

"You've got it."

"Watch Betz," Paula cautioned. "If he pushes for your source, you could still wind up with contempt problems."

Wilson suddenly turned serious. "I understand you wouldn't reveal the name to Paula. I'll accept that for now, Palmer, but I'm warning you not to fuck this up. Get us the name of Treaster's killer before the *Times*. Don't let that A.J. Egan beat us on this story again."

"I'll try."

At the door I glanced back. "Thanks, both of you."

"It better be a fuckin' good story," Wilson said loudly.

Moses looked up from his terminal and grinned at me with pure delight. "Welcome back," he muttered, his bony Adam's apple dancing in the loose red skin of his neck.

20

THE MARLIN COUNTY MEDICAL examiner's office is caught in an odd ramp loop to the interstate, close to the police station. It's not easy to get there, but then not that many folks are trying to. It's certainly not one of my favorite spots, but that late in the day I couldn't afford to wait around for an autopsy report.

Dr. Rudy Shake seemed glad for a little live company. He rambled at me cheerfully as we leaned over the examining table.

"Compared to some you and I have seen, Palmer, this one's positively dainty, almost fastidious. Remember when Batman Dickson's head and body parts washed up on Marlin Beach during three days of high tides?"

I mumbled a reply and watched with knotted stomach as his gloved fingers carelessly spanned the red ragged hole in Kincaid Treaster's neck. The big prosecutor was chilled down by biological necessity and draped at my request. I'd never known Shake to worry much about modesty for the dead.

"Pure chance the man's gone. If his carotid artery was where it oughta be he'd be walkin' around right now with only a sore throat and a Bandaid."

"Are you saying his attacker was not trying to kill him?"

"Whoa, now, that's jumpin' a bit far, Palmer. After all, the man is dead."

I felt phony being on a first-name basis with the tactless medical examiner; I really couldn't warm to him. But he'd always taken a friendly stance with me because we're both Florida Crackers. So I didn't fight it.

"Had lunch at Rotary with Treaster the day he was killed," he rambled on, baring teeth that a man in his profession should have the money to fix. "Roast beef, cauliflower heads, and creamed asparagus. Treaster was still workin' on the beef when he got it. Wanna see?"

He flipped the sheet back like a 1930s comic doing the dinner table gag, revealing Treaster's resewn body. It looked like a huge laced boot.

"For Christ's sake, Doc, give me a break."

Shake snorted. "There's nothing left in there anyway except his own innards."

I stooped and peered at the neck wound to refocus his attention. "What sort of knife?"

"Not a knife."

"Come on."

"Look closer."

I was irked at the guessing game. "Okay, it's ragged but it's wide enough for a hunting knife."

The doctor grabbed a scratch pad with the logo of a local funeral home on it and drew a fair representation of what he believed had ended Kincaid Treaster's life.

"The wound's three centimeters wide at the surface, narrows steadily as it passes through tissue, nicking the bone and terminating in a rounded point ten centimeters below the surface. The epidermal layer is slightly bruised in a disc-shaped pattern, maybe from a rude hilt."

"You're saying the weapon's edges were blunt—like a letter opener?"

"A welding rod would be more like it, if it tapered. Or a screw driver." He glanced up at me. "He was killed in a cigar factory?"

I nodded. "A deserted one."

"Maybe the killer found an old tool lying around."

I knew he was wrong, but I couldn't say why.

Shake scratched his chin with a bloody glove. "The real odd thing about this killing is the angle of attack. It was almost straight down. Either Treaster was not on his feet when he was stabbed or this was done by the Jolly Green Giant—or you." He laughed, showing me those gray teeth once more.

"Who're you working for on this one, Doc?"

"Hah! Good question. The city and the county are paying my salary, but the Feds want this one bad."

"Yeah," I said, thinking of Priestly. I forced myself to look at his dead hero's face.

"Any signs of struggle?"

"No trauma, if that's what you mean, except where he fell to the floor. Back of his head's bruised, but it didn't kill him. His coat lapel and shirt were torn, like someone grabbed him, but there wasn't another mark on the big bugger. One jab did him in. He bled to death in a couple of minutes, but it took me forever to clean him up."

"What happens to him now?"

"Tomorrow we ship his body to Washington for burial. This wasn't his home, you know."

I left Rudy Shake shoving Treaster back into the cooler. When I reached my Jeep I sat in it, my hands folded over the steering wheel, and waited for the queasiness to pass. The image of Treaster's stitched-up body was hard to shake. Death looks better laid out in a Sunday suit.

It was too cold to sit still for long, so I cranked up the Jeep and negotiated the expressway loop for downtown. I arrived at the Federal Building five minutes too late. Civil servants were already pouring out when I drove by. My only chance to catch Deanna was at the parking garage down the block. As I pulled through the entrance gate I saw her amid the crowd pushing into the elevator. In a bad imitation of Mario Andretti I gunned the Jeep up the ramp, barely avoiding the stream of cars coming down. I screeched to a stop at the second level but Deanna didn't exit. I twisted up the concrete ramp three more times before I finally saw her step out onto the fifth floor.

She didn't seem happy to see me.

"What do you want?" she whispered at the Jeep's window.

"How about some dinner?"

"No."

So much for finesse. "Can you spare a couple of minutes?" Anticipating another refusal, I added, "He can't get you fired now."

She hesitated. "I don't know anything about how Ken died."

"I didn't think you did. This is about zoning."

She got in. I drove to the roof, parked, and shifted in the seat to face her. "How are you doing?"

"Fine, Palmer. What do you want?"

"Two things. First, Nick Darvin. I can't seem to find out much about him."

"Not much to tell. He wasn't a bad sort to work with, although his only interests were sports and food. His desk always smelled like a bakery."

"You really think he's on vacation?"

"He had a lot of accrued time. Look, Palmer, if you're trying to get me to say Nick was involved with the Alliance, forget it. As far as I know he did his job and went home and watched television."

"Do you know if any zoning petitions involving Joseph Contreras came across his desk?"

"Joe Sparkles? Why?"

"I'm just curious."

"I see. Well, you can keep on being curious. I'm sure that old mobster's behind any number of legitimate businesses in Marlinsport, but his name certainly isn't going to appear on any zoning requests."

"But you hear things, Deanna. There was a rumor last year that organized crime was behind the new dog track. Was Darvin involved with that zoning?"

"Gossip and rumors. Is that what you're after?" Deanna said irritably.

"No, I want to know who handled the zoning for the track."

"Check the records."

"I would if I could. Those records are among the missing. Like Darvin."

Deanna looked at me strangely. Then the irritation fell from her face. "I get it," she said. "You think Contreras killed Darvin to cover his trail, then killed Ken when he figured it out."

I laughed. "That's some scenario, Deanna. But I'm not thinking anything. Not yet. All I want is a little information."

"Sure, Palmer. I know how it goes. If Contreras is involved in Ken's death there's no way on earth it'll ever be proved. So stay the hell away from me. I don't want to end up dead, too."

I delivered Deanna back to her car and headed south to meet my crabbing buddy. Since it was a little early I stopped on the way for a pizza and to call A.J. She wasn't at home. If she was working late it could only mean trouble for the *Trib*, and for me.

At the pier, choppy swells were throwing up cold sprays against the pilings. I searched the horizon, but the lights of New Seville were invisible across the foggy bay. When I spotted Cy Betz I decided he was either getting cocky or forgetful. There was no sign of fishing gear, and he was shivering in a thin business suit.

"Very discreet, Cy," I said. "Who'd ever guess you were an attorney dressed like that?"

He took a pull of Bond Street. "I fit in better here like this than I would showing up at the office later in a slicker and a rain hat."

"Going back in, hunh?"

"These are long days and short nights for the good and the godly, Palmer. We'll be meeting over Treaster's body long after it's in the ground . . . Are things going to be all right for you at the paper?"

"There's hope."

He seemed embarrassed. "I have to play this thing through."

"I know."

"I wasn't setting you up, Palmer."

"That's reassuring. You have any idea who killed him?"

"Not a glimmer."

"What about the charges against the *alcalde?* Are you going to drop them?"

"I can't. At least not yet. It wouldn't look right."

"Poor Julio. He gets screwed by Treaster, dead or alive. What about the break-ins?"

Cy smiled wryly. "I've ruled out coincidence."

"Seems a reasonable conclusion. Any idea what Treaster had that someone would want that bad?"

"Evidence, I assume . . . Maybe I was wrong about him, Palmer. Maybe he was onto something real."

"You know which was burgled first?"

"No. But this has Washington's full attention. They want to know if organized crime's involved."

Deanna's fearful words echoed in my brain. "Why?" I asked.

"Getting into the Fed Building was no job for amateurs. In fact, both break-ins look professional. No prints. No witnesses."

"What did Washington say about his diary?"

"So you heard about that, hunh."

I nodded. "What's in it?"

"I'm afraid the things you and I only think about. Paranoia Rampant. Leaps of fantasy. He could take an innocent remark and see a conspiracy in it. Even in the office, failing to say good morning was tantamount to insubordination."

"Can I see it?"

"No way. I've shipped a copy off to Washington. If they analyze the thing for the next twenty years it won't lead anywhere."

"I don't see how you can say that, Cy. There have to be some real clues in it."

"You'd do as well finding his killer by reading the phone book."

"That many names?"

"Close enough."

"So you haven't drawn up a list of suspects from it?"

"If I did, your name would be at the top."

"Me?" I almost jumped.

'We spent half our time talking about you. Think about it. You followed Treaster to El Principe and had words with him that morning in this office. Priestly says it sounded like you had a score to settle."

"It's not very bright, Cy, wasting time going after me."

"Bright? Who wants bright? Action! That's the order of the day. I'm getting big-time pressure, not just from the regional office, but from

Washington and the FBI, to lodge you in the slammer until you reveal who sent you there."

"I can see how that could be a problem for you."

"Very funny, Palmer." He floated enough Bond Street downwind to trigger a foghorn.

"If they use hoses, I might break."

"If we really wanted to make you talk we'd tie you to a chair and drop big rocks on one of those million-dollar chariots of yours."

"You have a gift for imagery," I said flatly.

"Too bad it's only an act. I'm reduced to role playing in front of my subordinates and superiors alike."

"Then get on with the investigation. Since when does anything Priestly says carry any weight?"

"He also claims Treaster told you about an IRS audit."

"He threatened me with one. So what?"

Cy eyed me uneasily. "It was no idle threat. The IRS is running their records on you all the way back to before the farm sold, along with a search of your late wife's estate, to see if Uncle Sam got cheated out of some revenue in all that."

A surge of emotion overwhelmed me. I turned away and stared blankly out at the pitching waves.

"I thought you should know."

I pivoted to him. "Leave Betsy out of this."

He raised a hand. "Take it easy, Palmer. She owned half of that land. And you did make a fortune on it."

"Betsy died as poor and honest as Mother Teresa! She was gone a long time before that convention center deal came along."

"Calm down," Cy said, backing away from me. "Nobody as big as you should let himself get so angry. You're like a loose blade in a sawmill."

"Don't try that Cracker shit on me, Cy." My voice broke with rage, but I couldn't help it. "Not on this issue. Not on Betsy. You understand me?"

Cy sucked in air through the pipe clinched in his teeth, then nervously withdrew it. He tapped the bowl against his hand.

"It was a bad call by Treaster."

"But it's on the record. Isn't it?"

"To the extent these things ever are, yes."

"Betsy's name is in some sleazy dossier. By God, Cy, I'd like to punch your lights out."

"I can see that." He relit his pipe, fumbling.

I walked to the end of the pier. The salty wind stung my eyes. After a while I realized Cy had come up beside me.

"I'm gonna go on now," he muttered.

I nodded.

"I'll try to keep them off you. Not just for my sake, either."

"Sure."

"I may have to make some threatening remarks . . . you know . . . for the others, for the . . . press."

"Say what you must about me, but only me." My meaning was as clear as I could make it.

"You can count on that," he said and left. His hard-soled dress shoes reverberated on the deck as he hurried away.

I seethed on the end of the pier a long time, turned melancholy at last, and made my way back to the beach. As I neared the Jeep, the sounds of static reached my ears. I reached over and turned up the radio. Through the crackle I heard first Paula's voice, then Randy's. She said my name and I listened closer. Emilio Salgado, it seemed, was turning Marlinsport and the Alverez District on their ears. Looking for me.

21

WHEN I APPEARED AT his door, Salgado's satraps scurried outside like bugs running from the light. The little chief himself sank lower in his old leather chair.

"This is sticky, Palmer. Real sticky."

"I know, Chief. I'm almost sorry I didn't phone it in and run."

His eyes flickered in confusion. "You're talking about Treaster?"

"Aren't you?"

"Umm. No. Cesar."

Something had popped.

"You got a make on the fingerprints at the restaurant?"

"No. And we won't. Too many FBI smears. It's hard to believe they were that stupid."

He thumbed through stacks of papers on his desk, flat-handed like one of the old-time dealers at the Casino. He lifted one out. "Here's the report. But it no longer matters."

"Why?"

"Cesar jumped off that desk."

"Cesar committed suicide? You're saying that officially?"

"Not what I say." This time Salgado reached into his desk drawer. "But what this says."

The plastic-sheathed note he held up was written in long hand.

"May I see it?"

As he handed it to me, his sober, stiff expression was unsettling. I glanced down to the signature, then went back to the top and read slowly.

"The shame is too much to bear. I ruined everything. Dear *familia*, forgive me. *Alcalde*, forgive me. He did not mean those things we said, Mr. Trister. Please do not put the tax man on my restaurant. Father, pray for me. Cesar Armonia."

I read it one more time, then raised my eyes to Salgado, who was sitting as if he were encased in Lucite.

"Where'd this surface?"

"It was delivered here." His voice was almost accusing.

"Don't look my way. This is the first I've heard of a note. Anyway,

I try to be a principal in only one of your cases at a time. Who delivered it?"

"You should know."

I was puzzled. "Come on, Chief. Am I supposed to guess?"

He studied me the way a slaughterhouse hammerman studies a bull. "Considering last night, aren't you surprised I'm showing you this evidence privately, before anyone else?"

"I thought maybe you were sorry."

He came up from his chair and jabbed a finger toward me.

"I've got good cops sweating like Banana Dock stevedores over this thing while you sit here at ease because you've got hundred-dollar-an-hour lawyers."

A flush of anger started up my neck, then I got hold of myself. Salgado was pounding on me because somebody was pounding on him.

"What are your men worried about?"

He was seated again, his head and chest rising only a little way above his desk.

"Me!" he declared with a thumb to his heart. "I'm going to burn them if I find out . . . if I find out . . ."

I glanced back to the suicide note.

"Un-hunh! Un-hunh! Now you're beginning to get it, aren't you, Mr. Kingston?"

Damn. He must really be steamed to call me that.

"All I get," I started carefully, "is that this is a note written by Cesar before he committed suicide. And the first officer on the scene — "

"Officers."

" — found no note."

"They say they didn't," Salgado corrected.

"Maybe the note was under something."

"Maybe the Pope will be named Archbishop of Canterbury!"

"So, you don't believe them." It was half a question and certainly not meant to offend, but up he came again, a finger in the air, this time jabbing like a nineteenth-century orator.

"But I *do* believe them. That's the point. I know they didn't find a note, but I don't dare say that publicly because the first words out of the press will be 'police whitewash' and 'bungled investigation.' "

"Maybe you better tell me how this note got here before you come over the desk and clobber me."

Slowly he sat down again, like a jack-in-the-box on a hard spring. His voice was equally tense.

"The chief executive of Marlinsport turned it over to me a couple of hours ago."

I could only gape at him.

"And well you might be speechless. The one man who benefits most from this document suddenly comes up with it."

"The *alcalde* brought you this?"

"He was not happy about it, but, yes, he gave it to me."

"How . . ."

"He says it was in the interoffice mail at city hall. He went there today—after hours—to clean out his desk."

I handed back Cesar's last sad communication with the world. "You sound like you might not believe him."

"I have only his word."

"Why would he lie?"

"To protect someone. We still don't know who found Cesar's body and called us." His brows lowered on me again.

"Well I, by God, didn't."

"Didn't say you did."

"You were thinking it."

"No, Palmer, you better stick to reporting, because you're not much at mind reading."

He gauged me for an uncomfortable period of time. "Don't you want to ask me why I'm letting you in on this before your fellow reporters?"

Stated that way I suddenly saw why the chief was so put out. "Julio asked you to call me."

"Right. When I balked, he became highly agitated. Said he'd acted in good faith, bringing the note straight to me, but it was important to him for you to know about it. He even picked up my phone and threatened to call you himself if I didn't cooperate." The chief's face twisted into a nasty scowl that I didn't like. "What are you doing, Palmer? Branching out into private detective work for the mayor?"

I kept my mouth shut. Whatever Salgado concluded he'd get no help from me.

"Okay," he snarled, "play dumb, but we both know the rest of the press is going to have a field day when they find out the *alcalde* came up with this note."

"Maybe, but at least Cy Betz will be forced to drop the bribery charges."

"Don't count on it."

"What do you mean? Cesar admits he set up the mayor."

"Does he? What makes you think a federal prosecutor will read that note the same way you do?"

"What you're saying is it doesn't matter a tinker's damn about Julio. The law's going to cover its own ass."

The show of anger on my part seemed to take the bite out of Salgado's own. He let out a loud, wistful sigh. "I can do nothing about that. Nothing."

"I know, Emilio."

We sat there and listened to the tick of the old Spanish clock on his wall. At last Salgado spoke in a dejected voice.

"Julio doesn't look too good, Palmer. Maybe you should talk him into seeing a doctor."

"Was he going home?"

"He oughta be there by now. He was stopping first at the Salvation Army to check on his worthless brother-in-law."

"Rojas?" I asked. "At the downtown mission?"

Salgado was disgusted. "He's drying out. My men picked him up at a bar down by the river. I told Julio it was time to send that bum away again for the cure, but he . . . ."

The chief's last words faded behind me. I was already out the door.

▽

22

I PUNCHED THE EXIT button on my terminal. The story of the suicide note and Rojas's admission to me that he'd set up the bribe scam with Cesar was on its way to type and the front page of tomorrow's *Tribune*. When I found him, the mayor's brother-in-law was a blubbering mess. Ashamed, he'd refused to see the *alcalde* and had tried the same drunken act on me, but I knew better. He was sober enough. Perched on the edge of the Salvation Army cot with his head between his hands, he listened to me and soon realized his secret was no longer secret.

When he stopped sobbing about how he had no idea Julio would be hurt, I finally got some real information. He admitted that it was Howard Ketch who lured him into a poker game way out of his league and kept lending him money to cover his losses. When it was over Rojas owed the Balders Swamp developer ten thousand dollars. This much I was able to verify with others in the game. Rojas said Ketch later demanded cash, then offered a way out. The slate would be clean if he agreed to give one dramatic performance representing himself to Cesar as the mayor's bag man.

"No money's gonna change hands," Rojas quoted Ketch. "We're only putting a little pressure on Cesar—to show him he can't handle a certain business deal without us."

As I was leaving, Rojas called to me. "Cesar knew."

I stared back at him. "What do you mean 'He knew?' "

"Cesar came looking for me the day Julio was arrested. I told him the truth."

I stared at Rojas a moment longer, and then left.

At the *Tribune* I called Ketch and told him what I had. He claimed Rojas still owed him ten thousand dollars, denied offering him any deal, and called him a drunken liar. That was good for a few lines.

There was no way I could write about my suspicion that Ketch set up all three—Rojas, the alcalde, and Cesar—to lead Treaster away from the Alliance. That I had yet to prove. But one thing was self-evident. Ketch didn't lend an unemployed drunk ten thousand dollars because he was a good risk.

It was nearly midnight by the time I wrapped up my story. Although I was dead tired, I reread it. Concern for Cesar's family still swirled in my mind. I'd called Don to explain why I was quoting his father's sad suicide note, but he was too distraught to care. Finally I shut down my terminal, got to my feet, and stretched.

The room was nearly empty. With no windows, the wide expanse looked like a deserted cocoon. It's always struck me as odd the way newspaper buildings are designed. The newsroom, where the pulse of a community is taken every day, is usually tucked away on a second or third floor; reporters are inaccessible, and denied even a view of the skyline except through the occasionally raised blinds of the executive offices.

I stifled a yawn and looked down on the back of Moses' ribbed bald head. He was on the phone, patiently taking a story, asking questions to fill in the holes for a green reporter. When Moses was put back on the street it was supposed to be for a "dream" job, as Wilson put it, promising him free rein to come up with stories on his own. But promises in the newspaper business die between editions. After several really stupid errors about Marlinsport appeared in print, Wilson realized neither he nor Paula knew enough about their adopted town. So to cover their asses he put Moses back on the desk, on late rewrite, a thankless job not three people in the newsroom could do well.

I was slowly getting into my leather jacket when Randy Holliman came in. His face white as chalk, he haltingly headed for me. He had the look of a man with real bad news for somebody.

"Palmer, you need to come with me."

He took me by the arm as though to lead me away. It was like a rowboat tossing a line around Gibraltar and expecting to relocate it.

"Tell me first, Randy. What's up? I need to get home."

"Oh, Jesus. Just come, please."

My shroud of fatigue was sliced away by the alarm in Randy's eyes. His bad news was for me.

"What's happened?" I demanded.

"There's been a bad accident."

"Who was in it?" Somehow I knew that was the right question.

"They're not sure," he said, breathless. "A car's nose down in a phosphate pond."

"Whose car?"

"All they can see is the rear bumper. Everything else is lost in the murk." There was a tremor to the voice. "But it's a Volkswagen, and

116

it's got one of those stick-on badges for parking at police head-quarters."

"Where? What phosphate pit?"

"That played-out mine Agrichem is giving to the county for a water park. Where Route 395 skirts it. I'll take you."

I shook off Randy's hand and started running. To get by the delivery trucks I slammed the Jeep through a hedge bordering the *Tribune*'s parking lot, jumped the curb, and gunned toward 395.

I know it's not possible the cops were staying out of my way, even if they all do know my Jeep, but somehow I barreled through every traffic light in town without a chase, my hand glued to the horn. The Jeep whined its innards out as I got a steady, grinding eighty out of it.

Abandoned phosphate pits in this part of Florida claim lives every year. This one was particularly treacherous. Its banks were rough and steep and the water was slimy and dark.

Divers in black wet suits were emerging from the pit as I slid broadside almost to the water's edge. Their dive lanterns cast eerie rays on the rutted bank.

"What's down there?" I shouted over the squawk of police monitors, a bullhorn, and the squeal of the wrecker winch unwinding.

"A fucking mess," growled Wingate, the chief diver, lifting his mask. When he saw it was me, he shook his head. "Sorry, Palmer. There's nothing more we can do down there tonight — too murky."

"Then give me the light." I reached for it.

He put a hard wet hand on my shoulder. "The car's been under three-quarters of an hour. Another ten minutes for the wrecker to get it up isn't gonna matter."

I looked at him. He was right. Absolutely right. Going in that pit wouldn't accomplish a thing.

All I felt was the shock wave as my chest hit the surface. The water was cold as brine ice, but I hardly noticed. The blackness of it, though, was forbidding. The bottom was so stirred that it was like swimming in sludge. In the weak light A.J.'s little bug, standing almost vertical on its front end, was no more than a dim shadow. I felt my way down its side.

The vinyl top was up; the windows were down. I anchored myself on the door handle and swept the inside with the light I'd snatched. I couldn't see. The swirling sediment was thick as soup. I groped desperately about. My air was running out but I horsed myself all the way inside anyway. I ran my hands down by the pedals and over the seats, terrified I would not find A.J.'s body and terrified that I would. My knees tucked up, I pushed the top of my torso into the back seat. My chest was exploding with pain. Out of the darkness and the murk a hand floated before my face.

I reached for it but missed. My brain was shutting down. I'd been in the icy water too long. My body was chilled into inertia, and my ability to resist was gone. The hand seemed to reach for me as the air began billowing from my mouth uncontrollably.

Consciousness slipped away as the water rushed in to replace the escaping air. I felt myself and the cold hand settling back down, down into the lowest corner of the little car. And was content.

23

"BIG DUMB CRACKER, YOU better not be drowned!"

I opened one eye. Emilio Salgado was leaning over me. Above his shoulder, through the blur, I could see a ring of faces. Gravel bit into my back. Coughing, I rolled on to one elbow and shook water from my head. The only emotion I felt at still being alive was regret. A grinding noise and thumps told me the wrecker was hoisting the ruins of A.J.'s car from the slime.

"You find her?" I rasped.

"Wingate had his hands full getting you up, Palmer."

His words stabbed at my heart. The reality that A.J. and I were separated, she on one side and I on the other, hurt like a jet of fire on a raw burn. I couldn't believe I was going to be left behind again. I laid my forehead down against the cold ground. Salgado squeezed my shoulder and cursed under his breath.

I heard water sloshing as the Volkswagen emerged, rear first, from the pit. I raised my head and saw Wingate reach out for the driver's door handle. The idea of a last cold contact with A.J. possessed me. With Salgado bracing me as best he could, I struggled to the Volkswagen. Muddy water cascaded across the uneven ground as the door sprang open.

A murmur of surprise went up around me. The Volkswagen was empty. I sank to my knees.

At the edge of the pit Wingate called to the police boat out on the water to begin dragging the murky bottom.

Their spotlights zigzagged across the blackness.

"It doesn't mean she's in there," Salgado said beside me. "The witnesses don't know who was driving. It was pitch-black. They just saw the car churning toward the pit with its lights on. There's a chance A.J. could—well, maybe she's not out there at all." His optimism was strained.

"Call her apartment," I whispered, not trusting my voice.

"We did—there was no answer."

Shivering, I scanned the expanse of flat black water, then turned back to the VW. Already the interior fabrics were swelling and splitting. I took a step toward the pit.

"No, Palmer," the chief said behind me. "If she's in there, they'll find her. You never would."

The ambulance attendant bundled me into a blanket and led me to a seat. Throughout the rest of the night the harsh white lights glittered against the indigo waters. Cars passing on the highway slowed to a crawl, their occupants peering bug-eyed as police waved them past. An hour after dawn Salgado ordered me off the scene. It was a gesture of kindliness, I knew, but I shook my head and prepared to dig in. Salgado motioned to the attendant, who'd spent the night at my side, and the two of them put me in my Jeep.

"I'll call the *Times*," Salgado said as he slammed the door. "Someone oughta be there by now. You go on home."

"I belong here," I grumbled.

"No, you don't. Go home. I'll call you."

I nodded and started the Jeep. It was a long ride. When I turned onto my street the sun's rays were angling over the roof above A.J.'s dark windows. How was I going to tell her folks in Indiana?

Walking along the ivy-draped columns in the garden, I gazed at the swimming pool. Mists were rising from the water. The blues and golds and scarlet in the Spanish tiles blended into waves as I felt the tears on my cheeks. A.J. had loved the old monstrosity, one of the first built in Florida, its rectangular walls as thick and well built as Castillo de San Marcos. On long summer nights the two of us lazed on the marble benches cantilevered into its sides and listened to the night song of the crickets.

I knelt by one of the marble Art Deco maidens carved in the pool's rim. The first time A.J. swam with me she'd teased me about them. It was the night we found out that Archie Lameroux, the longtime editor of the *Tribune* and the man who taught me almost everything I know about newspapering, was dead. She'd said just the right things, shared a bottle of wine with me, and with the moon riding low over the trees, put her hands on my shoulders and kissed me. Falling in love for the second time had come as the most wonderful surprise.

I stood. What in God's name was A.J. doing on 395? On wooden legs I climbed the back steps to my kitchen door. It was unlocked. The smell of hot cinnamon rolls filled the room and my brain like the memory of a thousand Christmases.

At my breakfast table sat A.J. Egan, clad in corduroy pants and a shiny Miami Dolphins jacket. She was reading the *Times*.

"Palmer!" she exclaimed. "You'll never believe it. Somebody swiped — my God, you look awful. Where were you all night? I've been worried. When I didn't see your Jeep, I came in to wait for you."

It is strange how emotions play tag with themselves in your body when somebody you've given up on shows up alive.

I couldn't speak.

"What's wrong, Palmer? You look like you've been electrocuted."

I still couldn't find my voice. Her eyes grew round as I took her in my soggy arms.

"You're trembling! And you're soaked!" She freed a hand and put it to my forehead.

"Ewhh. You're clammy. Hey, what's the matter with you?"

I clung to her and buried my face in the hollow of her shoulder, her warm, thin neck so vibrant next to my lips.

"Don't, Palmer," she whispered. "It's all right."

Her arms tried to encircle me at the shoulders. She snuggled close, then with an effort pushed away.

"What's happened?" Concern turned her little face hard.

With an effort I loosened my grip and let her go. Water stained the front of her Dolphins satin, and her hair was sticking out in a sort of ebony horn on one side. She stepped back and glared up at me. I must have looked terrible, for suddenly I found myself the object of her nursing instincts. I was coaxed along to my bedroom like a drake by a goose girl.

Over the spray of the shower we had a shouted conversation punctuated with "What!" and "Gah . . . that's terrible!" A.J. mumbled a few words about being out of town when I told her the police thought she was dead. The search for her body didn't upset her nearly as much as the news about her car.

"My poor little Bug. Ruined, *ruined*," I heard her cry. "I can't believe it. If it's only water I'll dry it out — maybe a hair dryer on the seats all night — "

"Forget it," I called through the billowing steam. "That car's not even worth scavenging parts from anymore."

She sounded on the verge of tears. "I've had it since college."

"Don't get emotional," I yelled. "That's no good."

She came to the shower door. "Right. I'll just be indifferent like you would be. It's only a car, after all."

I opened the door, spraying her with water. "Sorry," I said. "About the crack — and the water too."

Her voice, fading and growing, told me she'd started pacing. "I called in a stolen car report hours ago. *Hours* ago! Why can't the cops ever talk to each other."

"They'll talk when Salgado finds out you're alive — damn, A.J. You better call him."

There was silence. Then I heard her arguing with somebody at headquarters. After a moment the receiver slammed into the cradle.

"They're mad because I didn't know that I was supposed to be drowned when I phoned before," she called.

"I love you," I yelled back.

It sort of sneaked out. I didn't plan it, but I couldn't stop it either.

There wasn't a single sound from the bedroom. I wondered if she'd left.

The door to the shower eased back and there she stood, Dolphins jacket getting more wet, her dark eyes fixed on mine.

"You do, hunh?"

I shut off the water and grabbed a towel. The place was like a steam room.

"I guess that's not the way to do it, is it?"

"Do what?"

I looked at her as steadily as I could, which is about as steadily as a locomotive sitting on railroad tracks. "To tell you that I love you."

"You've had a hard night. Maybe you better save that remark until later when things are calmer."

"No. I want to say it now. It was awful." My voice broke.

"That's exactly what I mean, Palmer — No — Keep your wet hands to yourself. And put on some clothes. It's time we both got to work."

I accepted her elusiveness. Her eyes told me she'd taken my blurted love song seriously.

"Eat those sweet rolls," she said as I slipped into fresh slacks and began running hot water over my razor. "I'm going to change, too. Give me a lift downtown?"

"Sure," I managed. I wanted to hold her, but something wasn't clicking.

Her steps echoed across the polished floor of the banquet room. I lathered up.

I'd finished shaving and was buttoning my shirt when she opened the front door and walked slowly across the dining room again. She was at one door to the kitchen when I came in the other from my bedroom. She stood there, leaning against the doorway, staring at a sheet of paper in her hand. I went to her and craned my neck to read: "You could just as easy been in the car."

Anger flashed in me like lightening strokes in a Van de Graaff Generator. I grabbed some serving tongs and laid the note on the breakfast table.

"There's a couple of holes in it."

"It was folded, and thumbtacked to my door."

"Where'd you lose your car?"

The briefest hesitancy told me she was deciding what to keep from me, but when she glanced at the *New Seville Times* lying on the table beside the letter she opened up.

"I left it at the airport. It was gone when I got back."

I snatched up the *Times*.

A.J.'s story was under a two-column head: "N.C. Deed Links Councilmen, City Zoning Clerk to Z Corp."

The dateline was one of those booming little mountain towns in North Carolina with gorgeous scenery that appeals to well-heeled Floridians who want to escape the summer heat waves. I read the first two paragraphs and glanced up.

"You found Nick Darvin!"

She smiled.

"How?"

"It's in the story. Baklava."

"Baklava. You're kidding."

"No, he has a thing for it. Had a box of it shipped to North Carolina from a bakery across from city hall. When I flew up there yesterday my only expectation was to talk to him about these zoning cases. But when I saw where he was . . . You wouldn't believe that resort. It has everything."

"Except a Greek bakery." I felt like an idiot. A.J. had outscrambled me once again. No doubt Zandell had stashed the zoning clerk away so he wouldn't have to answer any questions. But he hadn't been able to stash Darvin's appetite. I read on. Locating Darvin was only the first nugget. She'd spent the rest of the day in North Carolina going over land deeds and construction permits and hit the mother lode. Not only did she find Zandell's name — Ketch, and councilmen Jones, Stack, and Garland were listed in a limited partnership developing land adjacent to the resort.

"They got greedy and sort of careless," A.J. said. "It was a lot of land in an ideal location — their 'big killing' opportunity. I guess they had to pool their assets but didn't trust each other enough to let this one go with the usual omission of partners' names."

"This was the one where all the other little ten- and twenty-thousand-dollar deals paid off?"

"That's how I see it. They probably figured, 'Who the hell from Marlinsport will ever go through the land records of some little mountain town?'"

I stared at the newspaper. "I guess the answer to that is A.J. Egan. I'm surprised they didn't give this better play. It's a hell of a story."

"I dumped it from my portable computer at an Asheville phone booth last night past deadline."

"You think your story's connected to the job on your car?"

"Could be. I haven't been working much else."

"Did you know you were being followed yesterday?"

"Followed? No-o-o. But . . ."

"What? Tell me, A.J."

She frowned. "There's nothing to worry about. Other than the fact that I may have to get around town on a bicycle. I can't imagine my insurance is going to pay much on an old Bug."

I reached into my pocket and pulled out my key ring.

"Take the Thunderbird. Or the Packard. Take any of them."

She laughed. "You've got to be kidding! Me chug around in one of your precious antiques? If I wrecked one you'd never speak to me again."

"A.J., don't be ridiculous. Take a car. I don't care."

"I'm not going to do it, Palmer. I'd be a nervous wreck."

I jerked off a key and held it out. "Then take the Jeep. It's not worth a thousand dollars."

"And drives like a tank." She reached out and patted my hand. "Thanks, but I'll get by. Just give me a ride to police headquarters. I've got to talk to Salgado."

I looked back to the one-line note, scribbled carelessly in blue ink. There was no arguing with her, although my frustration level was high. If she thought telling me her own speculations about it would compromise her relationship with the *Times*, I'd stay ignorant a long, long time.

A.J. retrieved her note as a thundering sounded at my front door. I stalked to it. When the door swung open, Ed Priestly raised bloodshot eyes to mine.

"What do you want?" I asked.

"Betz sent me after you and the Egan dame."

"For what possible reason?" A.J. called behind me, her voice hollow in the high room.

"He wants to talk about your stories this morning."

I motioned the dour old agent in.

Slack-jawed, he took in my collection of neon signs. "What kind of place is this?"

I considered turning on the power and dazzling him, but distracted and weary as I was, it didn't seem worth the effort. His gaze switched to me. In one of those awful, intuitive moments I saw that he had read my mind and felt the slight.

"I'm calling the paper," A.J. said.

She ducked around the corner to use the kitchen phone, and I went to the hidden electrical panel and began throwing switches. The hum and glow of a hundred tubes of neon created an ambience like a theme park.

"I like the stuff," I said to Priestly.

My effort came too late. His eyes were cold now, hiding any curiosity that may have been under them, and his voice was indignant.

"Are you coming?"

Behind me A.J. walked across the hard floor. "I'll go with you, and I'll see the acting U. S. attorney without a lawyer but certainly not with him there." She raised a long, thin finger at me.

I smiled. "You two go ahead. Tell Betz I'll be along in a bit."

After they left I thought briefly about getting an hour or two of sleep, but I knew my surging adrenaline would prevent that. Not only was I still ecstatic over A.J. being alive, I was also angry, exceedingly so, at whoever was trying to intimidate her. Taking A.J.'s place at the kitchen table I reached for the *Times* and began eating cinnamon rolls. The telephone rang as I finished my fourth. The *alcalde*'s voice was choked with emotion and gratitude almost as much as mine had been an hour ago. He'd just finished reading both our stories.

24

C Y BETZ HAD SUFFERED since the last time I'd seen him. His eyes, usually scholarly and a touch mocking, now had a haunted look. I stood by his door while he finished a telephone conversation with the North Carolina Feds.

"I need a cup of coffee," he said, hanging up the receiver. "Let's go downstairs."

I followed silently. It wasn't all that amazing that Cy didn't want to talk to me in his office. In-between floors on the back stairs he stopped and while I waited packed his pipe.

"What took you so long?" he mumbled, lighting it. "I was expecting you hours ago."

"Business."

"Yeah? Sounds like you were as surprised at A.J.'s story this morning as I was."

"Maybe. What'd you find out from her?" I asked innocently but not innocently enough. He shot me a look as he settled back against the wall.

"I thought you two had some kind of code that keeps you from prying into each other's affairs."

"We don't tell each other what we're writing, but other than that anything goes. So what'd she tell you?"

"Ask her." His eyes, peering over his pipe, spared a moment for amusement before dropping back to their haunted gloominess.

I shrugged, "It was worth a try. What do you want from me?"

He sucked air past barely glowing tobacco. "A.J. wasn't the only one this morning with an interesting story. That stuff about Rojas was absolutely fascinating."

"I thought so. Kinda knocks the stuffing out of Treaster's bribery case against Julio, doesn't it?"

"The mayor's brother-in-law isn't exactly an unbiased witness. It'll take time to check out his story—and the mayor's."

"The mayor's? About what?"

"The suicide note."

"He got it in the office mail."

Cy pointed his pipe at me. "I know what your story said, but that old dog won't hunt."

"Salgado believes him."

"Yeah, I know the routine."

"You think I passed the suicide note to Julio?"

Color rose in Cy's face. "Nobody on earth has a better idea than I do of how devious you can be, or how loyal."

"Let's not go into that."

"Okay, but I need to know if you got that note from somebody and passed it to the mayor. I certainly don't think you took it yourself — did you?"

I stiffened. "Listen, Cy, you may as well know, I was late getting here because I was meeting with a lawyer. I don't intend to be backed into any more corners by anyone — and that includes you."

Cy looked like I'd struck him. "I'm not planning to press contempt charges against you. All I want here is a little help."

"If you doubt the *alcalde*'s story of how he got the note, ask him. You're wasting your time with me."

He laughed bitterly. "Why didn't I think of that? I'm sure he's eager to talk to the U.S. attorney's office."

"You guys made your own bed."

"I can't argue with that, but expecting cooperation from Montiega is out of the question and I need to know how he got that note."

"With a dead prosecutor on your hands I'm surprised you've got time to stew over Cesar's suicide."

"What makes you say that?" he asked. Something had reignited his suspicions.

"That's obvious."

"Did you give the *alcalde* Cesar's note?" he tried once more.

His tenaciousness surprised me. "Cy, I didn't even know there was a note until Salgado showed it to me."

"I can take that as gospel?"

"You can."

"You wouldn't try to con me?"

"Believe me or not. It's up to you."

"Okay. I'll believe you."

"That's all?"

"That'll do. Yes."

"Then let me ask you a question. In the past you've hinted rather broadly that Treaster fooled around a lot. Do you know who with?"

"Any female who'd fall for that line, and a lot of them did."

"Can't you do better than that?"

"I've talked to the secretaries in my office and city hall whose names cropped up with Treaster's. There's nothing there. Why are you asking?"

"How about the logbook downstairs. Have you checked it?"

"You know I have."

"And?"

"The day he was killed a woman signed out a few minutes before Ed Priestly signed you in. Her name was Norma Jean."

"Norma Jean!"

"Interesting alias, wouldn't you agree?"

"When did she sign in?"

"About nine the evening before."

"And the guard didn't know who she was?"

"No-o-o. In fact, he couldn't remember much about her except she was in a pink hooded raincoat." Cy sounded strangely disinterested, as bored by my questions as I had been by his. I suddenly realized he was marking time.

"I take it from your attitude you don't think Treaster's libido got him killed."

"That's right, I don't." He coughed. "If I could be sure it wouldn't get back to me . . ."

I couldn't believe it. The acting U.S. attorney was volunteering to be a source again. I eased back. "I hear a lot of scuttlebutt around town from a lot of people."

"I'm sure you do. There are at least a half dozen sources on the Marlinsport police force who could tell you this." His pipe had to be relit. After he went through the stagecraft of that the words rushed out in a stream of smoke. "We think — we very nearly know that Treaster had Cesar's suicide note with him at El Principe. Whoever killed him took it."

The smoke was rising now like Mount St. Helens and filling the stairwell. Through it he was studying my face as hard as I was studying his.

"How do you figure that?" I asked.

"One of Salgado's cops recognized it as the same kind of stationery as an empty envelope retrieved from Treaster's coat pocket. And the paper was creased to fit inside exactly."

"I'll be damned."

"That's not all. The lab report shows there are fibers common to both."

I thought out loud. "Why would Treaster be carrying around Cesar's suicide note? And where did he get it?"

"Good questions. Here's one more. What was Treaster going to do with it? I was with him just hours before his death and he didn't mention it to me. Of course, there's the possibility that somebody showed it to him at El Principe, then killed him to get it back."

"What you're saying is that one way or the other Cesar's suicide and Treaster's murder were connected."

"Had to be."

"So why are you telling me?"

"I must know how that note came into the *alcalde*'s hands. There's a chance somebody knows and is holding back out of loyalty to the mayor. If you were to mention the connection between Treaster and the suicide note in a story, maybe, just maybe, that somebody'll come forward. Not too many people will protect a murderer."

"I see."

Cy leaned toward me. "Just remember one thing."

"What?"

"You didn't get it here. Anywhere but here will be okay."

25

T HE MESSAGE ON THE *Trib* telephone slip jumped off the page at me. "Mama found the trunk. I'll be there at two today. Joe."

I checked my watch. With everything else going on I really didn't have time for this. But . . .

First I phoned A.J. at the *Times*.

When she heard my voice her own fell to a whisper. "No one's taking this well here. I'm beginning to wish I'd torn up that damn paper tacked to my door."

"What's the matter?"

"The city editor wants me to sit on the desk for a few days and leave the legwork to another reporter. Can you believe it?"

"I take it the police couldn't do anything with the note."

"They think the paper came out of my own car. And the only prints they could get off it were mine." There was silence, then she spoke so softly I could barely hear her. "They don't have the foggiest who drowned my Bug. Damn, I wish I knew what this was all about."

"What are you gonna do?"

"My job. I'm not letting them stick me on a desk."

"You have a way to get around?"

"I'm working on it . . . Palmer?"

"Yeah?"

"We'll talk later — about everything."

"Sure," I said, and heard the click on the other end.

I took off at a run. After detouring past my house to pick up the old Cadillac's keys I sped south along the bay. At the murky Eufaula River I crossed the bridge and turned east, bouncing roughly down the oak-shaded road through encroaching mucklands. A quarter mile down, behind a stone fence, there was a sweep of asphalt, crisscrossed with cracks and pitted with washouts.

The house was Spanish, built in the same era as mine but smaller and in nowhere near as good shape. Moss and oak leaves dotted the tile roof, once bright red, now stained with greenish mildew. Screens sagged as if potbellied men stood behind them. On my way to the front door I counted six cats drowsing on the damp earth.

Joseph Contreras, suited up all proper and gangstery, answered my knock. "She's in the living room," he said, leading me. There was no evidence of his bodyguards, although I didn't doubt they were nearby.

It was my second visit in a matter of weeks. Most of the dark-framed pictures of the family patriarch, Cat Man, in the company of old-time politicians and judges and movie stars, were already packed away. I searched for the big one of him standing with Al Capone before the Cadillac limousine now in my garage. Only a faded outline marked its place on the wall.

"Mrs. Contreras, good to see you again," I greeted the heavy, white-haired woman. "So it's getting close to moving day."

"Oh, it's here. Thanks to Sonny." She motioned me in with a hand weighed down by glimmering rings. "He's the one who came up with a place to display all my wonderful treasures."

"There was no way to get all this stuff in a condominium," Joe said, and sank uncomfortably onto a Queen Anne chair. "Even that old factory might not be big enough."

A sick feeling twisted my stomach. Mrs. Contreras laughed heartily. "It was the perfect answer for all of us. Poor Florence Armonia was going to lose everything before Sonny stepped in. Her sons agree some of this furniture will do very well as accent pieces in the shops."

"You've bought El Principe?" I asked. Joe's glance told me he understood my reaction and didn't like it.

"Let's just say the Armonias and I struck a deal."

Mrs. Contreras placed her hand on a stately armoire of deep-lustered mahogany and seasoned brass. "How do you think this would look against one of the factory's brick walls, Mr. Kingston?"

"Very nice," I managed, forcing a smile. "Look, I'm sorry to rush, but I need to get back to the paper. Could I see – "

"Of course," she interrupted, "the trunk! I had Joseph's men drag the heavy old thing under the porte cochere. Goodness knows what my dear husband kept in it."

Joe's eyes met mine for an uneasy instant.

"I'll go have a look," he said.

His mother shook her head. "Not without Mr. Kingston, you won't. It's locked and he's got the keys. Whatever's inside is legally his."

Joe gestured for me to follow him outside.

"So what are you doing about Treaster's murder?" he asked as we edged past stacked boxes.

This made me laugh. "Mr. Contreras, I don't report to you."

He sent me a look of bare tolerance. "The fact remains that the Feds have a buzz on about the *alcalde* and Treaster."

"In what way?" I asked with some distraction. We'd reached the handsome metal trunk, which was the same midnight blue as the Cadillac classic. It appeared to be in good shape.

"Treaster had Cesar's suicide note on him when he was killed. Because the *alcalde* came up with the note he's murder suspect number one."

I couldn't believe it. What Cy had so carefully laid out for me in the stairwell was already known by Marlinsport's old mob boss.

"Better let me open it." He extended a dark and splotchy hand for the keys.

Giving them to him I had a momentary image of Kincaid Treaster lying in his own warm blood. What if, as A.J.'s story suggested, he had gone to El Principe to meet someone? It could have been this man beside me.

There was a screechy protest as the piano-hinged top and side of the trunk opened for the first time in maybe fifty years. Inside was a leather-faced chest of drawers.

"Not a one of them big enough to hold a body," Joe said dryly. "Only silk socks and underwear. The old man sure dressed the part."

Neatly laid out in the top drawer was an amazing array. There were studs and cufflinks, scarves and a fur overcoat. I opened one of the lower drawers and almost jumped. Lying there was an old-time Thompson submachine gun in a case with two drums of ammunition. A gun out of history. Nobody used weapons like that anymore. With hardly a missed beat Joe shut the drawer, then closed the metal cover.

"Mother's right. We have no use for this crap. Do you?"

I was speechless. My pack-rat avarice was working on me. Maybe there were more guns in there, maybe knives and brass knuckles and sawed-off shotguns. But, I agonized, they were weapons that had done . . . what?

He glared at me. "Forget it. I'll have my men drop it in the bay."

"Oh, don't do that," I said, putting out a hand to protest, as if he could lift it. "The trunk makes the car complete."

He shrugged, "You paid for it. Take it."

I rapped on the trunk with my knuckles. "Okay, but if I think your mother'll want any of this stuff I'll give her a call."

The seams in his face were like dark canyons. "Old clothes and guns, yeah, that's exactly what she needs."

As I leaned down to pick up the trunk, Joe spoke again. "One more thing. Your girlfriend got a note, didn't she?"

I jerked upright. "What?"

"A note—after they pushed her car in the water."

I stared at him a long time. "How come you know about that?"

"Don't be stupid, Palmer. Or I may change my mind about telling you who did it."

"Who?"

"I have interests at the airport who keep me informed."

"And what did they see?"

"Three sweaty rednecks in a pickup truck jumping her wires. When they took off a fella who works for me tailed 'em. At the phosphate pit he saw them weigh down the accelerator, slip the car into gear, and let it fly."

"Where'd they go?"

"You want to know where they went or who they were?"

"You know?"

He laughed and his gold tooth glittered. "They were driving a Z Corp pickup. Three of 'em packed in a small cab like steers in a phone booth. Did I tell you they were big?"

A cold, hard silence stole over me.

I barely comprehended what he was saying. "I'll get the boys to help you with your trunk."

"Forget it," I grunted.

"Jesus!" he exclaimed as I hoisted it alone.

"Tell your mother I said good-bye."

I thought I'd go treat myself to the pleasure of another talk with Zandell. If he still had his golf club handy I was going to show him a new way to carry it.

"Palmer," Joe called as I threw myself into the Jeep and cranked it up.

"Yeah?"

"Don't you want to know anything more about those three guys?"

"I figured they were grunts for Zandell."

"They are that," he replied with a smirk. "But they've got a name."

"Which is?"

"Zandell. They're all Zandells."

"His sons?"

" 'As ye raise them up, so shall they bend' . . . That's in the Bible."

"More or less," I said and popped the clutch. Joe Sparkles quoting scripture was strange enough, but his quoting that particular passage was absurd.

133

2 6

A DOLPHINS TRAINING FILM I'd seen a dozen times was playing on Zacharia's giant TV.

" 'Lo, Palmer."

It was a familiar voice. I turned to a table, and as my eyes grew accustomed to the bar's darkness recognized Moses Johnson. There were few others there. It was a little early. The three who I'd been told back at the construction trailer usually stopped here after work hadn't shown yet either. Zacharia sat behind his counter, dividing his attention between the film and me, all the time fingering his baseball bat. The old buzzard had a way of smelling trouble.

"How're the oysters today?" I asked, easing onto a chair across from Moses.

"I'm not having any," he said, "only a little liquid refreshment. Help yourself." With long, slender fingers he raised the half-empty pitcher toward me. Moses had both the hands and temperament of a pianist. It's what he should have been. Everything—his creativity and sensitivity—would have fit together for him then. But, no, he became a newspaperman—the best writer the *Trib* would ever have, but not tough enough to rise in the chain, and thus to many on the staff, and to himself, a failure. "He used to be city editor," I'd heard new reporters exclaim on seeing that bald head glistening under deadline pressure. "Wonder what he's hanging around for." As if Moses should drop dead at fifty-five. I was still on the low side of forty, but having worked for the *Tribune* for more than twenty years I sometimes wondered if they said the same things about me.

I snagged a glass from the counter and poured myself a little of Moses' beer. "If Nettleman wanders in here and sees us drinking, it's so long, *Tribune*."

Moses grinned. "He'd can us both if he even saw us near this joint. But, officially I'm off today, even if I expect they'll want me when I call in. There's a lot going on." He was too much the gentleman to ask me why I was goofing off at Zacharia's when it was my beat where all the action was.

"You always call in on your day off?"

His fingertips rubbed the condensation off his glass. "When something big's working I give Paula a call."

"And she tells you to come in?" I knew since his divorce Moses stuck pretty close to the paper, but I'd never realized it was seven days a week.

The brown eyes were soulful. "Paula doesn't really know this town yet. Wilson never will, but it's Paula who'll pay if something else gets in the paper that's wrong."

"So to help her out you'll work every night? Come on, Moses, that's unreasonable."

"When was the last time you stayed home when there was a big story, Palmer?" he asked, and I realized it was time for me to shut up. I went over to the bar for a bucket of oysters. The door to Zacharia's squeaked open behind me. I jerked around, but it was only a young couple. They sidled along a wall, the girl giggling nervously. Probably this was the first time in her life she'd gotten up the nerve to come into a place like this. The lone waitress, in tight jeans and black T-shirt, was almost belligerent when she approached them for their order.

As I opened my oysters, Zacharia glared at me suspiciously. It was clear he didn't like my looks today. Not that I blamed him. I'm sure my expression matched my mood. The training film ended and he selected another tape and inserted it in the VCR. The big screen wavered, then the locker room interview of Don Shula after Super Bowl VIII began to roll. I'd also seen that one a time or two.

Moses laughed. "Watch Csonka behind him."

But I didn't get the chance. The bar door squeaked open again and there were the Brothers Zandell.

Three large editions of the father strutted in. They not only had his sour expression, they had his build, round and powerful like a sumo wrestler. Only in their case, much taller sumo wrestlers.

"It'd be a good idea for you to call the paper now, Moses," I said. "Better yet, drive on over there since you know you're going anyway."

"I've still got beer," he said. "What's up?"

"I'm going to talk to these guys."

Moses glanced over. The three beefaloes settled down at a large table and called for three pitchers of beer. One, staring at the young girl and her date, said loudly, "My nookie detector just started buzzing."

I'm sure I was smiling like Alice's cat as I crossed the dark room.

"Are you the Zandells?" I asked, toeing the leg of one of their propped-back chairs. "Larry, Curly, and Moe?"

"Who the fuck wants to know?" said the brother by me. The lucky one.

I nudged his chair out from under him, and he slammed to the floor with an enormous clatter.

He was up in an instant, as were his brothers, but they were on the other side of the table, and their brother, one paw making a slashing pass at my stomach, was right in front of me. I aimed a solid blow at his jaw, but he jerked away and I caught him hard and flat behind the ear.

He fell to the floor like a boneless walrus, sighing from deep inside, bubbly. I was stooping over to see if I'd killed him, when out of the corner of my eye I saw Zacharia, bat in hand, moving from behind the bar. I heard shrieks of "motherfucker" as the remaining Zandell brothers came at me, one around the table and one over the top of it. The girl and her date dashed for the door. The waitress, cursing, hounded after them for her tip.

A respectable set of knuckles grazed my cheek. Pride of ownership glittered in the close-set blue eyes.

His brother edged behind me as Blue Eyes took the frontal assault position. Clearly this was a drill they'd run before, but this time there were only two of them and I suspected I was considerably larger than their usual prey.

"Get his arms! Get his fucking arms!" Blue Eyes chanted, swinging again and connecting with my gut.

I wrenched loose from a grip on my arm and staggered toward the giant TV. I pulled up short. Zacharia had stationed himself before the screen, at the ready, protecting the only thing in the whole place he cared about. Whichever of us combatants came near it was in for a head bashing.

I retreated into a hard kick that sent me sprawling to the floor beside the senseless Zandell brother.

Blue Eyes dove. I rolled aside and he landed like a watermelon down a well on his brother's big stomach. The strange noises coming from those cavernous interiors convinced me I hadn't killed the first guy. A boot in the back of the head preceded a try for my kidneys from Brother Three before I could get to my knees.

Coming up I caught him with an elbow in the gut. His eyes popped in surprise as I let one fly at his nose, mouth, and chin. My fist is big. At that moment it was also messy, covered with blood and bits of teeth. My stunned adversary stumbled backward as Blue Eyes tried a head chop with his two fists locked together. I dodged sideways but helped him stay on his feet with a blow that split an eyebrow.

He lurched against a wall and decided that three against one wasn't good enough odds. Out of his boot he pulled a folding knife big enough to behead a shark and started for me.

But he wasn't my only problem. I saw him glance at his brother behind me. They were eager to make a sandwich, with me as the cheese.

A sound, half hollow, half like a cracking two-by-four, came over my shoulder at the same moment I kicked Blue Eyes right in the groin as hard as I could. His face was pale as Death's horse, and fluids and undigested food seeped from his mouth. He dropped with a heavy thud.

I twisted around and saw the last Zandell brother stretched out grotesquely on the floor. Over him stood Moses, his pianist's fingers gripping what remained of his seat.

"You swing a pretty mean stool," I said.

"Seems I do," he replied, dropping it. "I suppose I'll have to pay damages."

"Let them pay," I said, looking hard at Zacharia, back in place behind the bar. On his TV Don Shula was still holding forth on the philosophical pleasures of victory. "That right?"

"If they're the ones here when the po-lice arrive," old Zack rumbled, "they'll be the ones to pay."

"That sounds like a cue, Palmer." Moses was grinning now. "Who are these guys?"

"The birds who pushed A.J. Egan's car in the phosphate mine."

"Oh? Really?" He stooped beside his conquered warrior and re-trieved the shattered stool, and for a moment I thought Moses was going to hit him again. But he gave a twist and the stool fell apart, leaving only a single stout rung, like a billy club.

I heard a siren and glanced across the bar. The waitress was talking on the wall phone.

"Let's get out of here," I said.

Moses made for the door with me right behind him. We almost collided when he stopped suddenly and turned back to Zacharia.

"When these guys wake up tell them they're lucky we didn't throw them and their pickup in a phosphate pit," he said, sounding every bit like he meant it.

I looked at the detritus of our encounter with considerable satisfaction. Between them the Brothers Three looked to have lost a pint of blood and a dozen teeth. I knelt beside the only one still conscious.

"Tell your father Palmer Kingston will be coming over to show him what to do with that golf club."

The guy almost whimpered as he crawled away from me.

"Time to beat it, Palmer," Moses said dryly.

We roared out of the parking lot and passed the patrol car down the block. The last I saw of Moses he was lead-footing his Pontiac back toward town. On his face was a smile of satisfaction.

$\triangledown$

27

AFTER A QUICK SHOWER and change of clothes I headed downtown to the *Trib*. Although my right hand had a strong throb in it, as did my side and jaw, I was in a very good mood, and hungry. The tiredness and anger from my horrible night were gone, or at least submerged.

Moses was bent over the computer at the desk next to Paula's. Beside his right hand was the broken stool rung.

"Hey, Moses," I said loudly, "I thought this was your day off."

Paula raised fiery green eyes. "Where have you been, Palmer? The biggest damn story since I've been here is breaking, and you disappear. Where's your radio?"

"In the Jeep, I guess." Wilson bought dozens of them a year ago and we're all supposed to carry one on our belts, but I never have. "You need me?"

Paula took a deep breath. "Need you? We've got a murdered U.S. attorney, a gigantic zoning scandal that the *Times* has a lock on, and a mayor demanding charges be dropped against him."

"Sounds like you're going to be short on space. I'll try to keep it tight."

"Thanks, Palmer. I knew we could count on you," she said sarcastically. "Feed what you've got to Moses. He's going to pull everything together for me. And find that damn radio."

"You sound a little tense, Paula. How about we go grab some supper?"

"Supper? My God, Palmer, you just got here."

"I can't work on an empty stomach. And you shouldn't. Makes you crabby."

She was trying not to smile. "What did you have in mind?"

"Ortega's. We won't be gone long."

Paula stood and slid her jacket off the chair. I followed her out.

We were at the old riverfront restaurant in five minutes. Built when Marlinsport was no more than a terminus for Flagler's railroad, Ortega's used to be considered plain ugly. It's squat, with gray planks and a streaked tin roof. But after the high-rise offices went up on either side and the new money in town called it an eyesore, the old Crackers stuck their chins out and claimed it was picturesque, a historical landmark.

"I don't know what I'm going to do when this place shuts down," I said as we walked toward the door.

"It's closing?" Paula asked.

"Not today. But old man Ortega's in his seventies. He can't hold out forever."

The strong smell of fish greeted us. Paula stepped across the strange crater in the floor. Bare concrete was surrounded by rings of colored linoleum laid one on top of the other and worn down over the years. She sat down at one of the small butcher-block tables with a view of the river.

"Oysters okay?" I asked her.

"Steamed?"

"Raw."

Paula made a face.

"How about boiled shrimp?"

"Perfect!"

Ortega was taking all this in with a huge grin. When I approached the counter where he displayed his collection of oyster knives and fancy seashells he winked at me. "Does the black-haired one know about the redhead?"

"The redhead's my boss, Ortega."

He gave me a look that said every man should have such a boss.

"We'll take a couple of shrimp platters and coffee."

"Want me to shuck a few oysters for you?"

"Sure."

Ortega took my money with a gnarled red hand. "Go sit with your boss. I'll bring everything over."

"Another cold front's coming in," Paula said as I pulled out a chair.

Through a steamy window I saw the darkening sky. A couple of small shrimpers tied to Ortega's dock bobbed and jerked at their lines while the pelicans, feathers fluttering, stubbornly held to their perches.

I looked back to Paula. "There's something you ought to know about Treaster's murder. I don't know yet how it figures in, but I believe it will. A woman's involved. In a pink raincoat."

"A woman in pink?"

I told her about the hooded figure coming out of the Federal Building the Monday morning that I had been dragged in by Priestly to see his boss. "Chances are she spent the night with Treaster."

Paula's eyes never left mine. "How do you figure that?"

"She signed in and out at the guard station—under an assumed name. Also, Treaster was wearing the same clothes he had on when we met Sunday in Nettleman's office. And he was dry as a bone."

"Dry?" Paula laughed.

"Yep, although it was raining at dawn. In fact I was confused at first as to why the woman's raincoat was soaked. But it became clear to me when I saw what was on Treaster's desk—the bulldog editions of the newspapers, also wet."

"You're saying he sent her out at dawn to get the papers from a rack?"

"Right. Treaster must have thought a lot of her," I said.

Paula hesitated. "You didn't see her face?"

I shook my head.

"Too bad. But screwing Treaster doesn't make a woman a killer. Stupid maybe."

"But it's a factor—one I thought you'd like to know about in case something develops with it. What I have for the paper tomorrow is a lot more substantial."

While we ate I told her about the suicide note being on Treaster's body, information that Salgado's chief of detectives, Bennie, had been good enough to verify for me. He even named the young policewoman who made the discovery. It perked Paula right up.

She leaned across the table toward me. "Cesar's suicide and Treaster's murder are connected? Now that's a story. You think someone in Cesar's family is involved?"

"That's among the things we have to find out."

I could see Paula's mind clicking. "Treaster was killed at El Principe, he was there with a plat page of that block, and you think he suckered Cesar into going after the mayor. With the note, that's a lot of coincidences."

I went back to my oysters. When I glanced up Paula was staring at me.

"What?" I asked.

"Nettleman's not through, Palmer."

"What do you mean?"

"Our publisher still wants to know who told you to go to El Principe. He even sent Whitey Smythe to talk to Wilson and me. I'm glad you didn't tell us. It woulda put us in a hell of a bind."

"Paula, there's no reason to identify who it is and mess up a life."

"You're sure? Could your source be involved with Treaster's killing — in any way?"

My gaze slid form her face to the pelicans and back again. "At this point I don't think so."

Her words were barely audible. "You need to tell that to Whitey — tomorrow at ten. His office."

"I'll b there, but I'll let my lawyer do the talking."

"Your lawyer?" Paula's eyes turned sad. "I don't want to lose you, Palmer."

"I can only let Nettleman squeeze me so far."

"You're not thinking about going over to the *Times*?"

I found myself staring at the dumb pelicans again.

"They've been after me once or twice, but the truth is I don't see myself doing that, ever. It would seem too much like a betrayal. If I leave the *Tribune* I don't know what I'll do."

"As much as I don't want you to go, Palmer, the *Tribune* doesn't deserve that kind of loyalty," Paula declared with some emotion. "Not from you, not from anybody."

"Probably not, but that's the way it is."

Her fingers brushed the back of my hand, and I looked over at her. Color rose to her cheeks and she began to fumble with her purse.

"Should we leave a tip?" she asked hurriedly.

I summoned up a smile. "No, all Ortega wants is for us to clean up our mess. He hates to do that."

At the paper I made a few calls before settling down to write two stories — one on the meandering suicide note, the other on the future of El Principe. I was finished by nine and left with Paula's praises ringing in my ears and high hopes in my heart for a leisurely evening with A.J. At home I sat down on the corner of my bed to take off my shoes and laid back for a second. That was a mistake. My night on the bank of the phosphate pit caught up with me. When I woke at 3:00 A.M. I was still clutching my shoe. I dropped it to the floor and crawled under the covers.

$$\triangledown$$

28

MY EYES POPPED OPEN in the middle of another fight at Zacharia's. I fumbled for the telephone by my bed and dialed A.J., catching her halfway out the door. She assured me she was fine, only in a hurry, but there was tension in her voice. I wished I could tell her about the Zandell brothers. But that wouldn't go down well.

It wasn't just because she was a reporter for the *Times*. A.J. would be outraged at the thought of a man—"bozo" is the word that would more likely occur to her—duking it out in a bar over her affairs. I'd just have to let my encounter with the Zandells be for my own satisfaction, at least for now.

"If you give me ten minutes," I said, "I'll take you to breakfast."

"I can't. My ride's on the way." I could just see her fingers dancing nervously on the counter. "Randy Holliman did a short on my car and supposed drowning."

"I figured he would. Did it bother you?"

"Nothing like the *Times*'s coverage. They really overdid it."

"Write a letter to the editor." It was a poor joke, but I was in no position either to criticize the *Times* or to tell her they gave their top reporter the coverage she deserved.

A.J. laughed anyway. "I probably am going to have a few words with my city editor. After things settle down, want to go car shopping?"

"Sure. I'll bounce on the bumpers."

"Unh-unh, Palmer, not on my car."

We said goodbye, and feeling guilty over not telling her about the Zandells, I rolled out of bed. The more I thought about it, though, the guilt faded and another emotion took over. Anger.

Experience told me Zandell knew he couldn't scare A.J. off her story by destroying her little car. What he'd wanted to do was throw her off balance, torment her. And in that he'd succeeded. The sudden desire to see papa Zandell spurred me to shower and get out of the house in record time.

Z Corp was closed down tight even though it was after nine. I was circling the block, looking for a place to get a cup of coffee and kill a little time, when the radio came on. My foot eased off the accelerator briefly while I listened to Randy's excited words, then I floored it, made a U turn, and headed for downtown.

It seemed I was not going to get my hands on Zandell after all. Maybe it was just as well, I thought, as I raced to the Federal Building, where a new parade in chains was forming up. The three council members tried to brazen it out, but they lacked the *alcalde*'s sense of offended dignity. Jerry Stack and Link Garland sweated in the cold air as they made the long walk from the van to the door. Max Jones, grinning like a freshman at a fraternity hazing, made feeble attempts at repartee with the reporters lining the sidewalk. Passing me, he winked like I was either a fellow conspirator or one of his cronies. All I could manage in return was a stony stare.

Howard Ketch was next although few knew who he was. His head, hanging so low it almost reached his abundant paunch, was covered with a big white handkerchief.

Zandell's approach was different. It was tough for the television reporters to know if he, or one of the FBI men beside him, was in custody, so self-assured and contemptuous did he appear. A few questions were directed his way, but mostly the reporters were after quotes from the councilmen. That's the way it always is. Anyone arrested along with public officials is pretty much ignored, regardless of their level of sinning.

"Wave your golf club at them," I said as Zandell passed me.

He shot me a look of indignation. "Bastard," he mumbled.

I felt honored to be the object of his scorn, even if it was A.J.'s North Carolina story that had led to his arrest. Cy Betz was raining all over the Alliance on the basis of what she'd uncovered. Their parade in chains was probably Cy's idea of poetic justice, but for the mayor there was no such thing.

I searched the back of the crowd for a wreath of pipe smoke. I should have known better. The acting boss in the U.S. attorney's office would no longer hang around the fringes, making acid comments. I did see A.J. briefly with her young intern before they rushed down the street together toward a *Times* car pulling away from the curb. Strangely, their roles seemed reversed. Flushed with excitement, A.J. looked the younger, while her coed associate wore a mask of cynicism. She was learning at least the pose of reporting at the *Times*.

Ed Priestly appeared at the door with a fistful of press releases, and without so much as a cough, only a sour look, began to hand out Cy's statement. I glanced at it. Extradition procedures were also under way in North Carolina for Nick Darvin's return. Too bad for him. Baklava was not a staple of the city jail. I spotted Randy Holliman in the crowd and told him that as far as I was concerned the story was his. He looked so grateful a twinge of guilt rose in me. I wasn't trying to do him any favors. The idea of spending the rest of the day pounding out a story on the arrest of this bunch didn't hold much appeal — sort of like doing a play-by-play on last week's football games. Anyway, I had murder on my mind.

While most of the reporters in Marlinsport were racing back to their offices I cruised over to the police station. I wanted to pick the chief's brain before my appointment with Whitey Smythe. Instead, I got a surprise.

It would be an overstatement to suggest Emilio Salgado and Cy Betz were friends. But they'd gotten along for years with wary respect and a willingness to avoid stepping too far across the line into each other's territory. So when I pulled into the station parking lot and got a glimpse of Cy riding on the passenger side of Emilio's big black and chrome Chrysler, and the chief himself driving, I argued with myself on whether or not to follow. It really didn't cost me any time, since I automatically rolled out behind them — at a discreet distance — and held the debate en route.

Prudence, as usual, lost out to curiosity. It would take one hell of a topic to get the acting U.S. attorney into a private chat with the chief of police at the very moment three city council members and assorted bribers were being hauled into the Federal Building across town.

Following was not the problem I'd expected. Only a half dozen blocks from the station the chief pulled up beside a grassy riverbank beneath an expressway bridge. The two of them got out and strolled toward a copse beside one of the concrete monoliths holding up the interstate. When they were out of sight I swung around the Chrysler and parked farther down, on the other side of the trees. Walking back I had the dignity not to tiptoe, but I didn't kick rocks in the water, either. Cy's irate voice reached me first.

"That's the most amazing, outrageous goddamn theory you could come up with."

"Is that right?" Emilio sounded equally furious. "How about the evidence. I've got his prints, for the love of Christ!"

They were walking straight toward me. I stopped.

"Your ass will be in a Washington meat grinder if you go through with this. It's stupid and you're not stupid. You don't have shit for a motive," Cy said.

"Motive is for lawyers, like you. I've got Exhibit A."

"But you don't know what it means!"

"I know what it is."

"I'm warning you, Emilio. Go public with this and you risk your career. There's not a hair's breadth of room for error. You can't arrest him. You don't know he did anything."

"I'll tell you one thing I know."

"What?"

"That's Palmer Kingston's Jeep parked over there. I hope he isn't embarrassing himself by hiding in the bushes."

"Damn! I'll have his carcass crated and shipped to Atlanta for interfering with—"

I pushed noisily through the underbrush.

"Chief! Cy!" I smiled, red as a teenager at the beach on the first day of spring.

"Can it, Palmer," Emilio said. There was enough gravel in his voice to pave a causeway.

Cy Betz looked at him disgustedly. "You said not to talk in your car because the radio could be bugged. Now this."

"Palmer, I think I'm going to lock you up."

"For walking along the river?"

"For eavesdropping, goddammit," Cy boomed.

Emilio stomped away and walked back. "Ah, bull, we're not going to do anything with him, and he knows it. With the lab report, the prints, and the number of contacts Palmer's got, he was gonna get it anyway."

"If you've got leaks in your department you ought to plug them," Cy said tendentiously.

"I was talking about leaks in your department," the chief parried.

Cy's color deepened to match mine.

"Who are you after, and for what?" I asked Emilio. "One of the clowns the Feds arrested today?"

"Hah! He'd be smart if he did. Listen, Palmer, if we tell you what this is about, it's strictly confidential. Printing this will cause—" Cy stopped in midsentence and returned his attention to Emilio. For all the barbs directed my way I was obviously only a minor distraction from the dispute they'd been having. "Chief, I still don't think you grasp the magnitude of what you propose."

"Magnitude! Magnitude! You Feds indicted the mayor of Marlinsport on trumped-up bribery charges. Now you're questioning him like he's a suspect in the killing of a U.S. attorney, and you dare talk to me about magnitude?" The big word lost none of its authority issuing from the fireplug-size body of Emilio Salgado.

"You know goddamn well I'm going to lift those bribery charges as soon as I can. But Montiega did have a grudge against Treaster, he's the guy who came up with the goddamned note, and he has no alibi for the time of the killing. There's no getting around that."

"Ah, yes, back to the suicide note. I told you I'm willing to arrest the only other person whose fingerprints appear on that note besides two dead men and the *alcalde*."

"And the *alcalde*," Cy repeated.

"I'm satisfied he got it in the interoffice mail."

"Prove it." They were at it again, as if I weren't even standing there.

"You prove how those other prints got on it."

"We gave you the fingerprint ID," Cy protested with indignation.

This was weird. I couldn't even guess who they were squabbling over.

"But you offer no good explanation for how they got there! So I say they're the prints of Treaster's murderer."

"And he says Treaster showed him the note."

"He says! So what? You brought in the *alcalde* on less."

"So you admit this is a vendetta."

I stuck my head between them. "Bring in who?"

Cy raised a warning finger toward me. "One word, Palmer, one word in the paper before I say so, and I will jail your ass for obstructing justice. That, you know, I can do."

"Who?" I asked again.

Cy groaned.

Salgado sought assurances of his own. "Off the record, Palmer?"

"For now," I agreed.

Satisfied, he tried not to look like he was enjoying this too much. "We sent the suicide note to the FBI's lab. They reported back that the note had four sets of prints. Cesar's, Treaster's, one set where the *alcalde* pulled if from the interoffice mail and —."

"He could have mailed the note to himself," Cy muttered stubbornly.

"The other set of prints — whose were they?" I asked.

"Shit," Cy moaned.

The little chief drew himself up. "The other prints belong to Special Agent Ed Priestly of the FBI."

29

WHITEY SMYTHE AND MY lawyer, Rick Bryan, eyed each other respectfully and then sat down on opposite sides of the table. I stood by the window and looked straight down. The top floor of Marlinsport's newest high rise offered a checkerboard view of the grimy tops of the old two- and three-story structures that I'd admired so as a boy. Now they were stuck between skyscrapers like shims in a wall.

"Why did you want to see Mr. Kingston?" my lawyer asked.

Whitey took off his glasses, wiped them with a handkerchief, and pressed them back on his thin nose. His discomfort that I had shown up with the leading First Amendment lawyer in Florida was obvious to me. When Whitey at last spoke, his voice was the measured, even one he uses in the courtroom.

"Mr. Nettleman feels he should know, as publisher of the *Marlinsport Tribune*, the name of any confidential source Palmer has."

"Oh, he does?" My lawyer, a chubby short fellow fresh off the plane from Sarasota, sounded as affable as an Alfa Romeo salesman.

"Yes. Since he has the final responsibility for whatever the newspaper publishes, Mr. Nettleman must evaluate carefully the risks involved. His, after all, are the pockets that are deepest."

"He's a hireling just like me," I grumbled over my shoulder.

"Now, that's not the way—," Whitey began.

"Why don't we hear him out, Palmer," Rick interjected soothingly.

"Palmer, I really don't know if I can go forward with this meeting," Whitey said, closing the folder on the table before him. "This has the feel of impending conflict."

He nodded toward Rick. "Intruding your private attorney into the employee-employer relationship is provocation. I don't know how Mr. Nettleman's going to take it. And you and I have shared so many confidences over the years, I simply cannot ethically face you in an adversarial relationship."

"Very understandable," Rick said. "Of course, you'll agree that it was prudent of Palmer to get his own counsel, considering that his employer chooses to communicate with him not man-to-man, but through a lawyer of his own."

"I'm the *Tribune*'s lawyer," Whitey corrected him stiffly. I felt for Whitey. We had been through some storms together, long before Nettleman reappeared in Marlinsport, and Whitey could not possibly have liked the bind he was in.

"Palmer is nonetheless receiving communications from his employer through an attorney—that's usually taken as an ominous sign."

"Gentlemen," Whitey said rather lamely, turning to me—of all people—for support, "look at it from Nettleman's point of view. A volatile community, a United States attorney murdered a day after a nasty confrontation in the publisher's office between himself and the reporter who found his body. And considering who that reporter is—a man whose history—well, of course, Nettleman needs to ensure the interests of the *Tribune* are protected."

"What history are you talking about?" The suspicion and anger showed in my voice.

He tried to wave me off. "Let's not go into that."

"You said it. Explain what history you're talking about," Rick said.

I pressed Whitey. "Hammersmith?"

He nodded, eyes downcast.

They were never going to forgive me at corporate headquarters for that one, and apparently not in Marlinsport either. I'd pretty well made the case that our former publisher, Walter Hammersmith, killed the *Tribune*'s semi-retired editor to conceal a string of criminal acts dating back to the sixties. After I confronted Hammersmith, his yacht went down in Marlin Bay and he disappeared, assumed drowned, and Nettleman got his job. It had been my lot to insist the *Tribune* carry a story on the events, detailing as much of the truth as evidence permitted. My idea of loyalty to the newspaper I loved was not the same as the chain's. And the paper's profits were down, in spite of Nettleman's stinginess, or maybe because of it. Competing with a newspaper like the *Times* requires more vision than that offered by a man who thinks of the newsroom as the clerical staff.

"I did what had to be done with Hammersmith, and you know it, Whitey," I said.

Whitey didn't flinch but spoke directly to me. "I called Leland Hines this morning. It's his view that keeping the name of your source from Fred Nettleman serves no useful purpose and, in fact, shows a lack of trust in your employer. He thinks you ought to reconsider your position."

I was stunned into silence. Hines was right. I didn't trust Nettleman.

But I also didn't consider him my employer. I worked for a newspaper called the *Marlinsport Tribune*.

Thank heavens, Rick Bryan wasn't as tongue-tied as I.

"It is Palmer who should be receiving the trust and support of the *Tribune*. As one of Florida's best known and respected journalists, he deserves better than this from the newspaper you represent. Palmer's keeping his source secret, even from his publisher, is a position supported by some of the leading newspapers and journalistic institutions in this country." Rick leaned toward Whitey. "Until there is a time he needs to reveal the name to his editor for verification of the accuracy of a story in the *Tribune*, he need not give up his source. I'm sure Mr. Hines, distinguished journalist that he is, will not want to pursue this in court where his newspaper chain is put in the position of trying to undermine another distinguished journalist's rights."

Whitey stood abruptly and offered his hand across the table. "I will convey your position. Thank you both for coming."

I walked out first. I'd always considered Whitey Smythe a friend. Now I couldn't even talk to him. On the corner I thanked my new lawyer. His appearance alone had put Nettleman on notice to be careful.

30

"WE'VE GOT BETZ LIKING the mayor as a killer and Salgado liking Ed what's-his-name, a bona-fucking-fide G-Man?" Wilson asked in glee.

I nodded.

"Hot damn! That's wonderful," he gloated.

"Hold on a minute," I said. "I'm not going to write it. Not yet anyway. The chance either one of them killed Treaster is remote."

"Fuck it, Palmer! It's not your job to decide who killed him, just cover the investigation."

"Not with scattershot I won't. Salgado and Betz are only striking poses with each other. When they get serious, we'll reevaluate using the information."

"For God's sake, you're a newspaper reporter, not a lawyer."

We argued briefly, then it was over. Just as I didn't have the right to hold back from him this confidential information on the fingerprints, Wilson didn't have the right to order me to produce a story based on it until I said okay.

He glared at me across his desk. "For a change, Palmer, tell me what you are going to put *in* the fucking paper."

"I've spent the better part of the day investigating a select group of folks around town who really liked Cesar Armonia's ideas about revitalizing Alverez District. They just didn't want him in on it."

"Well, isn't that dandy," Wilson rumbled.

"Listen to me," I said, "then if you don't like the story I'll be glad to go home." He waited gloomily. "When Cesar first notified the city he wanted a zoning change there was a delay before he received a hearing date. A strangely long delay. It was weeks before he could send legal notifications to other property owners in the area about his plans."

"So?"

"Several pieces of decaying property around El Principe were put under contract at bargain prices during that period—before the owners knew they were going to escalate in value."

"You're saying someone in the zoning department was no stranger to corruption."

I nodded. "Nick Darvin's name appears on much of the zoning correspondence."

"Well. Isn't *that* a coincidence."

"Here's another. The names of two buyers of buildings near El Principe are the same ones I saw on the bloody plat under Treaster's body. That sporting duo, Zandell and Ketch."

"Holy shit. You believe one of these jokers did in Treaster?"

"It's a possibility. Or they could've had it done." I was thinking of the Zandell trio, but Wilson jumped to another conclusion.

"So the mob's involved," he said. "Contreras becoming a partner with the Armonias was not exactly an act of charity, was it?"

"That's true enough, but there's no evidence he was in on the deal to scuttle Cesar. At least not yet."

Wilson sat back and stared at me. "This is a hell of a story."

"There's more. I also learned at the real estate board that old poker-playing Ketch placed a back-up contract on El Principe, ready to go into effect the second the Armonias were forced out. Only Contreras ruined that for him."

Wilson jumped to his feet. "I'll tell the news editor to remake page one. We'll drop the fucking councilmen's arrest story to a three-column head and strip yours across the top. Make it good, Palmer, first time around. The libel lawyers will have to chew on this one tonight."

Poor Randy, I thought, as I followed Wilson out. I was screwing his chance for a page-one lead. But there wasn't a damn thing I could do about it.

It was after midnight when I finished with the lawyers. The moon was a cold glow in a field of blue clouds as I pulled into the back driveway at home. I closed up the Jeep and, passing my own quarters, entered the main entrance. Even though A.J.'s windows were dark, I rationalized it was possible she was still awake, watching Letterman. I really needed to see her — just to talk to her for a while.

That I'd made a mistake was clear when she finally cracked the door. Not only was she in pajamas, her hair looked like an explosion in a black thread factory. Sleepy eyes blinked up at me as if she was having a hard time putting a name with my face.

"You got any rum in there?" I asked sheepishly.

"Palmer," she managed at last. "What do you want?"

That wasn't exactly an invitation to come in, but since I'd already gotten her up I thought I'd try again. "I just want to see you, A.J."

"It's cold," she said, shivering.

"Why don't you ask me in and close the door?"

When my words registered, she stepped aside.

"You don't look very good, Palmer," she murmured as I leaned down to kiss her.

"Yeah, well . . ." I stopped, but not before she could read the rest of the sentence in my eyes. Her hands went to her hair, smoothed it, then dropped in a "what-the-hell" gesture.

"How about a drink?" I asked. "Might help you sleep."

She gave me a look and shuffled toward the cupboard.

"What time is it?" she grumbled, popping the top on a can of Hawaiian Punch. Carelessly she filled a tumbler with more-or-less equal amounts of rum and punch.

"Late," I said. "I'm sorry. This was probably a bad idea."

She handed me the glass without a word and collapsed on the wicker couch. I sat down beside her. Her violet eyes were on me now. "Is something the matter?"

I swirled the potent mixture around in my glass and took a long drink. "Give me a second or two to finish this and I'll let you go back to bed."

"You didn't batter your way in here for a drink. What's on your mind? Give. I'm awake." To prove it she arched her back and sat tall like a school child.

"Nettleman's still after my job. And he may get it this time."

"Not a chance," she answered, but for a moment I'd seen relief in her eyes and I didn't understand.

She went to the mini-refrigerator, opened herself a beer, and settled back into the wicker chair opposite me. Pale white legs stuck out onto a bolster. There's too much office work in reporting, I thought, looking at them.

"What'd Nettleman do?"

"He's . . . A.J., can I skate a little closer to the edge than usual? I can't dodge around so well tonight. I'm too tired."

"You tell me something I can put in the paper, and I'm going to do it."

Getting comfortable with A.J. can be like trying to take a nap in a burning fireworks stand. But, by God, it's never boring.

I smiled. "This isn't something to put in the paper."

"Don't act insulted," she came back. "After those things you said in the shower I don't know which way your mind's going to turn next. What's your problem with Nettleman?"

"Er . . . ahh . . ." I had to stall for a moment. Her remark about the shower rattled me. I tried to focus on what I could safely say. "Nettleman doesn't like it that the *alcalde* and I have been friends for years."

"You're right. There's not much news there for me to steal."

"And he's gone to Leland Hines with tales, starting with my refusal to cooperate with Treaster in a meeting the day before he was killed."

A.J.'s eyes flickered with interest.

"And . . . ah . . . my refusal to tell why I was the one who discovered his body."

"Was Montiega the source that sent you to El Principe that night?"

"That was very well done, A.J., but I'm not that tired."

A touch of a smile brightened her lips, then faded. "You put us in this mine field, Palmer. Don't blame me if I look for a little ore."

"You're mixing your metaphors."

"I've had a hard day, too."

"Anyway, Leland Hines is reexamining the whole thing that brought him down here in the first place — oh, yes. He was here. In and out. Settling my case. Now he's got doubts."

"Because you didn't like Treaster, or because you do like the *alcalde*?"

"Maybe both." There was no way for me to bring up the old Hammersmith business. I was beginning to see that this conversation was as much a mistake as waking her.

She took a pull on her beer. "Maybe you should never have covered this story."

"You think I've given Julio Montiega gentle handling?"

"I think you've been easier on him than most reporters in town, yes."

"Well, I didn't accept Treaster's accusations as gospel. That's a fact. But easy?" That chafed a little. "I don't think that's the word I'd use."

"Oh, Palmer, I don't think the *alcalde* killed Treaster either, and I doubt if he's corrupt, but I'm not paid to put in the paper what I think is the truth. Only what other people say is the truth."

"Maybe so, A.J., but as reporters we still get to choose the questions, don't we?"

"Yes, Palmer," she said in a soft voice. "And that's why you're such a damn fine reporter."

In the brooding silence that followed all I could think of was her "that shower thing" remark.

154

"How hard on you will it be if the *Trib* lets you go?" she asked suddenly.

"What do you mean?" I countered.

"Well, you live in this big house and seem to have all the money in the world. You've got a car collection so expensive you're ashamed for anybody to see it and yet . . . you're worried about losing your job as a police reporter." She looked embarrassed.

"You forgot my signs," I said, injured to the heart. "My neon signs."

"You got them cheap. And don't give me that pained look. You came here to talk about this. So I'm trying to talk about it. Devil's advocate maybe, but believe me, Palmer, I know what your job means to you."

My pulse rate picked up. "Has all this anything to do with 'that shower thing'?"

It was like a fencer's touch. The tension went out of her face, to be replaced by a gentle look. "I handled that badly. This isn't when we were to have this talk or how it was supposed to go. I don't begrudge you your money. Your house — nothing. Not even those silly old-time cars of yours."

"But?"

"Right. 'But.' It's been a long haul for me from a farm in Indiana full of chickens and Mollie Egan's daughters."

"I'll admit you're one hell of a reporter."

"I work at it — hard. And my job at the *Times* means a lot to me."

"All I did was say I love you."

"Don't go cow-eyed on me, Palmer. I can get pretty emotional, too. We've got to keep this at a higher . . . lower . . . at a different level. If you love me and I love you then we get married, right?"

Her violet eyes probed mine.

"Are you demanding a proposal?" I asked, smiling.

"Well, Mollie would be the first to say you'd better not be trifling with me."

"I'm not. I give you a proposal. Let's get married."

"See? See!" she cried. So much for winding down after a hard day. A.J. came up again, this time as tight as a hunter's bow. "I've totally screwed this up. I wasn't trying to get you to propose . . . because I'd have to say no." She took a deep breath as if to fortify herself. "I didn't work this hard to wind up as a rich man's wife. Don't get me wrong. There's not a thing wrong with money, but I've got a career behind

155

me—and ahead of me—and I won't preside over a bridge club under those neon signs in the dining room."

"I'll get rid of the neon. Or, at least put them someplace else. Maybe the workshop."

"Oh, Palmer." You'd have thought I was a kid with a fever the way she said it. She set aside her beer and curled up beside me on the wicker.

"It's not the neon. Can't we go on as we have? At least a while longer. We get married and I'll have to leave my job. Right now I know what they're saying at the *Times* — 'She's living in Kingston's house, hunh? Think he's getting any of that? Heh, heh' and an elbow in the ribs. But that's all. If we get engaged, we talk marriage, we get married . . . my replacement would be in the police station pressroom before my shoes touched the aisle."

"They better not make any of their jokes where I can hear them."

"Put the Neanderthal back in the cave. Because you're as big as a gorilla doesn't mean you get to think like one."

With that remark I thought I'd delay telling her about the Zandells a while longer, maybe about twenty years. Instead I said, "How come I sit here feeling like an idiot because I told someone I love her?"

There was a long, painful silence.

"I figure I'm only the second person you ever said that to."

I swallowed hard. "You are."

She kissed me, a gentle brush on the cheek.

"I know I'm in good company," she said, her head against my chest. "I love you, too."

"Both of you . . ." I said, and paused.

"Leave it alone, Palmer," she whispered, and I knew she was unsure of her own voice. "We'll look for ways to work things out."

I lowered my face into her sweet-smelling hair. "All right. If Nettleman gets his way our problem will be over anyway. Maybe I can open a used-car lot. That won't interfere with anything." I stroked her glossy black hair, or tried to. It was so tangled I gave up.

"Nettleman's a fool," A.J. said. "From what I hear Hines isn't. Only a fool would doubt your honesty."

"Thanks," I replied. "I hope you're right."

I could feel her yawn against me, and my thoughts began to wander.

"Anything else before you leave?" she asked abruptly.

Well, damn. In her code that meant '*Adios*, Palmer. See you tomorrow.' A.J. never played coy about anything.

156

"I thought you might invite me to stay."

"Oh, you did, hunh? I thought you were tired."

"Not that tired."

A couple of hours later A.J. finally kicked me out, and I dragged myself off to my own place for what was left of a night's sleep. But it was a wonderful sleep.

$\triangledown$

3 1

W HEN I GOT UP the next morning and scanned the *Times* I realized what A.J. was worried about the night before – that my investigation of Treaster's murder was going in the same direction as hers. On that score her concerns were groundless. A source, whom she identified as "someone knowledgeable about the U.S. attorney's activities," indicated Treaster went to El Principe the day he was killed to confer with an unknown person about the charges against Julio Montiega. She said the Feds were investigating the possibility that whoever met Treaster showed him the suicide note, then in an argument over it, killed him.

For a terrible instant I wondered if Cy Betz could be playing us against each other. He'd told me Treaster was going to the cigar factory alone with the plat book. There'd been no mention of a meeting.

Without even opening the *Tribune* I hurried to take a shower. I wanted an explanation, and I wanted it as soon as possible.

I wrangled my way past the receptionist and straight into Cy Betz's new office. Although he'd given the word to pass me in, it was clear my appearance there wasn't welcome. He was as cold and brusque as when I'd seen him with Salgado. I tossed the *Times* on his desk.

"I heard nobody but you knew Treaster was going to El Principe the night he was killed." I was being coy since Cy himself had told me that. Just because he'd moved into the big office didn't mean it was de-bugged.

"What's your point?" he said. With a guilty start I realized he was nodding yes at me.

"My point is this morning's *Times* brings up this mysterious appointment again. Was Treaster going to meet someone at the cigar factory or not?"

"I have no comment for the press." And he shook his head no.

"I'd like to know where she – the *Times* – got this stuff."

"Then why don't you get on out of here and find somebody who'll talk to you?"

It was said in a very unfriendly way.

I was within a half second of telling him what I was thinking – that ambition sure does lousy things to people. But Cy spoke first, with evident sarcasm. "I thought you reporters cast your nets upon the water for information. Don't try pounding on me."

I wondered if he meant what I hoped he meant. He still sounded nasty.

"I'll go where I have to, Mr. Betz."

He grinned. "Don't let the door hit you in the ass on the way out."

I growled a few words and lurched from my seat. Heads rose as I stalked through the outer room. Priestly, leaning over Deanna's desk, whispered something to her. She glanced toward me, but there was no warmth in her eyes.

Wondering if I was making a fool of myself I drove straight to the pier. After thirty minutes in the blustery wind I was sure of it. After an hour I decided I'd give Cy only ten minutes more. Twenty minutes later he slid his gray motor-pool car into a parking place and stalked out—MacArthur-like, with tobacco smoke streaming like a banner— to meet me.

"Good thing you got here when you did," I said. "I was about to leave."

"Bullshit. It would've taken a tornado to move you off this pier."

"What was that dance in the office?"

"You know the steps."

"Maybe. But I don't like it."

"You think I do? I didn't keep you waiting here deliberately."

"Thanks. But I've noticed how the cynical-spectator role seems to be fading from your life."

Cy winced. "I'm sorry about the way I acted in front of Salgado. If that little character knew I'd ever been one of your sources I don't know what he'd do."

"Emilio's straight as a carpenter's rule."

"That's what I mean. Anyway, that was show. Like the office."

"What did you want to tell me, Cy?"

"It's about that little black-haired gal with the heartbreaker eyes who lives at the top of your castle."

"I assume you mean the *Times* reporter who rents from me?"

"That's the one. You know a big lug like you is at a disadvantage. With those looks, she has a far easier time getting stuff out of some people at the courthouse—meaning all the men—than you do. The question is how reliable is it." Cy chuckled softly. It was a superior chuckle, like college professors have. He was getting under my skin. I guess he saw it.

"Look," he continued, "she's wrong about an appointment. There was no appointment. I was at Treaster's side during the whole thing. All I can think of is maybe he'd called A.J. earlier and told her a lie about meeting an informant in an effort to shake some zoning information from her. I don't think he would have mentioned El Principe, but she's put two and two together and come up with five."

"Not likely," I said.

"Then you figure it."

"All right. You say you were the last person with him. Where?"

"His office, talking about El Principe and Cesar's plans. He sent for the plat book. When the book arrived he went over all the notations of surrounding property owners. From your story this morning I know you saw that when you found his body."

"I saw."

"It didn't take him two seconds after he had those new names to decide to go over to El Principe. He suspected they were in a zoning conspiracy with Montiega and he wanted to get a feel for how Cesar's plans might be expanded to include other buildings. Well, he might have been wrong about the mayor, but he was on to something, wasn't he?"

I smiled woodenly. A terrible thought had come into my mind.

Cy sensed something was wrong, and his prosecutorial instincts — or in this case, defense attorney's — sprang into action. "I've had the honor to be questioned at length by Salgado's minions. Very gentle handling it was, and oblique. But also very thorough. They don't think I had motive enough to bump off my boss, and my alibi, while weak, is considered marginally adequate."

I decided to follow Cy on the path he'd chosen, although he'd jumped to the wrong conclusion as to what I'd been thinking. "What's your alibi?"

"I was at my mother's."

"I see."

"But I'd also dropped a number with the desk so they could reach me there."

"Did they call you?"

"After you found the body. And I was there. If they'd called me earlier I'd have been there."

"But they didn't."

"No, they didn't."

He waited, but somehow I didn't feel like telling Cy I believed him.

"Thanks for coming," I said, and walked away.

$$\triangledown$$

32

DRY OAK LEAVES CRACKLED in the street as I eased the Jeep to the curb behind an American-made compact at Deanna's house. Rain was in the air. Brown wet spots were already appearing on the sidewalk at my feet. The silver Christmas tree in her living room window was dark.

Deanna peeked through the beveled glass panel beside her door, then opened it partway. "Second visit in a week. That's a lot more attention than I'd expect from you."

"We need to talk."

"Sorry, Palmer, I'm talked out."

"Let me in, Deanna."

"They're all in jail—where they belong. There's nothing else to be said."

"Deanna . . ."

"Go away, Palmer."

"It's about you and Treaster."

Her countenance changed from defiance to alarm. "What about me and Treaster?"

I knew I'd scared her. Getting your name linked to a dead prosecutor's in the prevailing atmosphere of Marlinsport would scare anybody. Her moment's hesitation was all I needed. Feeling every inch the bastard that I appeared to be, I pushed past her into the house.

"I have company!" she called after me, panic in her voice.

I scanned the living room. To say I was startled would be putting it mildly. Sitting on Deanna's snow-white couch, wearing a silky blue shirtdress, was Alice Jane Egan of the *New Seville Times*. She'd heard every word. I must have withered before her eyes.

"Big as you are, Palmer, you look like you'd almost fit in a shoe box," she said nervously.

"A.J., I . . ." It would have compounded everything to lie, and if I told her I could explain why I was bullying my way into Deanna's house I would have been lying. Only a notion had brought me here, a notion that came to me during Cy's recitation of Treaster's last afternoon.

Deanna's voice behind me was filled with stress. "You can see I'm busy, Palmer. What's this all about?"

"I'm not talking as long as she's here," I said with bravado.

A.J. sucked in enough air to fuel a blast furnace, and there was equivalent fire in her eyes. "You come pushing into the middle of our interview like a damned TV reporter and you have the gall — "

"A.J., wait in the kitchen," Deanna said. "Lynn's fixing coffee."

"I can't believe this," A.J. began, but a steady look at Deanna's ashen face was more than she could handle. "Okay. I'll do it, but I don't think you should let him intimidate you."

The violet eyes lit on me as she gathered up her open notebook and purse. I felt like tinder under flint and steel. When the kitchen door swung closed I took her vacated spot on the couch and Deanna perched stiffly on a chair facing me. My gaze drifted beyond her to the little wilderness statue and the photograph of Raymond on the shelf. The picture of the two of them at the cabin was missing.

"You're wasting your time, Palmer. I don't know anything about Ken's death," my reluctant hostess said in a hushed voice. She was no more eager than I to have A.J. overhear us.

"Treaster's last day alive . . . Monday . . ." I was fumbling for the right words.

"Yes?" A little huskiness slurred the word.

"You know the police and Feds both have figured his movements minute by minute. Talked to everybody. I suppose they talked to you."

"Briefly."

"The police believe that no one outside his top office people knew Treaster was going to El Principe Monday afternoon."

A gleam came into her eyes. "You knew."

"You think there might be something to Priestly's theory that I killed him?"

"You never did like Ken," she said testily.

"No, I didn't."

Our eyes met. The tense lines around her mouth softened. "Priestly's not very smart. But that doesn't change anything. I was only a city-hall stooge, brought in for paperwork and research. I couldn't help the police and I can't help you."

I took in a lungful of air and forced myself to speak in the disinterested tone of a reporter checking out a few details. "I've read Cy Betz's statement that there was nobody else in Treaster's office Monday afternoon, except for when you delivered the plat book."

She shrugged. "So? That was my job, fetching papers."

I let my breath out. As easy as that she'd confirmed my hunch. I'd been lying, of course. Cy had never mentioned her by name. He didn't even recognize the significance of the arrival of the plat book. But I did. And Deanna's own bitter words explained it: they considered her a stooge.

Very much aware that A.J. was in the next room, I plunged ahead. "You overheard Treaster say he was going to El Principe, didn't you?"

Deanna's face froze like a porcelain mask, but her hands gripped the chair tightly. "I see now why you've come barging in here. Well, you can forget it, Palmer. They weren't talking about El Principe while I was in the room."

"No? What were they talking about?"

"You," she replied hurriedly. "Cy was telling Treaster he ought to charge you with obstructing justice for interfering with their investigation."

I lowered my gaze to the plush peach carpet between my shoes. I knew for certain now who was lying. When my eyes raised to hers, Deanna motioned to me like a conspirator.

"Take it from an old friend," she whispered, "Cy's got it in for you. You'd better be careful."

"Forget Cy," I replied, my tone as blunt as my words. "Tell me about the reporter in the kitchen. What's she doing here?"

Deanna jerked back in her seat, then spoke tentatively, leery of me once more. "I can't keep a reporter from stopping by. Look at you."

"That won't wash. I know you're A.J.'s source. You fed her the whole thing—which zoning cases to investigate, the way the council members voted in rotation, how to find Darvin, and this business of a secret meeting at El Principe."

"You don't know a damn thing. You're guessing."

"Maybe so, but they're pretty good guesses, aren't they?"

She went to the window. Beyond it trees were swaying in the wind. Hoping that Deanna would level with me I waited while she thought it out. When she turned back, however, her expression was angry.

"Last week you were the one begging me for help. How dare you question me now because I've talked to another reporter? That's my business."

Still controlling the level of my voice, I said what we both didn't want to hear. "You lied to A.J. When you told her about taking Treaster the plat book she believed you. And when you told her you overheard him say he was going to meet someone she believed that, too. She trusted you. You'd given her a lot of good information. But there was no meeting. Treaster went there to survey the old cigar factory's layout and that of its neighbors. Treaster wasn't going to see anyone about the mayor. Why did you say he was?"

Deanna paled. Her words were barely audible, but I could read her lips. "I *thought* Treaster said he was meeting someone."

Her eyes asked me to let it go at that. The gusting wind rattled the window and distant thunder rumbled. "Believe me, Palmer. I wouldn't lie to you."

I hated the sudden phony sweetness in her voice worse than the earlier coldness. It said that what lay between us now was stronger than all our history together.

"Where'd you go?" I asked.

"Go?"

"When I stopped by the Federal Building Monday afternoon you weren't there."

My question didn't throw her as I'd suspected it would. Instead, she seemed ready for it. Her response was quick, and loud.

"What's the matter, Palmer? You don't like it that the *Times* beat you on a big story? If you want to know if I went to see A.J., why don't you ask her?"

Her words could be heard throughout the house. As I stared at Deanna in stunned silence, chairs scraped along the floor in the kitchen. The next second A.J.'s head poked around the doorway. Behind her another head appeared.

"I'm going on back to the paper," A.J. announced and walked into the room. Her piercing gaze caught the tension in Deanna's face and sent me the bill for it.

All I could manage to say was "It's raining."

From behind A.J. emerged the blue-eyed intern who'd embarrassed the press corps with Treaster. I was amazed. An intern along on a meeting with a source like Deanna?

"I'm going, too," she said.

"Take your raincoat," Deanna mumbled.

The girl frowned, but after peeking out the front window at the increasing storm, went over and opened a narrow closet door. She removed a pink hooded raincoat and slipped it on, holding a side for A.J. to get under. Together they dashed out of the house.

Dumbfounded, I looked back at Deanna standing at the window, watching her daughter leave. She spoke to me without turning. "I have nothing else to say to you. Please go."

I wanted to hug her, for her sake, for old times' sake, for my sake. For the pain I now realized she carried. But I couldn't. All I could do was leave.

The door clicked behind me, followed by the dead bolt.

Huge drops came down in a steady beat. As I walked to my car I did not know whether to bless the rain or curse it.

$\triangledown$

3 3

I STOPPED BY THE *Trib* before starting on my heartsick journey.

"What the fuck do you mean A.J. Egan's been had?" Wilson leered hopefully. Catching the *Times* in a big error—that was a coup to be relished.

I said it again for him. "No one had a rendezvous with Treaster at El Principe the day he died. Her stories were based on an unreliable source. A.J. was used."

"Then she's screwed and the *Times* is screwed," he chortled. "Well, tough shit. They spread their own legs on this one."

"You really can be gross," I growled.

"Come on, Palmer. Enjoy it! Your tootsie's been had!"

Paula's face lit like a roadside flare. "Damn it, Wilson, you sound like a cretin. A.J.'s not a tootsie, not in any sense of the word," she declared with a good deal more anger than she usually allowed herself around the *Trib*'s managing editor.

Wilson came to stunned attention. He looked as if Paula had his balls in one hand and scissors in the other.

"I was only saying it's nice when the competition stumbles." He was almost apologetic. "We've got to get this in the paper."

"No," I said.

"No, my ass."

"It's not time yet."

"Shit, Palmer. All you've done lately is tell me about stories we can't run. You sound like a Latin American censor."

"Look, I want it right, no mistakes, no screwup by the *Trib*, you understand? No stupid story saying my source says her source is wrong."

His reply was a tight-lipped glare.

Wearily I told him the rest. "I'm gonna be out of pocket for a while. Maybe a couple of days."

"Oh, no, Mr. Kingston, you just went too far," Wilson bristled. "You're not dodging this bullet."

"What bullet?"

"A.J.'s fuck-up."

166

"I don't care about that."

"The hell you don't."

"I've got something else on my mind."

"The hell you do."

I glanced toward Paula, who was playing with Wilson's acrylic nameplate on his desk.

"Okay," I said to her, "he's got me figured. I'm taking a couple of days to avoid having to write a story that contradicts the *New Seville Times*. I've only spent my entire adult life fighting those sanctimonious bastards and now that there's a chance to nail them a little, I've turned faint-hearted."

"Pussy's done worse than that to guys," Wilson mumbled.

Before I could react, Paula did. She stood and whacked his nameplate on the desk. It sounded like a headsman's axe on the chopping block. The hostility in her expression as she looked down at her boss would have made a sword melt.

"I've got to redo my schedule if Palmer's going to be away," she said, and turned to me. "Keep in touch when you can. I presume you're working on Treaster."

"You're right, and I will." My eyes slid back to Wilson, who was still staring openmouthed at Paula. "Think what you like. I'm taking the time."

She left, and Wilson and I watched her move toward the city desk, a good, long walk away. Although she wore a loose jacket over her slacks there was enough sway to her walk that Wilson's eyes were riveted.

"Would you look at that ass," Wilson said with unconcealed hunger in his voice.

"So long, Wilson," I said, not trying to hide the disgust in my voice.

"Forty-eight hours, Palmer," he shouted after me. "After that I give the story to Randy."

His threat didn't even merit a one-finger salute, but I gave it to him anyway.

▽

34

MY DILEMMA WAS CHOOSING between loyalties. To the *alcalde*, my story could have brought immediate peace of mind. To Cy Betz, a permanent title. To Wilson, that huge headline. To Chief Salgado, avoidance of the embarrassment toward which he was hurtling. In the end, I went the way my conscience dictated. I went to Raymond.

At first I was puzzled why the photograph of my boyhood friend and Deanna in front of his father's cabin had been removed from the shelf. Before I left her house I knew why. She hoped to eliminate a clue to Raymond's whereabouts. But if there was anyone on earth who knew about that cabin it was me. The Shack, as we called it, was located so deep in the Florida scrub that when I was young I expected to meet Marjorie Kinnan Rawlings's ghost every time I went up there.

Primordial Florida, that's what it was, a place no developer would ever want. Black water, alligators, wading birds, lowland palmetto scrub, rattlers in the pine woods and moccasins in the marshes. There were deer up there, and marsh hens, and a world of mosquitoes. I thanked God it was wintertime.

The Jeep whined and bounced north out of Marlinsport and angled toward the coast — or as close to the coast as I could get. There is a break in the strip of beaches that encircle Florida like a broken strand of pearls. From the Georgia line above Jacksonville all the way down to Miami and the keys the glittering sands run, then circle back up the west coat on the gulf side until they get north of Marlin Bay. There they dissolve into marshes and twisted mangroves. On up to the state's big bend, the musk gland of Florida, trees and swamps ooze into the Gulf with only a brackish line on the dark water to separate them. In the Panhandle the beaches appear once more, sweeping up into dunes.

Gulf Hammock is at the southern end of the marshlands, below Cedar Key. Its unnamed islands are filled with mangroves so dense and wet the air is thick with their decadent smell. Here, too, is Teach River. Way up in the backwaters of that evil-named sluggish stream was the Shack.

A couple of hours of highway driving brought me to a barely marked intersection. Tucked in a palmetto patch, a crude wooden arrow pointed off toward the sunset. Hand printing spelled out "Reds' Camp." Three smaller words skewed sideways—"boats," "bait," "beer." The sign was a feeble gesture. Stuck there in the sand for at least twenty-five years, it probably hadn't lured a single tourist down the unpaved shell road. Like the apostrophe in Red's name it was in the wrong place and accomplished nothing. A person either knew where the camp was or didn't go there.

In this part of Florida a turn to the west is always a jolt to the kidneys. This one was bad. At the ragged edge of the pavement the Jeep dropped a foot. But that wasn't the worst part. In a few yards the shell and sand settled into a washboard effect that jostled my insides and made my teeth rattle like marbles falling on a glass tabletop.

I drove for miles through thin pine woods covered by a heavy sky. Armadillos, eager for night, poked in the underbrush and an occasional buzzard coasted over the treetops. After a few miles the scraggly pines gave way to mixed water oaks and cypress. The land softened and the sun was lost in thick, dripping branches and choking undergrowth alive with insects. Mangrove, palmettos, and reeds were woven together tight enough for a panama hat. In places the road was rimmed by pools of seawater left behind in pockets by high tide. The Jeep bounced up a slight rise, and stretched before me was the Gulf.

Its rocky shore was cluttered with coquina marls and detritus of marine and shore life. And beyond, an enormous orange sun hugged the horizon under dark lavender clouds. It immediately brought to mind a day I'd not thought of in many years. The first spring after we were married Betsy and I came up here, and it was while viewing such a sunset that we planned our lives. God, we were happy. But that was a long time ago and this was a different sunset.

I swung the Jeep north. When it began lugging in the sand, I down shifted and dropped into four-wheel drive. Around a huddled patch of seagrapes with waxed leaves as big as plates the Jeep dug in and Red's came into view.

It was a squat concrete-block structure designed to present as little surface as possible to the usually serene, but occasionally awesome, winds coming in off the Gulf. Whatever Red could not crowd into the building he sheltered under makeshift lean-tos of marine plywood and scrap lumber. These blew away with the periodic storms, but the sand-colored building, circa 1950, endured.

The last time I'd been here his rental boats were moored at a rickety dock. It had projected not into the Gulf but onto the Teach River north of camp where the river's bilious contents emptied into the sea. Now the dock was gone. Long gone, judging by the dilapidated condition of the spindly wheeled carriages he'd replaced it with. These contraptions were like boat trailers, except they had flat-rimmed wheels the size of bicycle tires.

I pulled up beside two parked cars — and one International Harvester pickup about the same age as the building. It was Raymond's truck.

Although I was wearing faded jeans and my weathered jacket, big old Red sized me up on sight as a man who didn't belong out on the backwaters of the Gulf. There was no way he could recognize me as the skinny kid who used to hang around. His own fashion statement consisted of a plaid flannel shirt over bulky long johns. Dirty brown suspenders held up his stained polyester pants.

"You look lost," he growled.

"I'm not lost. I want a boat." Ordinarily the way I'd handle the redoubtable old-timer would be with patient respect and enough conversation to let him learn that I was a Cracker, too. Today, however, I was pressed. Red would have to deal with me on my terms.

His white shaggy brows came together. "You ain't got no fishing gear."

"I'm not fishing. Raymond upriver?"

"Raymond?"

"Raymond Chancey. Fisherman. Oysterman. Lives upriver."

"No Chancey here."

"That's his truck out front. Come on. I'm a friend."

"Yeah? How come I ain't seen you before."

"How much for a boat? And a kicker."

He squinted at me with malice. "I ain't rentin' no boat at this time of day. You'd foul the motor up in the dark."

"Listen, Red, I've got to see Raymond. I'll be careful with the damn boat."

A big-knuckled red paw dipped under the counter and came up with a steel shark club.

"Raymond's got all the friends he needs around here. You hit the road."

I glanced at the shiny club on the cracked countertop. Red's fingers squeezed it rhythmically. He'd used that thing before, I could tell, and not only on sharks. He was intent on protecting Raymond, but he also intended to enjoy it.

I took out my billfold and found the sharply creased square of a hundred-dollar traveler's check I had kept there ever since Karl Malden told me to on TV. I unfolded it on the counter.

"I'm taking a boat, and a kicker, and two cans of gasoline. I'm leaving you this."

"You ain't doing shit," he said. The bat came up and started back in the windup for a roundhouse swat at my skull.

It appeared this was to be a hard week on my knuckles. I lunged over the counter and caught his head between my fist and the back wall like a pecan in a cracker. He sat right down.

Except for a little blood, and that was from his nose, my hand fared better this time. As he fumbled unsuccessfully to regain his feet I headed for the boats.

One, thank heaven, was not locked. After loading my supplies, I grabbed the roughly welded wheelbarrow-type handles and trotted it toward the rough ramp Red provided for launching.

In a few minutes I stuck my head back in his doorway. He was standing but still groggy. I saw a 30.06 leaning in a corner. I didn't want that to be his next recourse for handling me.

"Listen, I'm taking your boat, but you've got my hundred dollars and my Jeep's outside."

"Son of a bitch," he mumbled, but it seemed directed more at the back of his own head than at me.

"I'll be back."

"Son of a bitch." Now he was looking at the palmful of blood from his nose.

The little Evinrude started like they always do, and I headed northeast between the wide banks of the Teach. Red would be no trouble now. Soon the swamps would close in on me, and the darkness of night.

35

CROOKED OAKS, DRAPED WITH wispy shrouds of Spanish moss, sagged like mourners over the black water. The boat's wide V wake closed down to little more than an arrowhead as I worked my way up the gloomy river. The temperature was dropping as the afterglow of day faded. I pushed the little Evinrude hard, trying to put as much river as possible behind me before the gathering darkness caused me to throttle back. Even now it was risky. If the boat ran onto a fallen tree at full power I could be thrown out. And at dusk the alligators feed.

The black of the water and the darkness of the night finally became indistinguishable. I slipped the power to slow. While the boat chugged forward I went through my pack. One thing that twenty years of covering cops had taught me was to be prepared for perils of the night. The little K-Lite I carried in my jacket was powerful for its size, but not powerful enough for this kind of venture. I fished out a two-foot-long flashlight with a head on it as big as a cougar's skull and stuffed with cadmium batteries. Rigged to the bow, its beam knifed through the blackness at the water line. Glittering rubies, alligator eyes, floated unblinking. Occasionally those red, hungry orbs sank below the surface, then reappeared a bit closer to the boat.

Even though it was December, mosquitoes settled on me once the boat slowed. But nothing like summertime. I found myself remembering the trip on which Raymond found the clay figure and I took the photograph now missing from the Chancey bungalow. Then, mosquitoes hung over the river in clouds. Raymond, Deanna, and I had come up for a day of messing around the river instead of a day of algebra and English and an art class of painting petunias on dime-store cups. Betsy couldn't come because by that time she was already working in the classified-ad department at the *Trib* after school and all day Saturday.

The sun was straight up when we made the river on our old red Cushman motor scooters. There were several fishing camps and a trailer park at the mouth of the Teach in those days. With our pooled resources we rented a boat. Arms loaded with Cokes and bags of peanuts we jumped in, and Raymond began poling us through the thick water hyacinths. I kept him alert by rocking the boat and Deanna alternated between laughing and cussing me.

"Blood Loaf's Knob," she yelled as the bow labored through the purple water blossoms and under a sagging palm. Cracker legend has it that Edward Teach, a.k.a. Blackbeard, buried his loot near or on the mound of earth. It was named, so the story goes, after he slaughtered the crew who did the digging and . . . well, dipped a biscuit in their blood and ate it. In the two and a half centuries since the scoundrel was hanged at Ocracoke, treasure hunters have turned a lot of mud on the banks of the Teach. As a youngster I turned a few shovels myself.

Most times going upstream we'd stop long enough to widen the apex of the volcano of shell and earth. It was Raymond who first noticed the absence of sound, and then we all realized we'd never seen a bird or rabbit or even a mouse there. Only mosquitoes.

Once Deanna found two tiny bird-hunting arrowheads and gave them to Raymond for his collection. I was an adult before I realized that the bones and shells and arrowheads we found on the promontory were part of a Calusa Indian kitchen midden, a waste heap.

I pulled out my K-Lite and played over the land mass as the boat eased past. Big as I was and old as I was, a shiver still ran up my spine.

Raymond's cabin was up ahead at the very end of the navigable waterway. On the south side of his camp shallow marshes stretched off for miles, and a low but drier area of hammock and scrub country extended to the north. It was a hunting and fishing paradise for those who didn't mind heavy doses of danger and misery.

Suddenly the kicker bucked and turned free in the air. I pitched sideways like a struck bowling pin. The only thing that kept me from falling overboard was my foot jammed under a support. I pulled myself upright in time to see my ninety-dollar bow light swing loose, roll, and drop overboard. Its powerful beam faded quickly in the organic soup.

I killed the Evinrude and lifted the kicker to examine it. The pin had survived, but I was reluctant to restart the motor. My K-Lite wasn't much. No matter which direction I cast, the narrow glow only revealed tangled branches flexing in the bitter wind. Beyond a few feet the river channel was undistinguishable from the swamp.

After unshipping an oar, I thrust downward from the stern. To my relief I didn't touch bottom. At least the boat was still in the channel. The water seemed warm enough while my arm was submerged, but when I raised the oar, the wind knifed through my wet jacket sleeve. I had been as careless as a teenage boy. Twenty years older, I realized with regret, doesn't mean twenty years smarter. After locking the motor up, I shifted seats and set both oars. Shivering, I started pulling against the sluggish current. The boat's deep hull, designed for Gulf fishing, made for awkward strokes. Intractable roots slowed me even more. As the minutes slipped by I was tempted to start the Evinrude, but caution dictated saving the little motor for the return trip. Whenever I paused to catch my breath, I flicked on the K-Lite, searched first for the river channel and then swept the thin white tunnel toward the shore. Finding a landing spot at night in woods I could barely see was not going to be easy. My right sleeve crackled from the cold. My arm was numb. Stroke after tired stroke, I pulled for what seemed half the distance to the Georgia border.

Finally a flash of reflected light — perhaps a window at Raymond's cabin — answered my probing beam and I rowed toward it with re-newed vigor, until it vanished. After that I stopped every few feet, searching the shallows for an opening in the teeming vegetation. At last I spotted a flat grassy area that looked enough like the old days to do. Besides, I was tuckered.

Edging the boat aground onto the soggy shelf, I leapt out. My feet took off in different directions in the slime and I almost did the first split of my life. Only a desperate grab for the bow saved me from a mud bath. Mumbling under my breath, I tugged the heavy boat further inland. Because of my bungling I not only was cold and wet and muddied, all I had to show the way through the swamp was a flashlight the size of a pencil.

My sneakers made loud sucking noises in the ooze as I stumbled along the bank. Somewhere in the weeds there was a footpath to the Shack, which stood on stilts a good quarter mile from the river. At a stunted sago palm with a crook in it my pulse quickened. It I recognized.

My eyes raised slowly to the thin line stretching away into the dark underbrush. This was the way to Raymond's.

Unbidden emotions rose in me. I had to talk to him, but I dreaded it. For a short distance the trail followed the river, but gradually it twisted deeper into the swampy woods. The concentrated beam of the K-Lite flicking from bush to branch to palmetto clump gave me no sense of direction. I turned it off, hoping to see the distant reflection I'd spotted earlier. It wasn't there. For the first time I considered the possibility that Raymond wasn't at the cabin. That I was wrong, or he'd run away.

The moonlight was dim, almost ghostly. I turned the light back on. The trail closed down to not much more than a lightening of shadows in the shaky beam, and I slackened my pace to study each step. Where my clothes were damp the cold cut through. I began to brood. The more I thought about it the harder it was for me to accept that Raymond chose to live in this desolate place with only his guns and tackle and sketch pads. As much as my furtive friend liked the outdoor life he'd not been a loner when we were young. He'd always liked to have Deanna, Treaster, me, and sometimes Betsy and the others from Station 500 trailing along.

"Nuts to that," I remembered Treaster saying to him on one of the weekend trips we made to the Shack. Raymond, an energetic gleam in his eyes, had asked us to go outside for a nighttime reconnoiter of the terrain.

"I'm certainly not going to become mosquito bait," Deanna declared. "And Palmer's not either. It's no fun playing cards with two."

Raymond brooded a while, then slipped out.

We settled in to play cards, but after a couple of hands I threw mine down and went outside. At the edge of the woods I called. There was no answer. Yelling his name, I stumbled around the perimeter of the camp for a few minutes and almost jumped out of my skin when he suddenly appeared in front of me. Without a word he signaled me into the woods after him.

Now I was back stumbling through those same woods. Only this time there was no Raymond to mark the trail. Thorns snagged my jeans and face. When my light caught the shimmering darkness of a spring, I paused, remembering. Alligators hid in the mossy waters and cottonmouths infested a marshy island on the far side. In the daytime they squirmed over each other competing for a spot to lie in the sun. Once, while I pleaded with him not to do it, Raymond rowed to the island to show me, or himself, he could walk barefoot among the warming snakes.

I struggled on. The soggy ground sloped down into a slough. A dam of driftwood and deadfall offered a dry crossing over the shallow water. Waving my arms in the air for balance, I started over the springy branches. My feet were staying reasonably dry, and I was feeling pretty good about that when a limb underfoot cracked loudly. I glanced down and then snapped my head up at a louder noise. Out of the darkness, like a lunging bear, an enormous log crashed through the canopy of foliage and slammed with an earth-pounding thump into the crude bridge. Mud spurted over me. I teetered, like a high wire artist determined not to fall in the abyss. Then the second blow fell. A sapling clawed my face. In an instant of nightmarish intensity my feet lost purchase. I slid sideways, arms flailing, and fell with a tremendous splash into the pool.

God, it was cold. I burst to the surface. With a sense of inevitability I saw my K-Lite's beam spiraling into the depths. Close enough to panic to be drawing in water with my air, I lunged for the bank.

The crack of a rifle nearly paralyzed me as the water exploded into needlelike projectiles.

"Raymond!" I gurgled. When I tried to shout again, water drowned his name in my throat.

Another shot slammed into the pool ahead of me. Involuntarily I recoiled, backing toward the far marsh, but I still couldn't make myself swim for it. Desperately I wanted to crawl out onto the path, not among the awful morass of Moccasin Island. A volley pounded the water by my face sending shock waves to my brain. I floundered under the surface. Water flowed in my mouth and nose.

Good God, I thought, I'm going to drown in a pit full of alligators and snakes. If that was how I was meant to die I wished it'd been in A.J.'s little red Beetle. As I again struggled to the surface I wondered if snakes eat dead flesh.

Another bullet hit the water flat and spun with a wasp's hum by my ear. To hell with this, I decided. With my clothes dragging me down I sluggishly made for the snake-infested island several yards away. In the middle of the pool my right calf banged into a hard object. A submerged log, I told myself, but then it moved, rolling and bending back on me. I slashed at the water with suddenly agile legs and churned through hyacinths to the tiny island.

A jarring pop from the rifle sent a bullet through a tree with a noise that stabbing a drum would make. I plunged into the thicket until I reached a knobby cypress. Panting, I sagged behind it.

The panic had nearly subsided when something slid across my sneakers, lost in blackness as if I were standing in a river of tar. A shiver wracked my body, but that was because wind was passing through my soaked clothes—at least I told myself that was it. As I concentrated on moving my feet ever so slowly in order not to alarm whatever was slithering in the grass, I felt a creeping on my scalp.

"Raymond!" I yelled, with some force behind it this time.

A bullet thumped into the trunk of my sheltering cypress. Whatever was on my head departed, leaving only an extra damp spot behind.

"Raymond, for Christ's sake."

I heard a bolt action slam home in what was obviously a big-bore rifle. From the sound of it I'd put him maybe two hundred, two hundred fifty feet away. There was a long, long silence. I was freezing.

"Raymond!"

"Palmer?" he murmured in my ear.

I jumped like a shot armadillo.

He was standing next to me. With a sick sensation I realized a rifle muzzle was resting on top of my belt buckle. In the moonlight Raymond's eyes glittered with a dangerous look I'd never seen there before. He appeared under some form of compulsion.

"What the hell are you doing here, Palmer?"

"I wanted to see you." My shivering was worse.

"You coulda got yourself shot sneaking up on me like this."

"No shit."

"You got no business coming up here." His voice was losing its wonder and turning hard.

"Are there still cottonmouths on this island?" I asked and cursed the timbre of my voice.

"Why are you shaking like that? You scared?"

"Feel my clothes, Raymond." There was a good strong dose of contempt in my voice. "I'm freezing."

"Yeah." There was a vacantness in his own. It alarmed me because it told me he didn't care very much about the state of my health.

"Point that thing someplace besides my gut, will you?"

He didn't answer. And he didn't move it away. He only stared at me as if he couldn't decide whether or not to pull the trigger.

"Let's go to The Shack." It was the first thing I'd said in a normal voice.

He eyed me a long time, then without a word his rifle barrel nudged me in the right direction. Consciously aware of each step, I weaved through the cypress knees. Moonlight broke into waves on the black water. On the island's far side, where the pool was only a dozen feet wide, Raymond pushed me toward a log bridge crossing back to the woods. My teeth rattling, I gingerly slid a foot onto it.

Right behind me, Raymond whispered, "No deadfalls here."

It took me a second to realize he'd said that to hurry me along, that the trunk that sent me into the pool was a trap he'd rigged. Back on the path he nudged me right and left around sharpened sticks I'd have rammed into my bowels if I'd kept following the path to his cabin without a guide.

"You didn't mean to overdo the welcome, did you, Raymond?" Moving had helped get my shivering under control.

"You shouldn't have come here, Palmer."

"The same thing occurred to me when the alligator went for my leg."

" 'Gator get your leg he's got all of you." He poked my side. "Shack's to the left. Don't you remember anything?"

"Damn, Raymond, it's been a long time."

"Nothin's moved."

I thought of his rigged tree trunk, but decided to pass on mentioning it. Instead, I asked, "Am I bleeding? That damn branch almost took my head off."

"Shit. I don't know. Wait'll we get inside."

"Are we almost there?"

"Christ, Palmer, you've been in the city too long. The step's right in front of you."

$$\triangledown$$

36

THE SCREEN DOOR SWUNG open and I entered the cabin, but it was meager shelter for the state I was in. The visibility was poor in the dark interior, but my sense of smell brought it back clearly. The aromas were familiar: kerosene, coffee, burnt wood, oranges, shrimp. It had always been the same. Now I could spare no thoughts for all that. My shaking was getting worse.

"I heard you cut the motor a couple of miles down river," Raymond rumbled. "You really think I'm so dumb you could just row up to my door?"

The rifle barrel nosed me toward a wooden chair. I pushed it aside and made my way to the little wood stove.

"You better do as I say," he threatened.

"Go screw yourself," I shot back, peeling off my soggy clothes. "I've got to get warm. Got any towels?"

He backed over to a shelf and tossed a couple at me. I rubbed myself dry and, with his rifle leveled on me, stripped the army surplus blankets off his bed. Wrapped up fit to receive General Custer I returned to the chair he'd picked out for me.

"Satisfied?" I asked.

Raymond didn't reply. Instead he peeked out the door, then the front windows, seeing infinitely more in the black of night than I ever would, even with a flashlight. At the moment the only thing sharp to me was the thin orange outline of the stove's door.

"Any of my buddies show up yet?" I called.

"This isn't funny, Palmer. Nobody on earth is going to pen me up in a cell." He fixed his gaze on me long enough to make sure I knew he was serious. "A man could die just trying to get his hands on me."

"The kicker hit a snag. That's all. I was worried about shearing a pin so I rowed. Can we have a light?"

"What do you want a light for? You came upriver without one."

"My God, Raymond, I lost it when I hit the snag."

The shaking was subsiding. I pulled my legs up to get my feet off the cold floor.

"There's nobody with you?"

"Nobody."

"Who knows you came?"

"Nobody." It was the truth. The note I'd left under A.J.'s door said only that I was going to be out of town.

He peered out the windows again. In spite of my disclaimer he held his rifle ready. The dimensions of the room were lost in shadow. I pulled the coarse, itchy blankets tighter. Without any reason I could understand the long scar on my back went from a cold dull ache to feeling like a hot brand. I set my teeth and waited.

Raymond crossed the room, pulled up a chair, and straddled it backward, facing me. The rifle pointed straight at my heart. I shifted so a bullet would have to pass through two layers of leg first.

A rustling in the leaves outside and a high-pitched, frantic squeak testified to a night hunter's success. At least the owls weren't put off by the cold.

My old friend craned his neck to check outside again.

"They're not on your trail, Raymond."

"They're not, hunh?"

"Nobody's coming."

"Just you."

"Just me."

Against the pale moonlight I could see his lank frame shift in the hard chair. The rifle muzzle drifted off to a far corner of the room, but only briefly. Not very subtly he trained it back on my slow-thumping heart.

"If there's nobody coming then what are you doing here? It's awful late at night to come sneaking up on me."

I adjusted the blankets to cover a gap letting in cold air next to my shoulder. "We go back about thirty years—"

"Miss Commander's class," he interrupted. For an instant there was a glitter of teeth. He'd smiled in spite of himself.

"We were a couple of pissers," I said.

"What's your point?"

"The point is that since we were in first grade I don't think I've ever seen anybody catch you unawares. Only a fool would even try it."

"You're right about that." Pride was in his voice.

"So what's sneaky about my splashing around in a boat and shouting your name?"

His eyes were lost in the shadow of his face. By some quirk of the stove's vague light the cold steel muzzle of the rifle was in stark relief.

Its single black eye stared at me with the motionless menace of a pit viper.

"Nobody else is coming?"

"No."

"So what are you doing here?"

"I want you to come back to Marlinsport with me."

"Visiting?"

"I want you to tell them you killed Treaster."

There was a short, mirthless laugh. He opened the bolt on his rifle and jacked a heavy copper-cased bullet onto the wooden floor. It landed with a thump and rolled like a marble. Raymond looked at the breech and rammed another round home. The unblinking black eye of the muzzle settled on me again.

"I had to check for ammunition," he said. "I couldn't believe anybody was stupid enough to talk that way while staring at a loaded rifle. I was wrong."

"Look, Raymond, why don't you quit dickin' around with that gun and put some wood in the stove?"

"I'm not moving. I want to know what you're after."

"And if you don't like it" — I got up and, clutching my blankets around me with one hand, rummaged in the dark with the other for firewood — "you're gonna shoot me and bury me out here in the swamp?"

"Feed you to the gators, more likely. Only trouble is, once they have you they'll look at me with different eyes."

I chuckled as I shoved quartered pine chunks in the familiar old stove. "You got something I can dry my clothes on? I don't want to leave here naked, no matter how it goes."

"Use the easel."

I found the empty artist's stand and moved it beside the stove. Raymond watched as I wrung water out onto his floor, snapped my wet garments in the air, and hung them on the wooden frame. My back to him, I picked up another wood chunk for the fire.

"Don't try some sudden move to throw that at me," he said hurriedly. "You'd be dead awful quick."

The stove door opened with a screech and I tossed in the wood.

"I wasn't going to throw it at you."

"Un-hunh. I heard about you stranglin' that guy in the circus train for stabbin' you. Played dead and then choked him."

"That's not how it was and he didn't die."

"I'm not going to, either. Sit back in the chair."

It seemed a real good idea to keep Raymond from becoming alarmed. The shock from the impact of those bullets on the water was still vivid in my mind.

The blazing pine popped loudly. Raymond and I both jumped. Soon the stove was cherry red, and my two blankets were more covering than I needed.

"Put enough wood in the stove, Palmer? You plan on barbecuing a razorback hog?"

"Sorry. I've gotten used to pushing a thermostat when I want heat. This stove was old-fashioned when we were kids."

"I've had all the twentieth-century advances I can handle," he mumbled. "Marlinsport's nothin' but asphalt and crowds."

"Everything changes."

"Not for the good. Forget it, Palmer. I'm not leaving here."

I peered through the shadows at Raymond's sad face. "You can't hide in these woods for the next forty years, shooting every fisherman who blunders in, because you think he may know your secret."

He seemed to be considering my words.

"I wish you'd put that rifle away."

His voice came back quietly. "Don't get confused, Palmer. I'm no ignorant pinewoods Cracker you can dazzle with bullshit."

"I know."

"And I'm quicker than you are."

"Yep."

Light dancing through a bolt hole of the stove glimmered upon a deer's head on the wall. A seven-point buck. We'd started out impressed with it, all of us. Somehow the older I got the smaller the dead buck became. Now patches of its hide were falling away. Raymond saw when my gaze fell on the gun cabinet under it.

"They're all loaded," he said. "But making a dash for one would be a good way to get your spine severed. The rack's locked."

"I'm fine here, thanks."

"How'd you know I did it?"

Confirmation of all my speculation. Justification for my being out here after an agonized examination of my own soul. Easy as that, he admitted it. Still I knew I had to choose my words carefully.

"It finally occurred to me that Treaster's death somehow revolved around Lynn."

"Bullshit!" he declared, and shifted so nervously that the rifle barrel made circles in the air around my nose.

182

"Now, Raymond —"

"Lynn is out of this! I'm warning you, Palmer, leave her alone or they'll be scraping your brains off the wall."

"You're saying we get to talk about everything but what happened?"

"Damn you!"

"It's okay. Quit waving that rifle at me. You don't want to talk about the truth, I can't make you."

"Not as long as I've got this gun."

"Or the oyster knife."

The light played dimly on the small leather sheath at his belt from which protruded the bone handle of his handmade oyster shucker.

"Yeah. Or as long as I've got the knife."

"That's what you killed him with?"

"Yes." His voice was low.

It was a puzzle. He'd admit the act but not the motive.

"I only wanted to talk to Ken. I didn't mean to kill him."

"With your rifle stuck up my nose I take that as good news."

"You think I could stab somebody in cold blood?"

"I have difficulty seeing you doing it in hot blood, Raymond. Your whole life's evolved toward withdrawal from the most ordinary contact with us other humans. I guess it must have torn at you having to confront Treaster over your daughter."

"I told you to leave that alone."

"Right. Anything but the truth."

"I tried to reason with Ken. I told him . . . I told him . . ."

"You told him to stay away from your daughter. What'd he do, laugh?"

Raymond's dark eyes flared, but his resistance was drained momentarily. There was pain in his face.

"Can we stop dancing, Raymond? You told him to leave your daughter alone. My guess is he told you she was twenty years old — or whatever she is — and old enough to make her own choices."

Raymond sprang from his chair, but not toward me. He began pacing in the dim illumination of the stove. Red and yellow spots of light slid across his face as he prowled. Like a long-caged bear he retraced his path about the room — his feet fitting almost exactly in the same steps. Ducking each time on his course by the window, he nervously checked the swamp for unwelcome visitors.

"I already told you. They're not coming. There's nobody after you."

"Except you, hunh?"

"You think I'm after you?"

"Better not be." He shifted his rifle in a way meant to be menacing. "You're really dumb, you know that, Palmer?"

"You're not plowing any new ground, telling me that."

"I mean, goddamn! You come out her unarmed, you sit there bare-assed naked telling a man with a loaded rifle you're going to take him in."

"I haven't said anything like that."

"Then what the hell are you doing here? Renewing old friendships?"

"We are old friends."

"Dumb as a stump."

"Un-hunh."

"If it hadn't been for Betsy you'd probably be holed up here yourself, scared of the way people are. Except for Betsy we'd be neighbors."

"Yeah, Betsy put me to work and to farming." I watched his routine. "You must pace this cabin a lot."

"Yeah, yeah, I do," he admitted. "Look, Palmer, if you figured out it was me, so will the others. Won't they?"

"I don't think so."

"I wish I could believe that."

"You can."

"Why are you telling me this?"

"You asked me."

"If they don't know, then I'm safe up here."

"Except for me."

"You?" He turned, his eyes vacant, as though I was hardly even present.

"I'm the only person, besides Deanna, who knows it was your daughter who was with Treaster in his office the night before he was killed."

"No! She didn't do that."

"Yes, she did. Fetched his papers in the pouring rain at dawn so he wouldn't get wet. Then he sent her scooting just before an FBI agent and I arrived for an appointment. Not quite quick enough, though."

"Then the FBI guy knows?" There was a certain archness in his voice, as though he figured out something I hadn't seen.

"I doubt it. He arrived after Lynn left."

Raymond looked at me, waiting. So I talked. "I figure Deanna was up when Lynn got home and forced the truth out of her. Poor Deanna. I saw how upset she was when she came in to work. I guess she was in a hell of a predicament. Her boss was messing around with her daughter.

I figure she asked Treaster to leave Lynn alone, and being the bastard that he is, he refused. So Deanna ran you down and asked you to talk to him. Later that afternoon when she overheard he was going over to El Principe, she contacted you to let you know that that was a good place to find him alone."

Raymond had stopped pacing. "That's close to the way it was, all right . . . I guess you wanna know what happened."

"Tell me."

"When I got there Treaster was by a window lookin' at a paper, a big sheet — "

"A plat book page."

"He reached in his pocket, like for glasses or a light, but instead comes out with an envelope. Looks at it and shakes his head. Like he knew it was there but was pissed about it. I came in while he was reading it."

"I bet that gave him a start."

"Yeah, although he was glad enough to see me, at least at first . . . until I told him to leave Lynn alone."

"You know, Raymond, times have changed since we were kids. It's not so unusual any more for there to be some difference in ages. It happens."

The rifle, carelessly pointed at the floor, again found my heart. Raymond's eyes were lost in the deep sockets of his face, but flecks of light, like phosphorus, blazed at me.

"Cut the crap, Palmer."

"Right." I had blundered into acutely dangerous territory.

"Just be careful."

"What about the note?"

"Treaster dropped it, dropped all the papers and grabbed me."

"Did you have a gun?"

"Shit. Like I said, I was standing there bare-handed, trying to talk sense to him. He wouldn't listen. Sounded like you, in fact. 'What's a few years?' he asked me. The fool."

Poor Raymond. He'd never get over the values of his youth. Then, neither would I.

"You know I never liked Treaster," I ventured. "Not from day one. I wouldn't want him foolin' around with my daughter if I had one . . . but maybe he really cared about Lynn. Maybe he wasn't just using her."

My intention was to calm him, try to reach him, but it didn't work. His anger surged into fury. Resuming his bear walk around the room, Raymond shouted at me. "You and Treaster sure are a pair, Palmer —

big as fucking dray horses and brains the size of oysters!"

I got up and quietly turned my clothes on the easel. They were still too damp to wear but they were getting there. I'd never before heard Raymond disparage anything about Treaster, especially his intellect.

"Goddamn!" Raymond shrieked. "Fuckin' idiot!"

I couldn't tell whether he was referring to me or Treaster.

Abruptly he leaned within inches of my face. "Why do you think I have this rifle, Palmer?"

"To keep me in line."

"Bet your ass!" he said and started in pacing again. "No big fuckin' walrus is going to push me around. Not you. Not Treaster. Jesus! I told him as easy as I could . . . I tried to explain but I couldn't hardly get the words out. You know how I always liked — how I always admired him. And there I was a burned-out hooch of a man, trying to explain to this grand . . . you saw his clothes."

I nodded.

"He called me an oyster-sucking, half-crazy recluse. All I was trying to do was talk to Ken for his own good. He wasn't the kind of man to live like that. It wasn't him — I tried to tell him."

The wind outside was picking up. Palm fronds clashed against the shack. I knew the clouds were moving, for suddenly the dark outside paled with moonlight.

Raymond's thin shoulders jerked as he moved nervously about the room. "Finally I told him straight out. He screamed I was a lying bastard, but his eyes betrayed him — he believed me."

I was confused. What could Raymond have told Treaster to upset him that much?

"He yelled at me, 'I'll throw your lying ass to the rats!' Hell, he picked me up and was going to drop me head first out the window."

"That's when you stabbed him." This much I understood.

Raymond nodded. "I was trying to lash at his face. God, I couldn't even see, the way he was holding me."

"What happened then?"

"He let go. I banged against the floor and he staggered back, clutching his neck. God, it was awful. The blood was pouring through his fingers and running down his sleeve. He had the most horrible look on his face. I cried out I'd help him and started to get to my feet, but he pulled out a pistol with his other hand and fired off one round. The bullet must have gone out the window because I heard glass shattering across the way."

"It hit the neon dancers," I muttered, but I don't think it registered. Raymond was in his own tortured world.

"I huddled up in a ball," he rambled on, "and waited for him to kill me, but there were no more shots. After about a minute I looked up. He was lying a few feet from me. I pulled myself up and just sat there. I knew he was dead."

Right in front of me Raymond stopped pacing. His eyes were those of a hurt animal. "Damn, Palmer, it can happen in a hurry. Doesn't matter what the hell you want. Or maybe it becomes instinct to survive. I don't know. How could I let myself kill Kincaid Treaster? Kincaid Treaster."

I kept silent. He had to get it all out.

"On the floor by my side was the note he'd pulled from his pocket. I don't know how long I stared at it, but at some point I realized I was reading Cesar Armonia's name and I knew what it was. Then I heard you coming, stuck it in my pocket, and got the hell out of there."

"Out the window?"

"Yeah, I squatted on the ledge until you went for the cops."

"If you didn't go to El Principe expecting trouble how come you wore gloves?"

He stared at me. "How'd you know that?"

"Because your fingerprints weren't on the window, or the note."

"Oh." He seemed relieved by the answer. His teeth even flashed faintly. "In case you forgot it's December. I had on work gloves."

"Was it Deanna's idea to send Julio the suicide note?"

He didn't answer.

"Treaster's office and apartment were both broken into that same night. You did it?"

"Break into the Federal Building after I killed Treaster?" He seemed shocked at the idea.

"But the apartment? To make sure none of Lynn's things were there?"

"Leave it alone, Palmer."

"What about Lynn, Raymond? Are you planing to just drop out of her life, never tell her what happened? After all, it was self-defense."

"No one's telling her anything, ever."

I didn't let up. "You can't hole up in this marsh, any more than you can stop being her father."

A flash of raw pain filled Raymond's eyes. "Shut up, Palmer. For God's sake shut your dumb mouth."

187

He was in agony. Intuition as much as logic told me that I was seeing something in the wrong way, like those trick pictures of a goblet that turns into two faces if you stare at it long enough, and just right.

My heart began to pound so hard it was reverberating in my ears. I sucked in a ton of salty damp air as the core truth of the whole thing struck me. No wonder Raymond kept calling me dumb.

"My God!" I exclaimed. "That lousy son of a bitch."

Raymond looked sick. The rifle barrel drooped at his side, almost resting on the low sill of the cabin window.

For a long time neither one of us spoke. Finally I did. Raymond would never say it.

"Lynn isn't your daughter. She's Treaster's. That's what you had to tell him. To stop him. That's what he was so mad about and what he hadn't the character to admit when you finally confronted him."

Raymond was a scarecrow figure against the misty moonlight through the window. In the swamp, fog was building up, the way it often does on frigid Florida nights.

"You and Deanna covered over Treaster's sins out of some screwball loyalty to him, didn't you?" My voice trembled with anger. "Were you afraid it'd ruin his career? Damn it, Raymond, I can't believe you screwed up your life for that pompous ass."

"It wasn't just for him," Raymond muttered. "I loved Deanna ... but she couldn't love me."

My emotions in shreds, I watched silently as he dragged his chair to the front window and settled into it. The rifle lay across Raymond's lap as he stared out into the pale night, but it pointed my way. I stared at his skinny, rigid figure. A couple of times I tried to get him to talk about it, and about what he was going to do now, but Raymond became agitated each time, telling me to shut up. It seemed wise to back off and not rush him; a little time to think things over might be exactly what he needed. I leaned my head against the chair back and closed my eyes.

But neither of us slept. When I stirred he noticed. About three o'clock I felt my clothes. Raymond was alert as I tossed aside my blankets and dressed. My jeans were warm and dry, and stiff. Moving slowly and deliberately I folded the blankets and, after shaking my still-damp jacket, stoked the fire and plied it with sticks. I wanted to talk to Raymond again, but I didn't. All my words seemed inadequate to his pain. I sat there, bones growing numb in the hard chair, and listened to his breathing and the breathing of the night.

37

THERE IS SOMETHING PRIMORDIAL about waiting for dawn in the woods. Whether you're in a cabin or outdoors the dark lifts ever so slowly. And then like magic a moment comes when it's light enough to see. The interior of Raymond's cabin came to view, not unlike a stage setting as the curtain slowly rises. A scaly remnant of a big bass was still nailed to the back wall, right where I remembered it. I glanced toward the far corner, where the bunk beds we once used were joined. Only one still functioned as a bed. The others were storage racks for a galvanized tub, a big chest that rivaled Cat Man Contreras's for size, if not splendor, and stacks of canvases and sketch pads.

There were hundreds of sketches and full-blown oil paintings. One face appeared over and over as I shuffled through stacks. Lynn. He'd sketched her repeatedly in the years he'd been in exile. But never with her in a formal pose. It came to me slowly and sadly that he must have stolen peeks at Lynn, unsure of himself as a father but still caring for her — and she'd probably never known.

He shifted in his seat, and I looked toward him.

"Better check your jacket," he said.

I did as I was told. "Still damp."

There was enough light outside now for me to see the grim expression on Raymond's face. His eyes, drawn and hollow, had a dry look of resignation in them. "There's one on my bedpost. Put it on."

"Sure," I said. It proved too short and too tight.

Raymond turned and looked out the window once more. His voice was strange, almost detached. "Do you know that every morning Aldo Leopold measured the candlepower it took to start a bird's day?"

"No."

"He found it wasn't very much. And it never varied. Can you imagine anybody being smart enough to sit with a light meter in God's outdoors to see what it takes to wake up gulls and flamingos?"

"No."

Raymond got up and faced me. "Let's go," he said.

"Where?"

His answer was slow enough to scare me. "For a walk."

He gestured to the door with his rifle. His grip, I noted, was no longer loose. The muzzle no longer drooped.

"I'll freeze my ass off," I said. "My jacket's still wet."

Some vague light of sympathy came to his eyes. "Grab a blanket."

I did, and he followed me out the door. I wished I were in a mood to enjoy the sunrise building over the trees.

"This way?" I inquired, starting for the booby-trapped pathway where I'd left Red's boat the night before.

"No. Around back."

I found the path. The outhouse had been moved but it was still standing, the same decrepit shed where I'd sat side by side with Deanna as a joke once, long, long ago. Raymond gave me a moment to use it again, surely for the last time. He waited guard outside, then hurried me on.

This trail was more subtle than the other. After we'd walked a half mile I saw the boat. Behind me a clicking noise told me he'd checked to see that the rifle bolt was down, the safety off. He was expecting me to run.

"Go ahead and climb aboard," he ordered when I just stood there. "I'll cast off."

It was an old wooden shrimper from the days when they had a quarter the capacity of today's monsters. No radar or sonar. No loran range. Just throttle, ammeter, fuel gauge, and compass. I discovered all this while looking about the steering compartment for a way to get the thing started.

Raymond jumped aboard, landing lightly but balanced. He was as agile afloat as ashore. My time was running out. I'd never gotten the jump on Raymond in my life.

The old diesel throbbed to his careful ministrations and we dropped downstream. The boat edged out through a cut I hadn't even seen last night and joined the main channel. A quartet of crying seagulls circled overhead.

"Lie flat on the deck," he commanded. There was an urgency to his voice that wouldn't be denied. "Here." He pointed to his feet where he stood at the wheel.

I eased down and he rested the rifle barrel on my temple. By straining my eyes sideways I could see him staring purposefully downstream while holding some of the weight of the rifle off me with the grip. A finger was wrapped around the trigger.

I felt panicky. My mind swarmed with the vivid memories reporters have of forlorn bodies in the woods or in abandoned refrigerators, or in banks where some self-obsessed subhuman freak has blown brains around like spilled chowder. I closed my eyes and tried to remember that this was Raymond Chancey.

Even in his awkward pose he negotiated turns with ease. There were no snags, no jerking movements, and when I opened my eyes a narrow pink streak lightened the sky overhead between the overhanging trees. I saw Raymond touch the bell. As if at his command the water and the sky changed at once—the sky opening and the water heaving. The bell had been for Red, then, and the sky and water marked our entry into the Gulf of Mexico. A single screeching gull swooped in beside the pilot house and flew effortlessly above us, his gimlet eye revealing to him the strange drama inside, a drama about which he cared nothing at all.

I shifted my weight and the rifle came down harder on my temple. I lay still.

"If you just hadn't come, Palmer. How stupid can one man be? Hell, why didn't you storm in and kill me in a firefight? That would have been okay. I'm not scared of dying. Don't want to, but I'm not scared."

"Ease off on that rifle, Raymond. It feels like a lance going through my skull."

He ignored me.

"But you come dumb-assing up, unarmed, with nobody even knowing where you are, and expect me to say 'Great, old buddy. Take me to jail.' "

"Raymond, I didn't come to put you in prison. I pretty much figured how it happened, I was just wrong about the why. I knew you killed Treaster. I never thought you murdered him."

"Don't give me that. You've put me in a hell of a bind. I've seen too much brig duty to choose prison for myself—ever."

I inched my hand toward his thin leg.

"You know what death is, Palmer? A man goes from life to death in a twinkling, if he's lucky. Maybe you'll be lucky. I guarantee it if your hand comes any closer to my leg."

I sighed. "Let me up."

"Lie still."

I did not like the roll and pitch of the boat. From what I could see the Gulf was in a pregale condition. No rain yet, but soggy clouds and heaving seas.

"How far out we going?"

I could tell by the wheel's position and the thrust of the bow we were still headed due west.

"Far enough," he said.

I lay still again. Once I let my hand sneak a quarter inch toward him, but the pressure of the barrel increased so painfully I gave up trying to take him unaware.

At last he throttled back a little, spun the tiller into a slow turn, and looped a line over the wheel. Abruptly the rifle lifted. Dazed from all the pressure on my head, I struggled to my feet.

"There's a spare anchor in the locker. Get it." The rifle was pointed straight at my right eye.

"Jesus Christ, Raymond." My heart convulsed. Adrenaline coursed through me like the sting of a wasp.

"It's your own stupid fault."

"It's my fault you're gonna kill me? You're sure being kind to yourself."

"Get the goddamn anchor."

"I've done all the getting and sprawling I'm gonna do for you."

"Don't turn stubborn now. It's too late."

"Get your own anchor. I'm not moving, unless it's to run that rifle up your ass like a ramrod."

He pulled the trigger — after swinging the rifle to one side so the shot would go harmlessly across the foam-topped waves. The concussion alone was enough to make me glad I'd visited his outhouse.

"Get the anchor and tie it to your leg."

I was rattled. I did it. At least, I went for the anchor. Some forlorn hope that I could throw it in his face half motivated me. Until I saw how heavy it was. It was an anchor meant for business.

"Take it to the stern," he told me, and I lugged it there, stumbling over blocks and nets and oyster tools. My eyes darted back and forth in a frantic search for something to defend myself with, but there was nothing that would do, not against a woodsman with a rifle.

Great waves rolled out from under the stern, oily green waves with salty foam fizzing on their surface.

We stood at opposite ends of the well: me, with the Gulf only a rail away, facing Raymond with his back to the cabin area, his rifle trained at my chest.

Reaching out to brace myself my right hand found a pathetic weapon, the sawed-off stump of a forgotten oar lying in a trough on the transom. It weighed perhaps a half pound and fit my hand nicely, but it was the wrong weight for throwing, or even for slugging him if I could get close enough. Worse than that it was spongy with seawater. But it was all I had.

"I'm not putting on that anchor, Raymond. I'm not doing another thing you tell me."

I held my little club at the ready; looking for all the world like an old-time football player executing the Statue of Liberty play. While Raymond stared at me in disbelief, one of the sentinel seagulls dropped down and tried to wrest the chunk of wood from my grip.

"You fool," he said.

"Come on! You and your rifle."

"You goddamn idiot. You're gonna take on a deer rifle with that?" He started laughing, low at first, almost a moan. Then he threw back his head and laughed, loud and free, toward the heavy sky.

I let my hand fall slowly to my side. The diesel kept up its steady thump as the shrimp boat slid down the back of one wave and nosed up the rolling front of the next one.

"Raymond, I—"

"Just shut up," he said with sudden weariness. "Let me be for a minute."

I did as I was told. The stump slipped from my fingers to the deck.

"How many friends can I kill to save my rat's nest of a life?" Raymond said aloud, but not to me.

I took an unsteady step toward him in the pitching sea. The sky was taking on a greenish hue. "Let's head back, Raymond. It's getting rough out here."

He shook his head sadly. "I want you to know I'm glad you came, Palmer . . . just understand . . . I can't choose between the hell of prison or the death of my best friend."

I knew he wasn't talking about Treaster. "It's not that way, Raymond."

"Yes, it is. But I've known what the solution is ever since you showed up last night. I just couldn't admit it to myself."

With the stoicism of one meeting his destiny, Raymond turned the long gun toward his own forehead and his thumb groped for the trigger.

"Good-bye, Palmer," he said.

I leaped, crashing against him as the rifle went off. The impact of our bodies sent us hard against the wheel and then we both tumbled over the railing. I heard a strange, gulping noise as we sank into the cold sea. Opening my eyes, I twisted and turned, looking for Raymond. He was sinking below me, no sign of life in his limp body. I dove after him.

My hand closed on his hair and I held on, kicking hard toward the surface. My heart was pounding in my chest, demanding that I breathe.

When I broke the surface, I sucked in air and forced Raymond's head up. He sputtered and coughed and I cried out in relief. Shifting my hold under his arm until Raymond's body was half on mine, I lay back to conserve my energy in the choppy sea. The cold water was already taking its toll, and I realized how lucky I was not to have on my jacket.

Blood was pouring down Raymond's face, but the best I could tell his head was intact. A swell broke overhead, causing us both to swallow seawater. Choking, I frantically assessed our situation. We were miles from shore, and the odds of another boat picking us up were worse than my chances of winning the Florida lottery.

"Take it easy, old buddy," I said as Raymond stirred in my arms. "Looks like we're in for a long swim together. A long, long swim." My voice trembled, belying my encouraging words.

I felt the chill intensify in my bones, knew this was the prelude to the inevitable hypothermia of winter sea. There was no sound except the whine of the wind and the caw of a gull overhead. It was only slowly that I realized I was hearing far away, but coming closer, the throb of a motor. I tried to see, but we were down in the well of a wave. I waited for the upsurge to carry us to the crest and then I raised my head into the air as far as I could, letting Raymond slip a little. He moaned as I fell back into the sea. I hugged him to me.

"Hang on, Raymond," I gasped, and began swimming side stroke. We're going to catch a boat."

What I'd seen when I'd peered out over the horizon was his old shrimper, circling back. Its rudder was holding in the secured position, bringing the boat around in a giant circle. All I had to do was get in its path.

I pulled with one arm and kicked as hard as I could, as fast as I could. Making headway in the choppy sea was difficult, and I wasn't sure how well I was doing. I found myself wishing I'd jogged more this winter. My legs were slowing their strokes regardless of how I willed them to move. Doubt began to fill my brain that I was going to have the strength to hold us above water, much less intercept the shrimper. At the top of another swell I searched for the boat. It was closer, a lot closer. With renewed hope, I shifted Raymond to my other arm and stroked harder.

For long minutes I propelled us through the water, the sound of the boat growing stronger and my muscles growing weaker. And then, glancing off to my left, I realized that all I had to do now was tread water. I'd cut its course. Lying back once more, I tried to gather my strength for what was going to be the greatest challenge of all, getting us both back on the boat. It was possible: a ladder ran down to the water's edge at the stern. If I timed it right, when the boat passed I could grab on. But there would be only one chance. If I missed, I wouldn't have the stamina to last until the boat made another slow circuit. Holding Raymond tight, I waited.

The boat was moving at dead slow. It barely made a wake. I tensed as the red hull sliced through the water inches from my head.

Taking a deep breath, I watched the stern ladder draw nearer. I lunged, too hard. My nails scraped along the wood, but my fingers grasped the rung and I prayed that it would hold. I should have known it would be solid as a rock. Raymond always took care of his equipment. The boat tugged us through the water.

I brought my other hand to bear, trapping Raymond between my legs, and tried to decide how I was going to get us out. I attempted several times to lift our bodies, but it was useless. My energy was nearly gone.

"Damn, Raymond, help me. I won't leave you." Then I realized that's exactly what I was going to have to do. If I was going to save him I was going to have to save myself first. With one hand I managed to undo my belt and slip it out of my pants. I looped it around Raymond's thin body and snugged him up against the rung. His head was barely out of the water, the blood glistening in the bright morning light.

I clutched at the higher rung. Then the next. The icy air shocked me. My forehead dropped against the side of the boat and my breath came sharply. Gasping, I reached again, and again, and finally touched the boat's rail. Ever so slowly my body eased over it. After a moment facedown on the deck I crawled over to the blanket I'd discarded earlier and wrapped it around my shoulders.

When the pain eased in my lungs, I went back for Raymond. I leaned over the railing and undid the belt with one trembling hand while holding onto his jacket with the other. When he was free in the current, I tightened my grip and fell backward, pulling my slight friend on board by the sheer mass of my own body.

We lay side by side in a huge puddle of seawater. I got to my knees, turned Raymond facedown, put a small barrel under his stomach, and pressed my hands low on his back. Seawater gushed from his mouth and nose. I pumped him dry, then turned him over for a clumsy attempt at CPR. He barely stirred. After a while I crawled into the small cabin and radioed for help.

$\triangledown$

38

MAYBE IT HAD BEEN a mistake to turn on my signs. With the Christmas tree twinkling and the house lights off, the glowing neon gave the great hall the illusion of a city of sin, and tonight of all nights, a sense of gloom. The others felt it, too. Christmas Eve parties seldom last very late, but this one was closing down extra early.

There was a brittleness in the air, only partially caused by the winter weather. Everyone talked and sang and ate enormous amounts of shrimp and A.J.'s stuffed mushrooms, but there were too many things to avoid talking about and too much lingering pain. And there were those who should have been there, but weren't.

The *alcalde* did come, wearing a fixed smile, the once-gregarious politician in him now elusive and quiet. He left early, he said to attend Christmas Mass. Neither of us mentioned Cesar.

As the last of my guests crowded the door with their good-byes around midnight there were two I asked to stay. Salgado grumbled, but I pressed him. Cy Betz needed nothing more than my pouring another drink of single-malt scotch for him to settle back. A glance from A.J., after taking in Salgado and Betz, asked if she should leave and come back later. We still had our Christmas to celebrate.

I shook my head. What I had to tell them she might as well hear, too. Her deadline was long past. Nervously she busied herself with collecting glassware and emptying ashtrays.

"If you kept us to gripe some more about Raymond Chancey," Salgado rumbled, "forget it. As soon as the doctor gives the okay it's in the lockup for your old buddy. We wouldn't want him killing Cy here over a 'misunderstanding.' "

"I don't consider being dangled beside an open factory window a misunderstanding," I responded.

"A U.S. attorney is dead," Cy declared with the proper indignation. "That won't go unpunished."

"Treaster's death had nothing to do with his being a U.S. attorney," I said. "All the posturing in the world isn't going to matter when a jury hears the evidence."

"You're right, Palmer." Salgado sighed wearily. "Ultimately it will

196

be up to a jury, but there's no way Raymond's going to face less than a charge of involuntary manslaughter regardless of what you say."

"Okay, we see this one differently. But both of you know Raymond is more victim than perpetrator. This tragedy didn't begin on the second floor of El Principe, and it won't end there. Not for Raymond, or his family. Or for Cesar's family. Or Julio's."

I turned to Cy. "Did you take a good look at the mayor tonight? The man's aged twenty years in two weeks."

Cy's voice reflected the soothing effect of the liquor. "Treaster may have erred on the *alcalde*, but he was on target with the others."

"Nailing those clowns on the council won't put the *alcalde* back where he was . . . ever," Salgado groused.

"Arresting him was a mistake, I admit," Cy said, "but don't forget Cesar came to us — outraged at what he perceived was a betrayal. I'm not sure yet how or when Treaster came by the suicide note but once he had a chance to absorb the old Cuban's words Treaster would have dropped the charges."

"No. That's not true." My words echoed from the high beams. Three sets of eyes fixed on me. A.J.'s showed keen interest. Salgado's and Cy's were wary.

I tried unsuccessfully to speak without emotion. "Treaster knew Cesar committed suicide even before the police found his body. I have a story going in tomorrow's *Trib* saying so."

A.J. rattled china with fidgety fingers.

"That's outrageous," Cy protested. He fumbled in a tweed-jacket pocket, produced a pipe, and started packing Bond Street into it.

Salgado traded the trapped expression he'd had since I bullied him into staying for one of rapt interest. "You can't say that just because he had the suicide note at El Principe."

"I'm not. Raymond also told me he went into Treaster's apartment later that night to make sure no letters or pictures of Lynn were there."

"That's supposed to be news?" Cy asked. "We already figured that. But give Raymond credit for neatness. It was tough just telling he'd been there." Bond Street billowed around him like a badly made campfire. "The same thing happened to Treaster's office. A door with three alarms was bypassed without a trace of tampering."

"Come on, Cy. If Raymond could slip by electronic locks like Houdini why would he then smash the two-dollar lock on Treaster's desk with a crowbar?"

Salgado's eyebrows rose like startled geese. "That's a good question."

A.J. came near and stood beneath the Casino's blinking sign while I continued. "And don't forget that convention after Cesar's suicide — the police and Feds were stumbling all over each other. Who called whom?"

Dead silence ensued as Cy and Salgado eyed each other suspiciously. After a moment Cy shrugged. "I have no idea who called our people. But the locals were there first."

"Now wait just a minute," Salgado said. "My men responded to a distress report from an anonymous source. They called no one but Dispatch."

A.J.'s voice came quietly from behind me. "It doesn't matter, does it, Palmer? What you're saying is the cops who got there first actually got there second. Right?"

"You got it. The same person called both the Feds and the police — after he broke into Cesar's office and took the suicide note."

"Had to be," the chief said with dawning satisfaction. "My officers did everything according to the book, and that means there was no note when they arrived."

"That brings us back to a basic question in police procedure, doesn't it, Chief?" I asked.

"Yeah," he said, "who profited by concealing that Cesar's death was suicide?"

We all looked to Cy, wreathed in a sweet cloud.

"Get serious," he chided us. "The idea of Treaster swiping the note is asinine. I didn't like the man, but I can't see him skulking around."

Salgado jabbed a finger at him. "You can't deny he had the note. And he sure was pressing me to call Cesar's death murder."

"But he didn't take it," A.J. said. Her eyes were alight as she moved into the center of the group. "Treaster's desk was smashed some time during the night *after* he was killed. What Palmer's saying is that whoever did that knew Treaster had the note and was trying to get it. To protect him."

"Except Treaster took it with him to El Principe," I said.

"It was Ed Priestly," A.J. whispered.

"It was Priestly," I agreed.

"So that's how his prints got on the letter." Salgado was enjoying himself now.

"Wait a minute," Cy interjected. "Whatever his shortcomings, Treaster would not have authorized Priestly to steal evidence."

"Perhaps not, Cy," I said, "but there's no denying Treaster sat on it to protect his reputation as well as his case against the *alcalde*."

Cy was predictably quiet.

I continued to the bitter end. "Treaster threatened Cesar after Julio's arrest and then when the distraught old man disappeared, sent Priestly to find him. I figure Priestly saw Cesar's body through the restaurant's rear window, broke in, swiped the note, went to the nearest phone booth to make his calls, then showed back up with the rest of you."

Salgado pointed an accusing finger at Cy. "That's why Priestly was so careless about touching things at the scene later. He was covering his tracks."

"The sonofabitch," Cy muttered. "I'll throw the book at him." He headed for the door.

"What book?" I called after him. "It's not much of a crime to jimmy open a desk in an office you have the keys to."

"He tampered with evidence of a ..." Cy stopped in midsentence.

A.J. said what he was thinking. "Taking a suicide note's not a felony."

"There was the case against the *alcalde*," Salgado growled.

Cy hesitated at the door. "But that's been dropped."

He watched as Salgado, rumbling under his breath, put on his overcoat and scarf. "Sounds to me like Priestly's going to get a slap on the wrist."

"No sir," Cy declared as I followed them outside. "One way or the other I'm going to force the old bastard out."

They reached the fountain before I spoke. "I asked Priestly earlier today for a reaction to all this. He stumbled around with a denial but your appearance at his apartment won't come as a surprise. He'll know you're not Santa Claus."

When I came back inside, A.J. was in the kitchen brewing the night's last pot of coffee just for us. Trying to salvage a little Christmas cheer, I stood by the tree. A call from Raymond's lawyer earlier gave me some hope he'd be bonded out as soon as he was ready to leave the hospital. I'd stocked the refrigerator in an empty apartment on the second floor just in case. Next week I'd go back to the cabin to retrieve his paintings and art supplies.

I took the gold card from the fir branches where it had rested for days. My name was inscribed in A.J.'s spare but precisely feminine script. Looking at it I could envision her as a little girl struggling over a series of uniform *O*s in an Indiana public school copybook. Such perfection took practice.

Through the archway I saw A.J. approaching with a tray of coffee and butterballs. She set the tray on a side table and returned to the kitchen. When she came back again with the Myers Rum Cream from the refrigerator I was examining a place on the wall between two small signs.

"I can guess what you're doing," she said with a laugh and gestured for me to sit beside her.

"Is that right?"

"You're measuring for that broken dance sign across from El Principe."

"Maybe not." She didn't know about the lethal contents of Cat Man's trunk yet. I still planned to display them.

"Come on, Palmer. You've already seen whoever owns it. Right?"

"Well . . ." There was room, maybe, for both the guns and the sign. "I was in the neighborhood and I did stop by the dance studio. They're on their last legs, you know."

"A dance studio on its last legs?" She moaned. "Save your puns for Salgado."

I growled a reply.

"When will you put the sign up?" she asked, smart-assed, knowing she had me.

"If I got it I would certainly have new tubes bent . . . if I got it, that is. Taking that monster down could be costly. I might not want it."

"Right."

As I poured coffee, A.J. cocked her head and stared at me.

"Palmer, you look like a mugging victim," she said affably.

"Just a bump in the dark," I lied. Raymond's booby trap had left a vivid welt on my cheek, and his rifle a dark red bruise on my temple.

She gave me a disgusted look. "You keep too many secrets."

"And you don't?"

I leaned back to the wall and flipped a few switches. Not all. The huge room with its clerestory windows now looked like downtown at 4:00 A.M., with lights on only where the action was. Except for the Christmas tree. That was ablaze. I spooned sugar into my coffee, along with a heavy dollop of Myers.

"Lynn called me this afternoon," A.J. said.

I stopped stirring and searched her face in the tinted shadows. "How's she holding up?"

"Not bad. She may make it as a reporter yet. An awful lot of immaturity got ground out of her in the last few days. She's beginning to realize what Raymond, and Deanna, sacrificed for her all these years."

"How is her mom?" I asked.

"She and Lynn will work things out. They know fate rolled the dice for them."

"Yes," I said. "Snake eyes."

I followed A.J.'s gaze across the room. She was focusing on the most sentimental piece in my collection, the neon flamingo.

"It's something for me, Palmer, to imagine you back then. Sometimes I wish I could have been with you and Deanna and Raymond, climbing those rooftops. Then I remember Betsy." She turned to me and her eyes were shining. "I'm glad she had you then, just like I'm glad I have you now."

I picked the gold card up from where I'd laid it on the tray.

"Oh! You're opening that?" she asked, jerking upright.

"It's time," I replied.

She was out of her chair in an instant, tucking her shirt into her slacks. Nervousness blossomed before my eyes like a night-blooming cereus.

"Whatever's in there, Palmer," she chattered, "it's just for the thing itself, not anything else, like maybe transportation."

"Fine." I fished around the table for a knife to slit the envelope.

She walked to the tree and fussed with the lights, although they were all on as far as I could see. She spoke to me over her shoulder.

"Overnight accommodations I maybe can take care of, or go fifty-fifty."

I found a cheese knife, wiped it on a paper napkin, and stuck it under the flap.

"And I guess I'll have to say that I was not altogether . . . candid . . . about Aunt Tot's farm sale."

"Oh?"

"I didn't lie."

I knew damned well there was something wrong with that deal when she first brought it up.

"All I said was there was gonna be a sale of her stuff and that I wanted you to get the third Monday in January off."

I sliced open the envelope.

The front of the card was blue sky filled with crystal snowflakes. Maybe not a good Florida card but a beautiful one to a homesick

Hoosier. Inside on a plain white surface were these words, written in Indiana schoolgirl script:

> Palmer. Thanks for making my first Marlinsport Christmas not so lonely. I have two tickets to the Super Bowl for us. Love, A.J.

"But —," I managed.

"I know they're not printed and it's not settled yet. But the Dolphins are going. I can feel it."

"Well, how—"

"There's this old man named Zack. He's got connections you wouldn't believe."

"That nasty-tempered old saloon keeper! You know him?"

"He's a nice old man and he guarantees my tickets are good."

I looked at her affectionately.

"If Zack says they're good, you can by God believe they're good. But how in the world did you meet that old pirate?"

She thought a moment before saying, "I just did."

So. Competitive secrets reared their heads once more.

"Is it a good present?" she asked half-timidly.

I was grinning. "You said you love me."

The violet eyes were open and honest and a little bit surprised. "I never denied it."

"You never asserted it, either."

The eyes were level and would brook no contradiction. "Oh yes I have."

I swallowed hard. Then I got up awkwardly and kissed her on the polished-coal hair she'd pulled back and swept up for the party.

"You're right. You have. And it's a great gift."

I saw the violet eyes begin cruising the room.

"Did you get me a present?" she asked bluntly. Loving a reporter has its unromantic side, too.

"I did."

"It's not under the tree."

I laughed. "You're right."

"Where is it?" she demanded.

"It's not here. We'll have to go for a ride."

Her brows joined in puzzlement. "What kind of a present would I go riding for?"

"You'll see."

She grabbed her jacket. "Okay! Let's take your Jeep. That rental car of mine's got something wrong with the heater."

"Well, the Jeep's kinda drafty. How about if we take one of the others?"

"You mean you're gonna let me peek in that garage? I don't believe it."

"Well, maybe this once."